AN UNSUITABLE FEELING

Lord Peterbloom turned and gazed deeply into Miranda's eyes. "You appear to be finding my talk of plants and herbs quite entertaining, Miss Miranda."

Although his gaze upon her lips seems fiercely intent, Miranda suddenly realized that she did not feel the least bit fearful. As always—of late, that is—he was behaving like a perfect gentleman.

Miranda found she had to drag her eyes from the dark pools of his in order to formulate a reply. "On the contrary, sir." How she wished to tell him she was desperately interested in growing things, and that she found his talk, and yes, him, or at least, the odd effect he was having on her, vastly intriguing, but . . .

To her chagrin, the viscount's only response was a deep throated chuckle.

"Spoken like a young lady who is far too polite to tell a gentleman he is as boring as paste." Lord Peterbloom's eyes continued to search hers. At length he inhaled a deep breath and said, "Perhaps a glass of rataffia and a slice of lemon cake would be more to your liking, my dear."

The seductively love tone of his voice sent an unwelcome ripple of delight coursing through Miranda. Without a word, she let the tall, elegant man escort her back through the fields.

WATCH FOR THESE ZEBRA REGENCIES

LADY STEPHANIE (0-8217-5341-X, $4.50)
by Jeanne Savery
Lady Stephanie Morris has only one true love: the family estate she has managed ever since her mother died. But then Lord Anthony Rider arrives on her estate, claiming he has plans for both the land and the woman. Stephanie soon realizes she's fallen in love with a man whose sensual caresses will plunge her into a world of peril and intrigue . . . a man as dangerous as he is irresistible.

BRIGHTON BEAUTY (0-8217-5340-1, $4.50)
by Marilyn Clay
Chelsea Grant, pretty and poor, naively takes school friend Alayna Marchmont's place and spends a month in the country. The devastating man had sailed from Honduras to claim his promised bride, Miss Marchmont. An affair of the heart may lead to disaster . . . unless a resourceful Brighton beauty finds a way to stop a masquerade and keep a lord's love.

LORD DIABLO'S DEMISE (0-8217-5338-X, $4.50)
by Meg-Lynn Roberts
The sinfully handsome Lord Harry Glendower was a gambler and the black sheep of his family. About to be forced into a marriage of convenience, the devilish fellow engineered his own demise, never having dreamed that faking his death would lead him to the heavenly refuge of spirited heiress Gwyn Morgan, the daughter of a physician.

A PERILOUS ATTRACTION (0-8217-5339-8, $4.50)
by Dawn Aldridge Poore
Alissa Morgan is stunned when a frantic passenger thrusts her baby into Alissa's arms and flees, having heard rumors that a notorious highwayman posed a threat to their coach. Handsome stranger Hugh Sebastian secretly possesses the treasured necklace the highwayman seeks and volunteers to pose as Alissa's husband to save her reputation. With a lost baby and missing necklace in their care, the couple embarks on a journey into peril—and passion.

THE UNSUITABLE SUITOR

Marilyn Clay

Zebra Books
Kensington Publishing Corp.
http://www.zebrabooks.com

ZEBRA BOOKS are published by

Kensington Publishing Corp.
850 Third Avenue
New York, NY 10022

First Printing: September, 1997
10 9 8 7 6 5 4 3 2 1

Printed in the United States of America

One

"Where is it?" Miss Miranda Fraser cried, her anxiety rising as she frantically riffled through the desk drawer. "It should be right here!"

A bewhiskered man stood in the doorway of the small room, his icy gaze following Miranda's every move.

"It has been here ever so many years," Miranda added. "Ever so many!" She shot an anxious glance at the elderly man, who only moments ago had appeared at the door to Fraser Cottage, an ancient half-timbered manor home situated in a pretty glen a few miles beyond the tiny hamlet of Halifax.

Today had begun much the same as countless others for Miranda and her sisters, who lived alone in the country now that both their parents had passed on. Soon after luncheon, Katie and Lucy had set off for the village and Miranda had curled up in her favorite overstuffed chair in the great room with a tattered copy of *Ellen, Countess of Castle Howel,* a widely circulated Minerva novel lent to her by their closest neighbor, Mrs. Willy-Harris.

Less than a quarter-hour later, however, Miranda's attention had been shattered by the insistent crunch of carriage wheels on the graveled drive in front. Thinking that perhaps a stranger had become lost in the tangle of country lanes and needed help in finding his way back to the main road, Miranda laid her book aside and proceeded to the front door of the cottage. Confused travelers at their doorstep were not an uncommon occurrence. Many were the times Miranda had listened to her papa, the late Vicar Fraser, steer lost souls back to the right path, both literally and figuratively.

Papa was the kindest man Miranda had ever known and she and her sisters dearly loved him. His sudden death just above one year ago, coming so quickly upon the heels of Mama's passing, was something the three Fraser girls had not yet got over. Still, despite their deep sorrow, the young ladies knew they had a great deal to be thankful for.

Although Papa had left them very little in the way of worldly goods, he'd always said that no matter what, they'd always have their home—Fraser Cottage. Though not the official rectory in the parish where Papa had held his living, the right to occupy the lovely manor home had been granted to Great-grandfather Fraser and any, or all, of his descendants who wished to remain there. Many times throughout her one and twenty years of life, Miranda had watched her papa carefully withdraw the aged yellow parchment from the top drawer of his desk and solemnly read over each and every word, then nod his head with satisfaction and slowly return the ancient document to its resting place.

So, why—Miranda frantically flung open another drawer in her father's large desk—could she not find the document now?

"A fortnight, Miss Fraser," said the gentleman darkening the doorway. "You and your sisters have a fortnight in which to vacate the premises."

"No!" Miranda cried. She flung another frightened gaze at the unfeeling stranger. The solicitor, named Mr. Fitch, had traveled all the way up from London to personally deliver the wretched news to whomever was currently occupying the cottage. It was clearly apparent to Miranda that the man did not believe in the existence of Papa's grant.

But it did exist! *It did!* Miranda's heart thundered wildly in her breast as she turned her attention again to her search. *Where had the document got to?* Already, Miranda had scattered the entire contents of three long drawers onto the desktop. Now, stooping over the row of smaller drawers to the side of the kneehole, she frantically worked her way to the bottom of them.

It must be here! It must be!

A mere week before Papa's passing, he'd again gathered his three daughters together and shown it to them once more. Miranda tearfully recalled the hollow sound of her papa's once-strong voice as he solemnly reiterated the terms of the agreement made between his great-grandfather George Fraser and . . . Miranda's stomach clinched fearfully as she valiantly tried to recall the *other* signature that appeared alongside that of George Fraser, but she was too overset now to remember what the other name was. It was obviously a distant relative of the gentleman who had sent this Mr. Fitch up from London to deliver the terrible news to the Fraser girls that the dilapidated estate upon which their home sat had been sold and the new owner meant to take immediate possession of the cottage himself!

"I assure you, Mr. Fitch . . ." Miranda tried to remain calm as she pulled herself to her full five-foot-two-inch frame and addressed the man again. "My sisters and I do have a legal claim to occupy our home. Fraser Cottage is called Fraser Cottage for the simple reason that it has always been—"

A sharp tone cut her off. "The estate has been sold, Miss Fraser. No entailments to it exist. Any verbal agreement made between your father's predecessors and those of the former owner are null and void."

"No!" Miranda gulped down her terror and fought the sudden rush of tears that sprang to her eyes.

The solicitor turned to make his way back to the foyer. Numbly, Miranda followed the cold-hearted man. She watched as he paused before the arched opening that gave onto the sunny great room. Blue chintz curtains fluttered at the mullioned windows, three of them standing open, a bright swath of afternoon sun spilling onto the freshly scrubbed hardwood floor and the hand-woven rug before the hearth. A breath of fresh air, rich with the heady scent of cool, dark earth and the new growth of spring, reached Miranda's nostrils. Her heart lodged fitfully in her throat as she watched the man's gaze calculatedly assessing her beloved family home.

She and her family loved every nook and cranny of the quaint old house, from the strong beamed ceilings overhead to the sturdy oaken floors beneath their feet. Never in her life had she contemplated living anywhere but here. She and her older sister Katie, three years her senior at four and twenty, had already accepted the fact that they would live here forever. With few to no likely candidates for marriage hereabouts, neither she nor Katie had given much thought to becoming any man's wife.

Lucy, of course, would marry. The youngest of the three Fraser girls, at sixteen, she was by far the prettiest and most outgoing of the three. Lucy was like Mama. Papa had always said that he had only to take one look at Maryella Brantley and he knew he would spend the rest of his life with her. It had been love at first sight for Mama and Papa. Miranda expected the same sort of romantical thing would happen to Lucy. She was *that* pretty.

Not so Miranda, or Katie. Not unattractive, they had both inherited Papa's even features, slender build, and brown hair, though Miranda's eyes were a lovely shade of sea green, whereas Katie's were brown, like Papa's and Sir Oliver's, his older brother. But Lucy, with her thick auburn hair and bright blue eyes, was much more vibrant than either of her sisters. Lucy already stood a good head taller than they and her figure was more rounded, one might even say buxom. Lucy would indeed marry, but Miranda and Katie would stay right here, the same as they always had, enjoying the simple, peaceful life they loved at Fraser Cottage.

Although, without the precious document in hand, how was she to convince Mr. Fitch of that?

A fierce longing for the life she had always known gripped Miranda. She could never leave their home! *Never!* Despite the family's reduced circumstances now, she and her sisters wanted for nothing. So long as they had their home and one another to love and care for, they were happy. They were safe. Even with Papa and Mama gone, life had changed very little for them. For the past year, the girls had managed quite well on Papa's pension, and there was still the hope of someday receiving the money Uncle Oliver, a baronet in his own right, had left to them. Although lately, Miranda had begun to seriously doubt that Uncle Oliver had had any money at all when he passed on. Given his penchant for excess, it seemed far more likely that he'd have exited this world with all his pockets to let than with anything to bequeath.

Oh, dear Lord, what was to become of them?

With no other living relatives, at least none that would welcome them, they truly had nowhere else to go!

Miranda thought again of her papa's disordered desk in the study. Surely, in her haste to find it, she had simply overlooked the precious parchment. Surely, once Mr. Fitch was gone, she would find it. *She must find it!*

She hurried after the gentleman, who was now making his own way through the heavy front door that still stood ajar where Miranda had left it after the solicitor had so abruptly stated his business. One gloved hand resting on the latch, the man flung a backward nod at her. " 'Twill make a fine hunting lodge," he said, then letting the door slam shut behind him, he was gone.

Miranda gasped aloud.

A hunting lodge! Not *their* home! Papa would roll over in his grave; Mama, too. They were the kindest, gentlest people to ever walk the earth. Papa would never condone the unnecessary killing of any living thing!

And . . . and . . . neither would she!

"Mr. Fitch!" she called after the man. She heard his boots crunching on the pebbles beneath his feet as he made his way again to his carriage. Darting onto the drive after him, she shouted, "My sisters and I will *not* be turned from our home, Mr. Fitch! Not *ever!*"

The man from London did not even glance up. Glaring at his retreating backside, Miranda's nostrils flared with fury.

After the coach door had snapped shut, a swirl of dust and pebbles filled the air as the dusty black carriage made a wide turn, then hurled itself down the lane, headed toward the fork in the road that, unless one was paying close attention and did not miss the sharp turn back to the left, would *not* take one straight to the main highway.

Miranda's small breasts heaved with anger. She hoped Mr. Fitch's driver was as clunch-headed as he was and had not noted the markers on the way here. She hoped the pair of them became hopelessly lost in the thick woods that lay north of Fraser Cottage and that they never made it back to London! She hoped—

Oh! What was the use?

She felt her chin begin to tremble as anguish and yes, *hatred!* for the bearer of the bad news filled her to overflowing. She fought the flow of hot, stinging tears that of their own accord began to trickle down her cheeks. But, a scant second later, she bit down hard on her trembling lower lip and squared her small shoulders. Self-pity was not in her character. She would find the proof of their claim to Fraser Cottage and take it to the new owner herself! London was not so very far away.

Two

An hour later, Miranda was still searching. She had begun methodically, sorting through all the papers in the desk, coming across notes and parts of sermons her father had written, as well as various receipts for goods and supplies he had purchased throughout his lifetime. But, after looking through all the desk drawers—even discovering a secret compartment she did not know existed but which, nonetheless, was empty—she still had not found the familiar sheet of aged parchment.

Just as she was about to give up, she heard the gentle murmuring of her sisters' voices drifting through the opened window at her side. At the sight of her sisters coming down the lane, Miranda's heart caught in her throat. Lucy's auburn curls were gleaming like burnished copper in the sunlight and the fresh spring air had brought roses to Katie's cheeks. Her soul ached as she wondered how to tell them the awful news?

Suddenly, Lucy broke away from Katie and came running into the cottage. "Miranda!" she gaily called to her sister.

Miranda gulped back a sob. Dear Lucy. She had already suffered a great deal in her young life, the loss of both her parents . . . and now this. Miranda pulled herself to her feet as Lucy burst into the room, lightheartedly swinging her old straw bonnet by its frayed blue ribbons. As always, the pretty smile on Lucy's lips nearly took Miranda's breath away. Lucy was so very like Mama.

"Miranda . . ." Lucy's smile vanished the minute she dashed into the study and spotted the mess strewn atop the desk. "Why, what have you done to Papa's desk? Katie! Come and look. Miranda has torn up Papa's desk!"

Shrugging from her brown stuff pelisse, Katie's brows drew together when she, too, caught sight of the rubble. "Oh, my, Miranda . . ." Katie lifted a concerned gaze upward.

"It's . . . gone, Katie," Miranda murmured. Feeling her knees buckle beneath her, she slumped again onto the chair behind her, her small body not filling the larger imprint left on the seat where Papa had sat, poring over his Bible, year after year. "I've looked everywhere."

"But, what are you looking for, Sister?" Katie's tone was gentle as she hung her pelisse on a hook outside the door, then advanced into the room.

"Oh, she is probably looking for another of Papa's sermons," Lucy said with some dismay, "which she will have you read to us tonight after supper. It appears to me we get enough churchifying every Sunday, I don't see why we also have to—"

"Do be still, Lucy dear," Katie said absently. "Miranda, pray tell us what is amiss."

"Oh, Katie." Miranda felt hot tears well up again in her eyes. *How was she to tell them?*

As Katie's look of concern grew, Lucy asked brightly, "Did a gentleman call on us while we were in the village this afternoon, Miranda? Mr. O'Malley at the mercantile said a stranger had asked directions to the cottage only minutes before we arrived."

Miranda's eyes were still fastened on Katie. "We . . . did have a caller this afternoon."

"Did we, indeed?" Katie asked with interest. "Who might have called on us, Miranda? We so seldom have callers this far out." She waited expectantly, and when Miranda said nothing, she asked again, "Who called, Miranda?"

Miranda gulped back her terror. "A . . . a gentleman from London."

"From London!" Lucy cried excitedly.

"Lucy, do be still."

Again, Lucy paid her older sister's gentle scold no mind. "Was he dashing and handsome? What did he say, Miranda? Had he come to tell us that Uncle Oliver's affairs had been settled and we are now rich as kings? Oh, that must be it!" She began to dance about the small room, her blue eyes shining, her cheeks aglow. "I am to have a Season, after all! Mama always said I should have one and now I shall!"

"Lucy!" Katie's tone, though still contained, was considerably firmer this time.

Miranda's solemn gaze had not left her older sister's face. "The gentleman's name was Mr. Fitch. He is a solicitor in London and he had come to tell us that we . . . that we . . . must leave." Her tone was barely above a whisper.

"Leave? Leave where? Leave what?" Katie moved closer to the desk. "I do not understand what you are trying to say, Miranda."

"Oh, Katie . . ." Miranda's fingers sifted listlessly through the pile of papers scattered atop the desk. "I have looked everywhere and I cannot find it. It has simply vanished."

"*What* has vanished?" Lucy demanded. "I declare, you tell me to keep silent so Miranda can explain and she has not yet said one sensible thing." With an impatient toss of her auburn curls, she flitted from the room. "I am near to famished," she announced to no one in particular, but the sound of her footfalls echoing in the corridor told the older girls that she was headed for the pantry in search of a biscuit or a slice of cake.

"What have you been searching for, Miranda dear?" Katie asked quietly.

"The document. Papa's parchment. The one that says—"

"Oh." Katie smiled sweetly. She stepped to the bookcase and pulled down a large black book. "I put it in Papa's Bible for safekeeping. Here it is." She withdrew the faded piece of paper and handed it across to Miranda.

"Oh-h, Katie!" Miranda sprang to her feet and hugged the tattered page to her breast. "We are safe!" Her eyes quickly scanned the familiar missive, then she carefully slipped it again into Papa's Book. "I shall take it to London straightaway and show it to Mr. Fitch. Otherwise, we shall be obliged to remove ourselves from the cottage within a fortnight."

The pronouncement did not appear the least bit alarming to Katie. "But, Miranda," she said, the ever-present smile of serenity still upon her lips, "we've only to present our claim to the new owner when he arrives and I am certain the gentleman will honor it. Frasers have always lived at Fraser Cott—"

"The property has been sold, Katie and—"

"But the gentleman and his family would not wish to live here. The main house on the hill would be far more to their liking. True, it needs a bit of attention, but it is much more grand and even now lies vacant."

"Mr. Fitch said the new owner intends turning Fraser Cottage into his hunting lodge!" Miranda blurted out. "I have no choice but to go to London and present our claim to him at once!"

"But, Sister, surely such a trip is unnecessary."

"On the contrary, Katie, it is imperative!"

"But this has always been our home. Surely this Mr. Fitch was mistaken in his assertion that—"

"He said the property was unentailed, Katie! We must present *proof* of our claim." Miranda sat back down again and began to straighten the assortment of papers she had strewn about the desk. "I am aware that such a trip will be quite costly, but this is an emergency and I can think of no better way to spend the money we have set aside. I shan't be gone above—"

"No, Miranda," Katie said firmly, "I cannot let you go. A young lady traveling alone on the post . . . Why, what would Papa say if he—"

"We have no choice, Katie. I am certain Papa would do the exact same thing I am doing."

"No, Miranda. He would not. Papa would settle the matter his way, through prayer and supplication. And that is precisely what I believe we should do." She reached to take Miranda's hand. "Kneel with me now, Sister, and we shall ask our Heavenly Father to show us the proper way to go."

Miranda snatched her hand away. "I see no reason to trouble our Heavenly Father with this, Katie, when the proper way to go is already perfectly clear to me. I could not find the document when Mr. Fitch was here. Now I have found it. I shall simply go to London. It is the only way."

"But do you know where the gentleman's place of business is situated in London, or which law firm he is associated with?"

"Indeed I do. He is a partner in the office of Fitch, Fitch, Abercrombie and Fitch. I confess I do not know which Fitch he is, but I expect any Fitch will do." She paused to draw breath. "The journey should not take above five days, including the time it takes to get to London and back again. Once the gentleman sees that we do, indeed, have a legal right to occupy our very own home, that will bring the matter to a close." She turned again to the task of putting the desk to rights. "I shall remember to thank our Heavenly Father in my prayers tonight, Katie dear, for showing me where you had hidden, er . . . that is, where you had put the document."

Katie's lips pressed together as she watched her younger sister work. Presently, she said, "Miranda, I do not feel that this is the wisest course for you to take. In fact, the more I think on it, the more confident I am that the Lord would want me to accompany you to London. I am the eldest, after all."

Miranda did not look up. "And what of Lucy? If you mean to accompany me to Town, who shall look after our baby sister?"

"Lucy may stay with one of her bosom bows in Halifax. Prunella Fitzhugh springs to mind, or perhaps Caroline Wright."

"Yes, well, I suppose Lucy would like that above all things, but I cannot think it the wisest course for her. Lucy is quite easily influenced by her friends these days, and not always for the better, I might add."

"You said yourself it would only be for a few days. I hardly think a few days sufficient to ruin our Lucy."

"It is not necessary that you accompany me, Katie. I am perfectly capable of—"

"Is Miranda going somewhere?" asked Lucy, strolling back into the study, a thick wedge of cinnamon bread in her hand.

"She is determined to go to London," Katie replied absently.

"To London!" Lucy squealed. "Then it *is* true! I am to have a Season! It is what *I* have been praying for these many months! Every night I ask our Heavenly Father to please settle Uncle Oliver's affairs so that I might have a—" She halted abruptly, a sheepish look flitting across her face, "I-I mean, I . . ." Her voice trailed off again as apparently she realized how very selfish her pronouncement must have sounded to her sisters.

Indeed, a pained look had appeared on Miranda's face. It was true, Mama had promised Lucy from the time she was a little girl and it was quite clear to all of them that Lucy was destined to become a famous beauty, that she would have a Season, but none of them, except perhaps Lucy, had really believed it would ever come true. Even Lucy had ceased to speak of it until word reached them some months back of Uncle Oliver's passing. Dear, sweet Lucy. She was so very pure and innocent, so full of youthful dreams for the future. In the past year, Miranda and Katie had done their best to fill the gap left in Lucy's life by their parents' passing. Neither of them, most especially Miranda, wished to deny their baby sister anything.

"Lucy, dear," Miranda began patiently, "none of us are going to London for the Season. We've merely a . . . a pressing business matter in Town that must be settled straightaway."

"Oh, Miranda!" Lucy pouted prettily. "I never get to do anything I want! Why, only today, Katie refused to let me have the lovely new bonnet I saw in Mr. O'Malley's window when it is plain as a pikestaff that my old one is in tatters!"

"Plain as a pikestaff!" Miranda gasped. "Lucy! Wherever do you hear such vulgar talk?"

Katie's brown curls shook. "She hears it from the village lads. There were at least half a dozen of them hanging after her today, every last one of them making sheep's eyes at her. Theodore O'Malley among them," she added, it being common knowledge that this week, Teddy O'Malley was Lucy's favorite beau. "It was quite a shameful display, if you ask me."

"It was nothing of the sort!" Lucy cried. "Can I help it if the boys think I am pretty?"

"Lucy!" Miranda sputtered afresh, while Katie piously intoned, "One must endeavor to guard against becoming vainglorious, Lucy dear."

Lucy shot an indignant glance at her older sister. "But the boys all tell me I am the prettiest young lady in Halifax. What would you have me say back to them? Tell them to hush, that I wish not to become vainglorious?" She thrust her chin up. "I am only being friendly. I like to talk to gentlemen and I . . . I like it when they look at me."

Miranda gasped anew, then turned to Katie. "We shall all be going up to London, Katie. We've no choice but to take Lucy with us."

A whoop of joy escaped Lucy's pretty lips while both her elder sisters regarded their delighted younger sister with worried frowns.

Two days later, all was in readiness for the young ladies' trip. A quick visit to the posting office in Halifax the day before had netted them three seats on the morning stage to London, which on such short notice, was fortunate, indeed. Less costly than traveling on the Royal Mail, the public stage was also less comfortable and far less dependable, the frequent changes and stoppages along the way making it unable for anyone to exactly determine the time, and sometimes even the day, of one's arrival. Mr. Willy-Harris, the girls' closest neighbor, was set to drive the young ladies to the inn in Halifax early that morning to catch it.

At half past eight, Miranda stood in the foyer, hurriedly drawing on her gloves after she'd scribbled a hasty note to Mrs. Willy-Harris asking her to please water the new seedlings Miranda had planted only that week. Tending the kitchen garden and growing fresh flowers each summer was one of Miranda's most pleasurable pastimes.

She propped the note up on the commode by the door where Mrs. Willy-Harris would be sure to see it, then stooped to make certain that she had, indeed, tucked the three five-pound notes, which was all the money she and her sisters possessed in the world, into the secret pocket of her valise. The additional coins they would need for meals and constant tipping along the way she'd already secured in a handkerchief in her reticule. She dearly hoped that in the course of the next week they did not require more, for there would be no more money for them until next quarter day, over a fortnight away.

Having assured herself that all was safe, she rose again to her feet. Glancing through the opened front door, she spotted Katie, standing alone on the graveled drive, patiently awaiting the arrival of Mr. Willy-Harris. Miranda sighed. She hoped she could remember to borrow a leaf from Katie's book and remain as collected and serene as Katie always was when next she encountered the arrogant Mr. Fitch.

With a sigh, Miranda turned toward the stairs, expecting to find Lucy scampering down them. Lucy's things had already been packed, along with her sisters', in the one large valise the girls shared between them.

"Lucy!" Miranda called. "Make haste, dear." Gathering up the fairly bulky portmanteau, she called again, *"Lu-cy!"*

When no reply was forthcoming, Miranda called to Katie, "Katie, where has our Lucy got to?"

"She has gone on ahead, Miranda. She is to meet us at the inn in Halifax."

Emitting an exasperated breath, Miranda pulled the door shut behind her. "I do hope she is not late. The stage waits for no one, you know."

Katie smiled her assurance. "Lucy is quite atremor about our journey, Miranda. I expect she is awaiting us even now at the inn."

But, a half hour later, they discovered that Lucy was not at the inn. The next quarter hour was a frenetic blur as other travelers gathered in the busy inn yard, swelling the noisy crowd of ostlers, stablehands, post boys, shoeblacks, and other hangers-on who frequented the place, if for no other reason than to ogle the coach drivers, who swaggered about the inn yard in multicaped coats, freely dispensing advice on road conditions, horses, and other subjects of interest to the male gender. To impressionable rural lads, these knowledgeable men of the road were heroes of the first order.

Waiting to climb aboard the large black-and-yellow coach, its wheels and windows picked out in red, Katie watched as each traveler's bag or bundle was secured atop the coach, while beside her, Miranda's eyes frantically searched the throng for their truant younger sister.

"We cannot leave without her, Katie! Perhaps I should go on ahead and you and Luc— Oh! there she is. Lucy, do make haste. You have given us all a fright."

Her bonnet tumbling down her back, Lucy breathlessly scampered toward the coach just in time to board it. With eight people squeezing inside, and a half-dozen or more set to cling to the rails on top, loading up was nothing short of a mad scramble.

"I simply had to say good-bye to all my friends," Lucy exclaimed to Miranda, who had ushered Lucy ahead of herself and Katie, "especially to Teddy O'Malley. I might never see him again, you know!"

"Of course you will see him again, Lucy."

"I shan't if some dashing London gentleman offers for me and I agree to become his bride," Lucy retorted, her tone near indignant.

Miranda's eyes rolled skyward as she settled herself between a portly gentleman whose diet she could already tell consisted mainly of onions and garlic and a young matron cradling a sleeping babe in her arms, although how the child could sleep amidst all the noise and confusion, Miranda couldn't think. Lucy and Katie took seats on the opposite bench and, at last, the heavy coach lumbered off.

Near a scant mile down the road, however, Lucy insisted on changing places with Katie so she could better see from the coach window. "I told Teddy I would wave good-bye to him as we drove past."

Miranda said nothing. On the one hand, she quite enjoyed seeing Lucy in such high spirits, for the girl had had little enough of late to rejoice about. She directed a somewhat sad smile at her pretty younger sister. Lucy looked quite fetching today in a lovely lilac cambric gown that Mama had made especially for her. Miranda felt keenly the responsibility that had fallen to her and Katie to look after Lucy. When Mama died, Miranda had vowed to do all that was possible to see that Lucy had a happy life. Now, it appeared that if things did not go well for them in London, Lucy might have to forgo love in favor of a good marriage. Lucy might very well be the sisters' only hope for the future.

The overcrowded coach made several stops that morning to change horses. Not until they'd disembarked for luncheon at yet another noisy inn did the girls have a moment alone to converse amongst themselves.

"Are we to call on Aunt Isobel while we are in Town?" Lucy asked innocently as she popped a buttery potato cake into her mouth.

Katie and Miranda exchanged guarded looks. "I think not, Lucy dear," Katie said quietly.

"But whyever not? Aunt Isobel sent a note to us when she learned of Mama's passing. Perhaps that means all is forgiven. We have never set eyes on Mama's relatives in the whole of our lives. I expect Uncle John is a regular swell. He is a 'lord' after all."

"And Papa's brother was a 'sir,' but that did not make him a . . . gentleman," Miranda retorted as she hurriedly scooped up a forkful of the tasty green peas on her plate.

"Papa must have thought so."

"Papa thought nothing of the sort."

"Then why did he insist on taking you and Katie with

him to London when our uncle Oliver needed Papa to keep him out of jail?"

Startled gasps escaped both Miranda and Katie, who looked quickly about in the hope that no one else in the tiny parlor where they sat had overheard Lucy's careless remark. "Our uncle Oliver did not go to jail, Lucy dear," she said, her tone a tad bit louder than it usually was, just in case. "He was merely accused of a . . . a misdeed and needed Papa to stand witness to his good character at the hearing. That is the whole truth of it."

"The charges against our uncle Oliver were dropped," Miranda added. Although, even back then, the whole affair had seemed a bit havey-cavey to her. Of course, at age fifteen, she had hardly been in a position to question the decision of the authorities. "It was a very long time ago, Lucy, I wonder that you even remember it."

"I remember it quite well. You've no idea how I envied you and Katie the trip. Mama promised me over and over again that to make up for it, I should have a Season in London when I grew up."

"I can assure you, Lucy dear," Katie began, her tone again calm and well modulated, "our short stay in London those many years ago was as unremarkable as this one shall be."

Miranda sniffed piously. She might have agreed with Katie's assessment except that, for her, that long-ago trip to Town had not been quite so unremarkable as Katie thought. But she chose not to enlighten her sisters on the circumstances of that unfortunate episode now. She had never revealed a word of it to a living soul, not even to Katie, and she had no intention of doing so now.

"Do you not agree with me, Miranda?"

The gentle sound of Katie's voice penetrated Miranda's thoughts.

"I said the weather could not be more agreeable for a road trip, do you not agree?"

"Hmmm." Miranda nodded.

"It tells me that all of us going up to London is, indeed, *His* will," Katie added softly.

Miranda nodded absently and, moments later, when the shrill sound of the guard's horn reached their ears, signaling that the twenty minutes allotted for the meal had elapsed, they snatched up their belongings, and after Miranda had paused at the counter long enough to deposit the three crowns due for their fare, they scurried again into the sunny yard and climbed into the waiting coach.

A short piece down the road, Lucy said, "I expect it would also be *His* will for us to call upon our aunt and uncle while we are in Town." She looked to each of her sisters for a reply, but Miranda merely flung a speaking look at Katie and both girls remained silent.

Undaunted, Lucy turned to the young man who had joined up with the travelers at the inn just now and who had quite clearly jostled for a seat next to her inside the coach. "Our aunt and uncle, Lord and Lady Heathrow, have a lovely home in Mayfair," she began conversationally. "I understand Mayfair is quite near Hyde Park. Are you familiar with London, sir?"

Miranda's eyes rolled skyward again, but instead of issuing a stern warning to Lucy on the impropriety of addressing a gentleman to whom one has not yet been introduced, she merely swallowed her displeasure as Lucy and the young man commenced quite happily to converse. Lucy, it appeared, had not the least notion how to go on outside the tight confines of their small village of Halifax. There, everyone was acquainted with everyone else so it hardly mattered to whom one addressed oneself.

That night, however, as they were preparing for bed, Miranda did deliver the warning, trying not to lace her words with too large a dose of censure. Of late, it seemed that either she or Katie were constantly ringing a peal over poor Lucy's head. She fervently hoped that this rebuke did not come a day after the fair.

Lying abed that night, Miranda allowed that, all in all, the events of their first long day of travel had, indeed, brought fresh insight to her. Earlier that evening, as they were entering the inn, the legion of gaping, even *lewd* looks, bestowed upon their Lucy by every last man they encountered had made her feel like a hen quite unable to protect her chick. In fact, she had opted to spend the few cents extra that it cost to have their supper brought to their room in order to further protect Lucy. Taking their meal in the common room could very well be likened to throwing her baby sister to the wolves. Odd, that she had not noticed till now how very grown-up Lucy had become.

Three

That following morning, after experiencing a particularly troublesome dream, Miranda awoke with her thoughts again fixed on her concern for her blossoming younger sister. She and Katie had awakened a good bit earlier than Lucy and were now lingering quietly over their tea while the least Fraser sister slept.

"It is not that I mean to dash any small pleasure Lucy may gain from our trip, Katie, it is just that we are not on holiday and I do not feel she should be allowed to view it as such. You observed her yesterday in the coach, nattering on to that young man as if she hadn't a care in the world—as if *we* hadn't a care in the world. And it simply is not so, Katie. It isn't."

"All the same, I cannot help but think you are making much ado about nothing, Miranda. I am certain that once Mr. Fitch is made aware of our position, this will all come to nothing. We have the right of it, and I am convinced that Divine Providence will see us through this trouble, the same as always. In fact, I am certain of it," she added, conviction firm in her tone.

Miranda heaved a worried sigh. How she longed for even a smattering of Katie's strong faith. But she would think on that later. At the moment, another matter was weighing heavily on her mind. That of protecting Lucy from the hands of unscrupulous men. If Lucy were indeed to make a good marriage, it was imperative that she remain pure and unspoiled. Katie, Miranda was certain, was still innocent to the ways of men less principled than their father had been, but Miranda knew from personal experience that frightful things could happen to a young lady when there was no one about to look after her. Fortunately, the horrid episode she had endured those many years ago in London had come to naught, but their Lucy might not be quite so lucky. Lucy was far prettier than Miranda had been at that age, or was now, for all that.

"It is just that I wish to protect our Lucy from . . . well, from herself, if you will, Katie. She is unwise in the ways of the world. And with my thoughts so very full of concern for our home, I have very little time left to worry over Lucy."

"I do not understand what you are trying to say, Miranda dear. What possible harm can befall our sister when she is beneath our watchful eye every moment?"

Miranda clamped her lips tightly shut. She could not tell Katie the whole of it. She could not. But the truth of the matter was, trouble had befallen *her* when she had supposedly been under the watchful eyes of both Papa and Katie, and even Uncle Oliver.

She had been younger than Lucy was now when Papa took her and Katie with him to London, and she'd been every bit as excited as Lucy over the prospect of going up to Town. In the beginning, the trip had proved all that she could have hoped. She and Katie had quite enjoyed their time spent with Papa. Though he had been engaged with Uncle Oliver a good deal of it, the girls had been allowed to take long walks about the fashionable square where Uncle Oliver lived and even venture into some of the shops.

But their last night in Town had been a different matter altogether. That night, Uncle Oliver had insisted upon inviting what appeared to be half of London to his town house in order to help him celebrate his victory at court that day. Neither Miranda nor Katie, or perhaps even Papa, had ever seen the like. The tall narrow town house was ablaze with light and every room in it was soon crowded with revelers. A group of musicians arrived and there was dancing and card playing and food enough to feed the whole of Halifax. Carriages were still bringing people to the house in the wee hours of the morning. Miranda had finally escaped to the far reaches of the garden behind the house, where she'd been pleased to discover an unoccupied bench upon which to sit and wait out the proceedings, since, by then, it was clear to everyone there'd be no sleeping that night.

Suddenly, her attention had been diverted by a laughing trio of young dandies who'd extricated themselves from the horde of others who'd also spilled from the house into the garden. Before she knew what had happened, one of the young men, having apparently spotted her sitting alone in the shadows, snatched her up, pressed her small body to his and, despite her cries of protest, had ravished her mouth with his own! By the time the brazen fellow released her, she was less alarmed, in fact, she was truly convinced he meant no harm, otherwise he'd not have said, "Thank you, miss, I quite enjoyed that!"

All the same, Miranda had fallen back onto the bench, shaken, and yes, *tingling* with the pleasurable sensations the young man's kiss had inspired within her! She still had not forgiven herself for that transgression. Now, she was determined that such an unconscionable act must not, *could* not, happen to Lucy!

"It is just that preserving our home must be uppermost in my thoughts, Katie. It is our primary reason, our *only* reason, for coming to Town. I feel Lucy should be apprised of the severity of our situation and cautioned against viewing this sojourn as a mere lark."

Katie chewed on her lip thoughtfully. "I—I am beginning to take your meaning, Miranda. Perhaps it would do no harm to alert Lucy to our . . . trouble, although that is not to say that I have lessened my steadfast belief that our Heavenly Father will see us safely through it."

"No; no, of course not," Miranda murmured.

Katie took another sip of her tea. "But I must say that I believe our Lucy has the right of it in regard to our calling upon Aunt Isobel and Uncle John. Indeed, it is time the breach between our two families was healed. That was Mama's dearest wish, you know."

Miranda nodded slowly. Truth to tell, she had begun to think along those selfsame lines herself. If for some reason, things did not go as smoothly as she hoped at the solicitor's office, it would not be ill-advised to have an ally in Town. After all, Uncle John must be a very powerful man. He had turned Mama's entire family against her when she opted to marry a penniless country vicar instead of the titled gentleman they had selected for her. And their aunt Isobel would be a great help to them if it turned out that they must, indeed, pin all their hopes on Lucy. "I suppose since we are to be in London," she conceded, "it would be the Christian thing to do."

"I quite agree, Miranda." Katie smiled serenely. "I am certain Mama's sister, our own dear aunt Isobel, is as kind and loving a person as Mama was. I cannot imagine that Aunt Isobel would turn us away. Not now, not with Mama gone."

Miranda nodded. "Perhaps it would be best to wait until tonight, Katie, our last before we arrive in London tomorrow, to tell Lucy the whole of it. I should not wish her nattering on to everyone in the coach today about our private affairs." Besides, she added to herself, with the three of them sequestered together inside the carriage all day, nothing untoward could possibly happen to Lucy before they reached London. Nothing at all.

"Very well, Miranda," Katie said with a smile.

Still, before they climbed aboard the stage that day, Miranda felt compelled to caution Lucy once more on the impropriety of striking up conversations with unknown gentlemen.

"Try to remember, Lucy dear, that a young lady is to first be presented to a gentleman before she is allowed to speak freely to him."

Because Lucy had again nodded as if she did, indeed, take Miranda's meaning, Miranda was doubly stunned when that evening at the Inn in Wolverton, just after she had signed their names to the register at the counter, she heard the unmistakable trill of her younger sister's laughter intermingled with a deep rumble of the same coming from what could only be a gentleman's throat.

Whirling about, Miranda's mouth gaped open. Lucy was indeed engaged in conversation with a gentleman, a gentleman who, judging from his looks and bearing, was . . . well, a *gentleman.* The tall, dark-haired man was dressed to the nines in a splendid maroon velvet riding coat, gray riding breeches and a darker gray embroidered waistcoat. About him was no air of tawdry shabbiness or the unkempt look of a village lad, or even the well-fed haughtiness of a country squire. No, this gentleman was Quality, every last, impeccable inch of him. Staring aghast at the handsome pair—for in her stylish lilac cambric, Lucy looked every bit the gentleman's equal—Miranda fought the alarm she felt rising within her.

She had not yet thought what to do to extricate Lucy from the man's clutches without causing a scene when, a scant second later, the handsome man flicked a gaze her way and she got a direct look at his finely chiseled features. Her eyes wide with shock and disbelief, she actually had to grasp Katie's arm for support. It was him! *Him!*

She had gazed upon that scoundrel's face too many times in her dreams—only last night, in fact!—to be unsure of the reprobate's identity. It *was* him, she was certain of it! Indeed, he had five additional years in his dish now, but still, there was no mistaking the bounder's identity. Many nights during the past five years she'd awakened with a start when she'd realized the handsome devil with the laughing black eyes had again invaded her nocturnal wanderings. And now, here he stood in the flesh, as tall, no, *taller,* than she recalled.

Still unable to speak or to move, she stood rooted in place, working valiantly to swallow past the wild hammering of her heart as her astonished gaze inspected every last detail of the gentleman's lean, muscular form. The curly black hair atop his head was as thick and full as she remembered, though it appeared to have been clipped a bit shorter than it had been the night Miranda had first encountered him in Uncle Oliver's garden. Fine lines of age now punctuated the corners of his eyes, which were as black as midnight, and his full sensuous lips. Miranda gulped with renewed alarm as, unbidden, a vivid memory of those lips pressed to hers sprang to mind.

Suddenly, as if in a dream, she heard her own shrill voice rising above the din and confusion that surrounded them in the crowded foyer of the inn.

"Lucy! Come away this instant!"

When her younger sister barely glanced her way, Miranda added sharply, "I have secured a room for us. We shall repair to it straightaway."

Miranda took a determined step toward the stairs, her sharp gaze flying to Katie, who stood quietly to one side, a shy smile upon her face, as she, too, stared with admiration at the tall gentleman her younger sister was openly conversing with.

"Katie, why did you not—? Oh, do come along, and please hurry!"

"Miranda! Katie!" Lucy called after her sisters. "This gentleman is from London and he is acquainted with our aunt and uncle, Lord and Lady Heathrow. Can you imagine the like?"

Miranda's breasts heaved with alarm as she whirled about. What was she to do? Did she dare . . . No! She could not look the man full in the eyes, not now! Not ever! But . . . he was quite . . . handsome. P-perhaps she and Katie might at least . . . speak to him. With resolve, she gathered all the courage she could muster and lifted a frightened gaze upward. But, upon meeting the man's dark, penetrating look head on, she was both astonished and relieved to see not the least hint of recognition in his eyes!

Still, as Miranda stood gazing upon the wastrel's exquisite face, the pounding of her own heart in her ears all but drowned out Lucy's gay trill as she presented both Katie and herself to the gentleman.

Extending her own small gloved hand to him, Miranda's knees nearly buckled beneath her when he actually reached to grasp her hand lightly in his own.

"A pleasure to meet you, Miss Miranda," the gentleman murmured politely. "Lord Peterbloom at your service."

Suddenly, Miranda wished with all her heart to turn and flee from the jackanape; instead, she again filled her lungs with courage and bravely tilted her chin a notch higher. He might have ruined her five years ago in Uncle Oliver's garden, but she refused to allow the rogue to soil their Lucy! And rogue he was. Anyone with half an eye could see that that had not changed. He was as handsome as ever, nay handsomer. "You must forgive my younger sister's forwardness, sir," she said, in quite an even tone, considering her agitated state. "I am certain she did not mean to trouble you this evening."

With a slight nod of his dark head, Lord Peterbloom murmured politely, "Your sister has been no trouble at all to me, Miss Miranda. I daresay, I find her . . ." at this juncture, the rakehell turned what could only be called an appraising look upon Lucy, a look that made the hair on the back of Miranda's neck stand up, ". . . guilelessness quite refreshing."

Miranda's nostrils flared as five years of pent-up fury came to the fore. For a farthing she would box the reprobate's ears and flog him till he begged for mercy with the shiny coiled whip that dangled from his own impeccably gloved hand. Still, despite the unbearable tightness of her stomach muscles, she managed to hold her temper in check.

"Miss Lucy tells me," the unsuspecting gentleman went on, "that the three of you are going up to London to visit your aunt and uncle, Lord and Lady Heathrow."

Though she tried, oh! how she tried, Miranda could now find nothing in the man's tone that could be construed as the least bit improper. Still, *she* refused to say anything that would further the conversation, although, standing next to her, she heard Katie murmur something that sounded like, "Indeed, we are going up to London for a short visit."

And, then Lucy, sounding quite grown-up, said, "Lord Peterbloom is a frequent visitor in our uncle's home in Mayfair. Is that not true, sir?"

Suddenly, Miranda did find her voice. "It appears that you have only just arrived at the inn, sir." A quick glance flicked over his person. This time, she noted the rather rumpled appearance of his trousers and the tiny splatters of mud upon his boots. "I expect you must be as eager as we to repair to your quarters. You will please excuse us now." With a swish of her skirts, she whirled about before the gentleman had a chance to reply. Though over her shoulder, she did hear him murmur, "As you wish."

And then she nearly choked when she heard Lucy call gaily to him. "I look forward to seeing you again in Town, Lord Peterbloom!"

In Town! Miranda's jaw dropped open once more. With

an angry grasp at Lucy's arm, she managed to shepherd her younger sister up the steep stairs ahead of her and down the corridor on the first floor once they'd gained it. The split second she slammed shut the door to their chamber, she blurted out, "You are not to see that gentleman again, Lucy! I forbid it!"

Lucy sighed dreamily. "Is he not the most handsome man you have ever laid eyes on, Miranda?"

"The gentleman's looks do not signify!" Miranda sputtered as she flounced into the small chamber.

"They do to me. I should not wish to marry a gentleman who was not extremely handsome or very well-put as surely Lord Peterbloom is."

"Stop it this instant, Lucy! Stop it, I say!" Miranda began to jerk off her gloves, yanking at the tips of each finger in turn, then angrily tossing the bits of cloth to the quilt upon the bed. "You shall never lay eyes upon him again, Lucy Fraser! Never again, I say!"

"Why, I most certainly shall, Miranda. I have decided to marry him. I am already top over tail in love."

"Lucy!" Miranda gave a jerk to the frayed pink ribbons that held her old Gypsy bonnet in place. "Katie, say something to her!"

Having quietly busied herself with dragging the girl's valise across the hardwood floor to position it conveniently at the foot of the bed, Katie now looked up. "It is unlikely that any of us shall see him again, Miranda. How is he to know where to find us in Town when we've no idea ourselves where we shall be staying?"

Miranda stared dumbly at her elder sister. "Oh." She turned a satisfied look on Lucy. "So, there it is. I wonder that I did not think of that myself. Thank you, Katie dear. It pleases me that at least one of us is able to keep her head in time of crisis."

"Oh-h!" Lucy wailed. "He will never find us if we are

to put up at an inn. Especially when I told him that we should be staying with our aunt and uncle in Mayfair."

"Well, I daresay you have told the gentleman a falsehood," Miranda retorted primly. She directed another sharp look at her pouting younger sister. Now, she expected, was as good a time as any to apprise Lucy of the seriousness of the situation they were in. "I do not mean to be constantly admonishing you Lucy dear, but . . ."

In minutes she had told Lucy everything, about Mr. Fitch and the document and the reason they were now on their way to London. Near the end of it, Katie joined in with several of her serene reminders that all would, indeed, turn out well. They had but to put their faith in their Heavenly Father and their footsteps would be guided safely back home to Halifax.

After considerable tossing and turning upon her third of the single narrow bed the three young ladies occupied that night, Miranda at last fell into a fitful slumber. The dear Lord had protected them tonight, perhaps He was indeed watching over them. That was certainly her fervent wish.

Still, before the sun dawned upon another new day, the three Fraser girls were to be presented with a new kettle of fish entirely.

Four

"Katie! We've been robbed!"

"Are you certain, Miranda? We've not left our room all night."

It was not quite dawn and the two older girls had again arisen early and were quietly dressing by candlelight while Lucy still lay slumbering upon the bed.

"But the notes are not here!" Miranda cried. "They were here last evening; I recall checking just before we climbed into bed."

"You must have overlooked them, Sister. Here, I shall help you search." She bent to take Miranda's place, riffling through the contents of the valise.

"I tell you they are missing, Katie. I've searched everywhere. We've no money left, unless . . ." Miranda snatched up her reticule and drew apart the strings. "Oh! Even the few shillings I tucked inside here are gone!"

Katie straightened, a puzzled look upon her face. "But there have only been the three of us here all night, Miranda. Someone would have had to enter the room and plunder through our belongings while we lay asleep." She glanced at the door, then crossed the room toward it. Grasping the handle, she gave a tug, and to both girls' surprise, the door pulled open with ease.

Miranda's eyes widened. "I am certain I secured the latch last evening, Katie. I am certain of it!"

A movement could be detected from beneath the lump of bedclothes upon the bed. Sitting upright, her tousled curls askew, Lucy squinted sleepily at her two older sisters. "What is Miranda shouting about now?"

"You'd best get dressed, Lucy," Katie said solemnly. "It appears we are in a bit of trouble."

"What are we to do?" Miranda cried. "We've no money to settle our reckoning and . . . and nothing for the remainder of the trip."

It was unlike Katie to take the initiative, but in a situation as dire as this, her composed countenance was far more suited to their needs than Miranda's overset one. As Katie hastened to complete her toilette, they decided that the fact that Miranda had attempted last evening to pay the innkeep in advance should bode well for them now.

"It proves that we had the money and our intentions were honorable," Miranda added. The innkeep had refused to take the money, saying it was the custom to collect at the end of the stay so that any additional charges, for meals, candles or bathwater, could be tallied when they departed.

"I shall simply tell the man the whole truth," Katie said. Casting a somewhat hopeful smile at her sisters' anxious faces, she slipped quietly from the room.

Miranda fought back tears of disappointment as she and Lucy hurriedly dressed. With no fire blazing in the hearth, and one not likely to be, since they'd no money now to pay for the luxury, the room felt quite chilly. As light began to seep through the tiny window at the top of the room, Miranda wondered again and again what was to become of them. Since the day Mr. Fitch had entered their lives, things had gone from bad to worse, with no sign yet of letting up.

Still, she was determined to see at least one of their difficulties through to the end. Their coach fares to London had been paid in advance, and even if they hadn't a cent to their names when they arrived, she intended to perch on Mr. Fitch's doorstep till she'd presented their valuable petition to him. Nothing would stand in the way of that. *Nothing!*

"We will walk back to Halifax if we have to," she muttered, more to herself than to Lucy, who, since they'd apprised her of their predicament last evening and she did seem to grasp the seriousness of it, had not said a great deal.

In quite a meek tone now, Lucy asked, "If we've no home to go home to, Miranda, could we not live in London? I have always wished to live in London, like our mama did."

Miranda tried for a brave face. "You mustn't be afraid, Lucy dear. I assure you we shall, indeed, be returning to our home in Halifax. I will allow no one to turn us away. No one." Suddenly, it occurred to her that in her frantic search for their lost money, she hadn't bothered to check and see if Papa's parchment was still tucked safely inside his Bible where she'd put it, on the very bottom of the valise. When a quick look told her that the document was, indeed, still in place, she offered a sincere prayer of gratitude for that.

Moments later, upon hearing the sound of footfalls heading down the corridor toward their bedchamber, Miranda hastened to the door, her green eyes wide as she awaited Katie's pronouncement of the innkeep's verdict.

When the click of the door latch sounded and Katie stepped inside, Miranda was unprepared for the glowing smile of relief now upon her sister's lips.

"We are safe!" Katie exclaimed. Then, swinging wide the door, Miranda was stunned by the sight of the tall gentleman hovering behind her sister in the corridor, his large, muscular frame dwarfing Katie's slight one. "Lord Peterbloom has generously agreed to discharge our debt for us," Katie announced happily. She directed a sweet smile upward and was rewarded with a polite nod of the gentleman's dark head. "I was certain you and Lucy would wish to thank him in person," Katie added.

A cry of delight at once escaped Lucy's lips, while Miranda only managed a small gasp. But during the few moments in which Lucy gushed her gratitude, Miranda was able to collect herself to some degree. "We are . . . indeed, grateful to you, Lord Peterbloom," she murmured at length.

The tall man stepped to the threshold as Katie advanced into the chamber, still telling her sisters what had transpired belowstairs.

"Apparently we were not the only travelers last evening to have been relieved of our money," she said. "There are at least a half dozen more even now attempting to reckon with the innkeep. When Lord Peterbloom caught sight of me amongst them, he gallantly stepped forward and offered at once to come to our aid." She glanced shyly over her shoulder at the silent gentleman, her innate shyness once again overtaking her. "We are greatly indebted to you, my lord," she said.

Staring fixedly at the tall gentleman, Miranda's nostrils flared with anger. In *his* debt was the last place on earth she wished to be! Thrusting her chin up, she announced sharply, "We shall repay every cent we owe you, Lord Peterbloom."

The handsome gentleman held up a gloved hand. "On the contrary, Miss Miranda. You and your sisters owe me nothing. The amount was quite negligible. In fact," he directed a concerned gaze at Katie, "if you feel you will be needing a bit more before you reach your destination, Miss Fraser, I shall be more than happy to—"

"Oh, no, sir, we couldn't," Katie said quickly. We shall be at our . . . our aunt and uncle's home long before luncheon. I am quite certain of it."

"Well, then." The gentleman, whose countenance

throughout the entire exchange had remained polite but impassive, suddenly flicked a look Miranda's way. "I wish you young ladies a safe and pleasant journey. Good day."

She had been trying hard not to stare at him but was painfully aware that she was failing miserably. He looked extraordinarily attractive this morning in a riding coat of deep forest green, his fawn-colored buckskins tucked into a pair of gleaming, black leather top-boots. His thick, dark hair was damp from his morning ministrations. One tendril still clung to his deeply tanned brow. Miranda knew a maddening urge to brush the errant lock back into place, but chastised herself roundly for the wanton thought, as well as, for . . . for looking at him. She squared her small shoulders. "Good day, sir."

When Katie at last closed the door on their visitor and he'd indeed vanished from sight, Miranda was struck by the odd notion that there was something *vastly* different about the man now, that is, five years after her last encounter with him when he was a much younger man.

It was not until she and her sisters had again settled themselves inside the ill-sprung black-and-yellow coach and it was jouncing down the dusty road toward London that she clearly determined what the marked difference was. The teasing, rakish look she'd grown so accustomed to beholding in Lord Peterbloom's dancing eyes in her dreams was . . . well, missing now. In its place was the polite gaze of a . . . a mature gentleman, a gentleman who was every inch the picture of well-bred respectability.

Absurd as it was, the realization unsettled her almost as much as the first sight of him had last evening at the inn.

Mere seconds after the crowded coach had rumbled into London and turned onto a wide cobbled street that was alive with dozens of other dusty coaches, rickety wagons, and elegant equipages drawn by high-stepping horses, Lucy turned to her sisters and declared smugly, "We've no choice now but to stay with our aunt and uncle in Town, have we?"

Though Miranda and Katie had refrained from discussing the matter, it was clearly evident to Miranda that with no money to their names, they did, indeed, have no choice but to throw themselves on the mercy of their London relatives. Despite the logic of that, however, she still said, "Perhaps we've time today to run Mr. Fitch to ground and settle our business straightaway. We might even be on our way back to Halifax before nightfall."

"No, Miranda," Katie said firmly. "I am confident that our aunt and uncle will take us in, at least for tonight. Perhaps Uncle John will even offer to drive you to the solicitor's office in the morning."

Miranda's lips pressed together irritably. This simple trip to Town was becoming very like a ripple in a stream with ever widening circles of trouble to which there seemed no end in sight. "Very well. But if we are too late to put things to rights with Mr. Fitch, it shan't be any of my doing."

"It will all turn out right in the end, Miranda dear." Katie reached to give the balled fist of her sister's gloved hands a reassuring pat. "You'll see."

The lumbering coach finally reached the Swan With Two Necks Inn and the girls set out on foot for the town house of Lord and Lady Heathrow in Mayfair. The walk was quite a lengthy one, made even more uncomfortable by the heavy valise that the girls took turns carrying between them. When they'd at last reached the doorstep of the fashionable town house, Katie stepped forward to lift the polished brass knocker.

"I do hope they are home," Miranda muttered from

where she stood on the flagway below the stairs. "It would be a fine turn to have walked this great distance and find no one about."

"London is quite vast," Lucy marveled, gazing about with round blue eyes. "I'll wager if Lord Peterbloom had seen us afoot, he would have given us a lift."

Miranda's eyes rolled skyward. For the past hour as they trudged onward, she'd been forced to listen to her younger sister rhapsodize over the paragon Peterbloom. Lucy was quite certain now that she would, indeed, see the gentleman again.

When the door to the town house at last swung open, a stern-faced gentleman dressed entirely in black peered the length of a long nose at them.

"We have come to see our—that is, to see Lady Heathrow," Katie announced brightly. Both she and Lucy smiled up at the gentleman.

A brow lifted. "And who may I say is calling, miss?"

The flicker of assessment in the man's haughty gaze did not escape Miranda's notice. Dressed as they were in their soiled and dusty traveling clothes, she rather expected they looked as if they ought to be ringing the bell at the servants' entrance instead of standing boldly here on the front doorstep. She half hoped the man himself would turn them away.

"Lady Heathrow is our aunt," Katie replied proudly. "We are her nieces come from Halifax."

"I see." The man's lips pursed but, nonetheless, he indicated with one white-gloved hand that they might step inside. "I shall ascertain if her ladyship is receiving today."

The girls advanced into the marble-tiled foyer, looks of wonderment replacing all others on each of their faces.

"Oh, my" was all Katie could manage.

"Gor', ain't this the grandest place you ever seen?"

Lucy cried, her wide blue eyes trying to take it all in at once.

Miranda was also gazing about, too absorbed in her own thoughts to chastise Lucy's lapse in proper grammar. Till now, she'd had no idea their mama had sprung from such splendor. Why, the silk-covered walls alone were priceless, as were the gilt-edged settees, and the elegant fruitwood commode just inside the front door. A huge pair of porcelain vases flanking the arched entrance that led to the interior of the house fascinated her in that they were every bit as tall as she!

"Aunt Isobel must be as rich as the Queen!" Lucy stated, gazing upward at the immense crystal-and-gilt chandelier that hung above their heads.

None of the girls noticed when the butler returned.

"Her ladyship will receive you now," he said primly.

Like a small parade, they fell in behind one another as he led them down a long carpeted corridor to a sunny sitting room at the rear of the house. But before he'd had a chance to discharge his duty by formally announcing them, the girls' aunt Isobel, Lady Heathrow, rushed forward, both arms outstretched.

"Is it really you?" cried the small, thin matron, whose once rich auburn hair was now liberally dusted with gray.

Miranda noted that her aunt's pale gray eyes were already swimming with tears. Aunt Isobel had been torn from her sister's side more than a quarter of a century ago. It had been a painful cross for Mama to bear; the same must have been true for her older sister.

Miranda's heart melted. "Indeed, we are here, Aunt Isobel," she said sweetly. "We have wanted so very much to meet you."

"And I you, my darlings." Lady Heathrow hugged each of the girls in turn. "Your cousin Elinor and I were just about to take tea. Walker," she addressed the prim-faced gentleman without looking at him, "do bring us another platter of sandwiches and a fresh pot."

"Yes, madam."

"Elinor, your three cousins have come to see us from Halifax!"

Miranda glanced toward the slim young girl, who looked to be about eighteen, reposing upon a lovely green silk Egyptian sofa in the far corner of the cavernous room. Advancing closer to her young cousin, Miranda nearly gasped aloud. Cousin Elinor, with her short brown curls and almond-shaped dark eyes, was . . . the very image of Katie! Apparently, Miranda was not the only one to notice the marked resemblance, for a split second later, Lady Heathrow remarked upon it.

"Why, I do declare, Katie," she said, still dabbing at the tears of joy in her eyes, "you and Elinor favor one another to such a extent you could be sisters!"

Katie turned a warm smile on her pretty cousin. "I am quite flattered you would think so, but I expect I am a good deal older than Elinor."

The younger girl stood and embraced each of her cousins in turn. Then she sat down on the sofa and patted a place beside her for Katie to sit. Miranda and Lucy each slipped into nearby chairs.

"I daresay my Elinor has missed having siblings," Lady Heathrow said. "I am so delighted you girls have come. I was devastated to learn of Maryella's . . ."

When Lady Heathrow's chin began to tremble, Miranda reached to comfort her aunt by placing a warm hand upon her arm. "Mama spoke of you often," she said. "She never ceased thinking of you."

"Thank you, my dear. I am . . . that is quite reassuring to me."

"We have all wanted to meet you," Lucy blurted out.

Lady Heathrow turned a fond gaze on the youngest Fraser girl. "Dear child, you are the image of your mother!" Her eyes filled with tears again but she sniffed them away when the butler appeared at her elbow just then with the tea tray.

Lady Heathrow turned to the matter at hand, but before the girls had all been served cups of the steaming brew or taken even a bite of the delicious-looking sandwiches or sugar-coated tarts on their plates, all of which Miranda had been eyeing hungrily as she and her sisters had not had a bite to eat all day, another gentleman came striding into the room.

A proud-looking gentleman, he wore a bottle-green coat over an orange silk waistcoat and a pair of close-fitting plum-colored pantaloons. More noticeable than his rakish attire to Miranda, however, was the decided scowl on the man's rather puffy face.

"I was informed we have callers," he said cooly.

"Indeed we do, John," Lady Heathrow replied, her tone growing suddenly contrite. "M-Maryella's girls have come up to London for a visit. This is her middle daughter, Miranda. And the pretty one, next to her, is Lucy." She laughed nervously. "Not that you are all not *very* pretty. But, oh my, when I look at Lucy, I can just see—" She bit a quivering lower lip as more of her composure seemed to slip away. "And . . . this quite grown-up young lady is Katie. We were just remarking upon her decided resemblance to our Elinor. Do you not think she and Elinor favor one another, John? This is your uncle John, girls."

As they each murmured polite words of greeting, Lord Heathrow's hard gaze flicked from one to the other, but not a single word escaped his lips.

"Won't you join us for tea, John?" his wife said. One hand fluttered nervously in the direction of the teapot.

He flung her a derisive look. "I wish only to know how long the young ladies intend to light here."

"John!" Lady Heathrow flung her husband a horrified gaze. "The girls are welcome to stay as long as they like!"

"Oh, Aunt Isobel!" Lucy gushed. "Thank you, ever so! We were quite frightened you would turn us away."

Miranda winced as Katie added, "We do, indeed, appreciate your kindness, Aunt Isobel, Uncle John. But we shan't be staying overlong. We shall be returning to Halifax straightaway."

Lord Heathrow fixed a hard gaze on Katie and snorted. "Good day, ladies."

Miranda's heart again went out to her long-suffering aunt and to her cousin, both of whom appeared quite shaken by the powerful man's rudeness.

Presently, Lady Heathrow said, "I pray you will please forgive your uncle John's harshness, girls. I was not aware he was at home; he is so . . . seldom about these days." She lifted a clattering tea cup to her lips. A bit later, in a somewhat stronger tone, she added, "I will not let John tear this family apart a second time."

Once the three Fraser girls had eaten their fill, Lucy again turned a sugary smile upon her aunt. "That was quite delicious, Aunt Isobel. We hadn't any of us had a bite to eat all day and I, for one, was prodigiously hungry."

Another horrified look crossed Lady Heathrow's face.

"We were robbed this morning," Lucy added matter-of-factly. "We haven't a penny to our names now and—"

"Lucy!" Miranda sputtered.

"Well, we *were* robbed, and we don't have a cent left, Miranda, you said so yourself."

"Highwaymen held up the stage in broad daylight?" Lady Heathrow exclaimed, her eyes wide with alarm. "Oh, you poor dears!"

"It was not . . . there were no highwaymen, Aunt Isobel," Miranda put in.

"All the same, it must have been quite frightful for you," Elinor said. "Do tell us about it. I have never known anyone who has been robbed before."

"Elinor! You were not harmed, were you, girls?" Lady

Heathrow's tone was again full of concern for their welfare.

"Not at all," Katie said quietly. "I assure you, there is no cause for alarm, Aunt Isobel."

"We were rescued," Lucy exclaimed, "by the most splendidly dashing gentleman in the whole of England!"

"Oh-h-h," intoned Elinor, her brown eyes growing large with interest, while across from her, Miranda emitted an exasperated sigh.

"As it happens," Lucy began importantly, "the gentleman who rescued us is an acquaintance of Uncle John's."

"Oh! Who-o?" Elinor asked breathlessly, although Miranda deemed the question quite unnecessary as it was plainly evident that wild horses would be unable to keep Lucy from revealing every last detail of their encounter with the illustrious rogue.

Miranda squirmed throughout the entire telling of the tale, and when Lucy, at last, revealed the gentleman's name, she was certain she noted a small, set smile appear upon their aunt's lips. Even a veil of *something* seemed to cloud Elinor's even features.

When Lucy had concluded her recitation, all Lady Heathrow said was, "I see."

Elinor said nothing.

Which seemed quite odd to Miranda considering how interested the girl had been at the outset. Even Lucy seemed crestfallen by the other's less than enthusiastic response.

After a pause, Lucy added, "I expect Lord Peterbloom will be calling on us soon. He said he would."

Lady Heathrow cast a wary gaze about. "Well, it was quite gallant of the Viscount Peterbloom to step forward, Lucy dear, but I—"

"He is a *viscount?*" Lucy squealed. "Oh! He must be quite an important man. A viscount . . . dear me. I am *ever* so anxious to see him again now. I declare, he is the most attractive man I have ever laid eyes on!"

"Indeed, he . . . is that." Lady Heathrow set her teacup aside and cleared her throat. "Still, I would not put a great deal of store in what the gentleman said, Lucy dear. Gentlemen often make promises to young ladies that they have no intention of ever keeping."

"But he . . . he said he would call!" Lucy looked so near to tears that Katie reached to pat her hand.

"We were quite fortunate to have met him, Sister," she said, "and none of us shall ever forget him."

A small squeak escaped Miranda's lips. It had been five long years since she'd first met the man and she hadn't been able to forget him. Now it appeared the reprobate would be inhabiting her thoughts for some time to come, at least until Lucy succeeded in putting him from mind.

She was grateful when the talk at last turned to other things, and presently Lady Heathrow rose to her feet. "I've a meeting with my Foundling Hospital Society this evening. Elinor will show you girls to your rooms, won't you, Elinor dear?"

Elinor nodded happily. "Yes, Mama."

"Well, then . . ." she turned parting smiles on each of the girls, "I shall leave you to make yourselves comfortable."

Surrounded by more opulence than they'd had ever known in all their lives, Miranda did not expect she or her sisters to experience a bit of difficulty in doing precisely as their aunt suggested. For one night anyway.

Five

"But, Miranda, it simply is not done," Lady Heathrow said early the following morning. "An unmarried lady simply cannot call upon a gentleman at his place of business."

She and Miranda had all but collided on the stairs, Miranda hurriedly drawing on her gloves, the ribbons of her bonnet already tied beneath her chin.

"In addition," Lady Heathrow added, "I doubt you will find a single gentleman in London up and about at nine of the clock. It is far too early."

"But this is not a social call, Aunt Isobel, I have urgent business to conduct with—"

"Nonetheless," the older woman stated firmly, "it will never do." She took Miranda's elbow and succeeded in guiding her back up the stairs to the landing. "We shall send a note to the gentleman and request that he call upon you here. We musn't let your uncle John get wind of the fact that you meant to . . . Indeed, it would not do!"

"But, Aunt Isobel—" Miranda protested weakly.

"Come along, dear." Lady Heathrow linked her arm through Miranda's and steered her to the private little sitting room adjacent to her own bedchamber. "I've pen and paper aplenty in here. Once you've written your note, a footman will deliver it for you. You may expect the gentleman to reply before the day is out. Although," she added with a half-laugh, "I shouldn't expect to hear from him before luncheon if I were you, dear."

Seeing nothing for it but to do as her aunt requested, Miranda reluctantly removed her gloves and took a seat in the dainty chair drawn up before a lovely rosewood writing desk. Reaching for the pen, she cast another anxious gaze at her aunt, who stood hovering over her like a governess bent on ensuring that her pupil set down her sums correctly.

"When you've finished, my dear, ring the bell for Walker. He shall see the note is properly delivered." She at last turned to go. "We breakfast belowstairs in half an hour, and then I have a surprise in store for you girls."

With a long sigh, Miranda dutifully penned the note and, after sealing it, entrusted it to Walker's care. Then she gathered up her bonnet and gloves and returned again to her own chamber. She and Katie had been assigned a pretty rose suite on the third floor of the large house. An exquisitely appointed dressing room separated their two bedchambers. Katie was now seated before a small delicate cherrywood dressing table leisurely completing her toilette.

"Aunt Isobel is determined to take us shopping this morning," she told Miranda, glancing at her sister's reflection in the oval mirror before her. "She wishes to purchase each of us something lovely to make up for a lifetime of missed birthdays and Christmases." Katie laughed gaily. "I daresay she'll do precisely that, for she'd hear none of my protests."

She rose to her feet and walked to the intricately hand-carved clothespress that completely covered one wall. Noting the long face Miranda wore, however, she said, "Do tell me what is amiss, Sister. Lucy is beside herself over the prospect of a shopping expedition. I'd have thought you'd find the diversion excessively pleasing, as well."

Miranda looked stricken. "Katie, have you forgotten our purpose in coming to London? I simply must see Mr. Fitch today. But Aunt Isobel would have none of it. She insisted I rather send a note round asking the gentleman to call on us here. I cannot be away when he comes." She paused before adding dejectedly, "If he comes."

"Of course he will come, Miranda." Katie was again peering into the mirror as she drew on a pretty green-and-white striped morning gown. "Though I rather doubt he will call straightaway; it is quite early yet."

"That is what Aunt Isobel said."

"And she has the right of it. Therefore, there is plenty of time for you to enjoy yourself along with the rest of us this morning."

Miranda chewed fretfully on her lower lip as Katie prattled on.

"Aunt Isobel will be quite disappointed if you are not with us, Miranda. She is a dear, is she not? And Elinor is quite agreeable. I, for one, am thrilled that we decided to make ourselves known to them. Things could not have turned out more splendidly for us. You really must come, Miran—"

"Katie, please!" Miranda's green eyes flashed angrily. "Apparently I am the only one of us that is burdened by the matter of our losing our home. I simply must see Mr. Fitch today! It is ludicrous to suggest that I cast aside our troubles and go shopping for a . . . a new gewgaw! I cannot do it, Katie. I cannot!"

The sound of the door to the dressing room being flung open behind them caused both young ladies to turn in that direction.

"Miranda . . . Katie!" Lucy cried, rushing toward her sisters with Cousin Elinor close on her heels. "Elinor says we have a caller! A gentleman!"

"Oh!" Miranda's expression brightened. "Why, it must be Mr. Fitch! And come so soon!"

She snatched up her reticule, into which she'd carefully tucked the document, and was halfway to the door before Elinor said shyly, "No, Miranda. It is the Viscount Peterbloom."

"Is it not thrilling?" Lucy cried. "He said he would come and he has!"

Miranda's mouth gaped open. Without a single word to either her sisters or her cousin, she turned and fled from the room. She did not know how she was to accomplish it, but she simply had to make it clear to Lord Peterbloom that his attentions upon them were not welcome. Lucy was a green schoolgirl and she, for one, would not stand idly by while that bounder ruined her! She would not!

Miranda reached the ground floor well ahead of her sisters or her aunt. Spotting Walker, she marched up to him. "If you will please direct me to Lord Peterbloom, sir?"

Walker nodded primly. "The gentleman and his lordship are in the library at the moment, miss. Perhaps you would like to wait in the—"

"Thank you, Walker."

An appalled look appeared on the butler's face as he watched the petite young lady hurry off in the direction of the book room.

While Miranda had no intention of barging in upon them, she did hope to intercept the viscount before he and Lucy met up again. Just as she gained the corridor, she was pleased to see both gentlemen emerging into it.

The sight of the viscount's tall, muscular figure, however, caused Miranda's heart to do a funny flip-flop, but she ignored the sensation and proceeded onward.

When her uncle saw her, he seemed about to speak when Miranda suddenly blurted out, "Lord Peterbloom and I have already met, thank you, Uncle John." She turned flashing green eyes upon the handsome gentleman, then, with a start, realized she'd clean forgot what she'd been so determined to say to him.

To behold him again, in the flesh, after so long a time was . . . well, it was shocking! She had never felt so . . . so powerfully distracted in all her life. It was as if she could feel all over again the warm press of the odious creature's lips on hers. And, in addition to that horror, she could also feel the same tingle of pleasure that had accompanied his kiss. It was most unsettling and she'd have no more of it! But all she could manage now was to stare dumbly at the man.

Lord Peterbloom, as well, seemed to have momentarily lost the ability to speak. Two nights ago at the inn in Wolverton he'd experienced the selfsame oddity when his gaze had alighted upon the sweet, heart-shaped face of this petite young lady. With her dark-brown locks and fiery green eyes, Miss Miranda Fraser was far more appealing to him than the lovely but bubbleheaded Miss Lucy, who, of her own accord, had struck up a conversation with him as they stood together in the crowded foyer of the inn.

Even odder to Peterbloom—especially when one considered the style in which he'd lived the past five years—was that he'd noticed Miss Miranda at all. Whereas he had once maintained a lively social calendar, one might even say a raucous, debauched social calendar, he engaged in nothing of the sort now. He attended no *ton* parties, no routs, no soirees, indulged in no gaming or betting at any of London's famed gentlemen's clubs, although he was still a member of one. In the past half decade, he'd attended no weekend house parties, accepted no drawing room invitations, nothing. The fact was, other than his official duties in Parliament, which he'd only recently begun to take seriously, he lived the life of a veritable recluse, shunning society and all its silly conventions.

The night he'd encountered the three Fraser sisters en route to London, he'd been returning to Town himself after an extended trip through the north country where he'd been gathering information for an in-depth study that Parliament was conducting on agricultural techniques, and enclosures and clearances. The subject was of especial interest to Peterbloom. He'd written up his report last evening and had been anxious to discuss it this morning with the senior committee member, Lord Heathrow.

Beyond the civility of inquiring after Heathrow's three nieces, which he had already done, he had no interest whatsoever in seeing the young ladies again. Or, so he thought.

"Indeed," he finally murmured now, upon realizing that quite a long silence had ensued during which he and Miss Miranda had been staring as if transfixed at one another. "As I mentioned earlier, Heathrow . . . your nieces and . . . I were . . . made known to one another . . . whilst the young ladies were en route to Town."

His gaze having remained locked with Miranda's throughout this exchange, Peterbloom did not realize how haltingly his reply had been delivered. He thought Miss Miranda looked quite fetching this morning in a simple sprigged muslin gown with a peach-colored sash tied beneath her breasts.

"Indeed, we did!" Miranda sputtered, the force of her reply startling Peterbloom to a new level of awareness. "And I daresay it is in the best interests of all parties for me to say straight out how I feel in regard to you, Lord Peterbloom. The truth of the matter is, I—"

"Ahem!" Lord Heathrow's baritone interrupted Miranda's tirade. "It appears my nieces manners leave something to be desired, Peterbloom. Raised in the country, don't you know. I say, step aside there, girl, allow us to pass. Just so."

Placing a restraining hand on Miranda's arm, Lord Heathrow fairly shoved her aside as he and the Viscount Peterbloom brushed past her.

"Oh!" Miranda fumed, staring after them. She parked both fists on her hips. *Manners!* Uncle John might be a powerful man, but so far as she was concerned, he had the civility of a barnyard goat!

Her lips a bow of disgust, she charged after the gentlemen, who were headed briskly down the carpeted corridor toward the foyer. Just as she rounded the corner and caught up to them, the men were set upon by the four other women in the household.

"Oh, my, Lord Peterbloom!" cried Lucy, rushing toward the men the second her feet hit the ground floor. "How simply splendid to see you again, sir!"

Peterbloom turned a disinterested gaze on the semicircle of women. "Indeed." He nodded politely in Lucy's direction, then fastened a cool gaze on Katie. "I trust you and your sisters met with no further mishap en route to London, Miss Fraser."

Lucy stepped in front of her older sister. "Not at all," she exclaimed before Katie could begin to reply. "Although"—Lucy giggled—"we did have a frightful time finding Aunt Isobel and Uncle John's house. I told Katie and Miranda that if we had seen you, you would have—" She halted abruptly as if it'd suddenly occurred to her that perhaps she might be speaking out of turn. She cast a sheepish gaze about, bobbed a quick curtsy and murmured, "P-perhaps I am nattering on a bit."

Katie moved a small step forward. "Allow me to again express our gratitude to you, sir, for coming to our rescue at the inn. I don't know what we should have done without you."

His handsome features impassive, Lord Peterbloom nodded politely. "My pleasure, Miss Fraser. I am glad I could be of assistance to you and"—a quick gaze flicked toward Miranda, who stood a bit apart from the others—"your sisters."

"I say, what's this?" Lord Heathrow boomed. "Help? Rescue? What's this about?"

Peterbloom turned to address the older gentleman. "Your nieces, sir, were the unfortunate victims of a—"

"We were robbed!" Lucy cried, apparently unable to hold her tongue a second longer.

"Robbed? I say, why was I not informed of this?" Lord Heathrow cast an angry glare at his wife.

Lady Heathrow stepped forward. "I judged it of too little consequence to trouble you with, John. Especially since Lord Peterbloom had already dealt with the matter, and in quite a satisfactory fashion, I might add." She favored the handsome gentleman with a sincere smile. "We are, indeed, in your debt, sir."

Peterbloom again nodded politely.

Beside him, Lord Heathrow clapped the younger gentleman upon the back. "Saved the day, did you, my boy?" Suddenly the familiar scowl he so often wore again marred his features. "Though I'll wager I'm the loser here. I've now a houseful of women to contend with. Say your good-bye's, ladies. Peterbloom has urgent business elsewhere. Splendid report, son. Thank you for coming. Good-bye. Ta."

A silent Walker moved to hand Lord Peterbloom his hat and cane and to fling open the massive front door and close it again behind him.

Lady Heathrow turned a perturbed look upon her husband. "You needn't have been so hasty, John. Lord Peterbloom is the first gentleman to wait upon the young ladies. You might have invited him to stay for breakfast."

Already on his way back to his study, Heathrow paid

little heed to his wife's scold. "Peterbloom called to see me. Considered it my duty to rescue *him.* No man likes being ambushed by a gaggle of silly females." Spotting Miranda, he halted before her, and in a considerably louder tone, said, "This one there—" he jabbed a thumb at her nose "—very nearly accosted him! Shocking display of impropriety. Upstarts, the lot of them."

"John!" Lady Heathrow cried. "Elinor dear, will you please take your cousins into the drawing room?"

Her brown eyes round, Elinor jumped to obey. The three Fraser sisters followed her from the foyer, all of them tossing wary glances over their shoulders as they went.

Gaining the safety of the drawing room, Miranda at last sputtered, "Well, I never! Our own dear papa would never have addressed us in such a fashion!"

"Not ever!" Lucy agreed, her tone indicating that she, too, thought Uncle John's outburst grossly unkind.

Katie stepped to Elinor's side. The girl stood with her chin now nearly touching her chest. Katie slipped an arm about her slender shoulders. "You must have borne a great deal in this house, Elinor dear."

Elinor nodded shyly. "Papa can be quite . . . formidable."

"Hummph!" Miranda muttered. "A more apt term springs to mind. Boorish, for instance."

Katie flung her sister a quelling look. "Your being ugly will not help matters any, Miranda."

"If you can't say something nice, don't say anything at all," Lucy added in a singsong tone.

With a long-suffering sigh, Katie led the way to a grouping of wing-back chairs arranged before the low-burning fire. "Let us all sit down and have a nice coze while we wait for Aunt Isobel, then we shall have a lovely breakfast and a nice tour of the shops."

Three of the young ladies sat down, but Miranda, who

still did not intend to accompany her sisters on the shopping expedition, turned to steal quietly from the room.

Near the foyer, the raised voices of her aunt and uncle reached her ears. Miranda hurriedly ducked behind one of the huge porcelain vases that flanked either side of the entry way.

"Your manner toward the girls just now was rude to a fault, John. They are my sister's daughters, for pity's sake."

"I refuse to countenance the upstarts, Isobel. Orphans or no, I will not take them in."

"They are not to be staying a great length, not nearly so long as your sister and her children do when they come to visit. The girls are all that is left of my family, John, and I will not allow you to treat them in so shabby a fashion." Her tone grew stronger as she spoke. "I have never stood up to you before, John, but I am determined to do so now. I—I have been giving the matter of the girls' future a great deal of thought and I've an idea where they are concerned."

Miranda could very well imagine the disapproving look that must have appeared on her uncle's face then.

"You know very well that women haven't the capacity to think, Isobel. You will refrain from doing so at once!"

"And you will refrain from speaking to me in such a fashion, John!"

Miranda nearly jumped at the strength she heard in her aunt's generally soft tone. She leaned forward so as not to miss a single word the brave woman said.

"The fact is," Lady Heathrow went on, "I consider it my Christian duty to see that at least one of Maryella's girls marries well. Then she will be able to see to the welfare of the others. Surely you can brook no objection to that, John."

Miranda's eyes widened. Perhaps Uncle John could brook none, but behind the vase in the corridor, she very nearly blurted out hers, especially if Aunt Isobel's plan had anything to do with that wastrel Peterbloom!

"If you think I mean to shoulder the expense of firing off those vicarage upstarts," Uncle John sputtered, "you can just think again! Bringing out three penniless chits at once is not good *ton,* Isobel. Not good *ton* at all."

"But John, I . . ."

"You have overstepped the bounds this time, woman! It would take a twelvemonth of tutoring before a single one of those girls is up to the mark. A good name is everything, madam, and I'll not have mine sullied by the likes o' them. Entire family is a set of dirty dishes, including that Sir . . . what's-his-name, the vicar's late brother. The sooner we rid ourselves of the lot of them, the better."

Miranda very nearly flung herself from her hiding place in order to oblige her uncle John at once! But, fearing a flogging or worse from him, she held her tongue.

"—the girls are all very pretty," Lady Heathrow was now saying in quite a cajoling tone. "Lucy is the image of Maryella, and you recall, she had quite a successful career."

Heathrow snorted. "Running off with a penniless vicar when she could have had a title? I hardly call that successful!"

"Maryella was deeply in love with Matthew Fraser. I, for one, should like to see her daughters as happily wed as their mother was."

"Yes, well. I am reminded that we are still saddled with the upkeep of our own daughter, and it appears, are likely to be for quite a spell. The chit is as come-at-able as a mouse."

"You are too cruel where Elinor is concerned, John. It is my fondest wish to also see our child happily wed. Elinor is thrilled beyond words to finally meet her cousins. Despite the fact that she . . . did not take last season, I am certain that her association with three such charming and pretty young ladies will serve to boost her confidence."

A long pause ensued, and then Miranda again heard the soft but now quite firm treble of her aunt's voice.

"Elinor has missed a great deal by being an only, John. Some of the happiest moments in my life were those shared with my sister." Lady Heathrow's voice grew almost hard. "I have never truly forgiven you, John, for what you did to Maryella and me. Splitting our family apart was . . . unconscionable."

Miranda waited with bated breath for her uncle's heated reply to that, but when none was forthcoming, she assumed that her aunt and uncle had quitted the foyer, perhaps gone abovestairs or down the second hallway that led to the rear of the house. Believing it safe now to continue on her way, she took a tentative step forward, but, at precisely that second, Uncle John himself came wheeling round the corner and the two nearly collided.

"What's this?" the huge man demanded. His sharp gaze flitted from Miranda to the immense vase and back again. "Eavesdropping, were you?" He spun about as Lady Heathrow came into view.

"Why . . . Miranda dear."

Lord Heathrow snorted his displeasure. "I'll wager this one was sent by the others to learn if their ploy to ensnare us was successful!" A black gaze pinned Miranda. "You may tell your sisters that I will not be swayed, missy! I shall not be swayed!" That said, he stalked off in the direction of the library.

"Oh, my." Aunt Isobel stood nervously wringing her hands together as she stared after her husband. "I fear your uncle John is quite angry now, Miranda." She cast another worried gaze after the large man. "I hope you can forgive us, dear."

Miranda's heart was still pounding wildly in her breast. "I . . . of course I can, Aunt Isobel, though I must confess I . . . had been listening. I hadn't meant to eavesdrop, but when I realized you were discussing my . . . my sisters and me, I . . ." Her small shoulders lifted and fell.

A sad smile wavered across Lady Heathrow's face. "Well, what if you were? I expect I would have done the very same."

Miranda bit her lower lip. "I—I should have made my presence known, ma'am."

"Nonsense. No harm done. Come along, dear. Let us fetch our bonnets and be off." She cast another fretful glance toward the book room. "I daresay a bit of fresh air will do us all good. We shall not let that disagreeable man spoil a single minute of our lovely day together."

Miranda gratefully fell into step beside her aunt, but despite the protests of Lady Heathrow—and later, those of Elinor—to the contrary, she could not be persuaded to join the young ladies on the shopping trip that morning.

"I simply must be here when Mr. Fitch calls," Miranda insisted. "I must!"

Six

"If the slight had been delivered face-to-face, it would constitute a cut direct. Are you certain you do not wish me to take the matter up with your uncle John, Miranda?"

"Oh, no," Miranda said quickly. "It is nothing, really. Thank you, Aunt Isobel." She smiled bravely as she tucked the folded sheet of paper that had just arrived from Mr. Fitch into her pocket.

Miranda had waited nearly the whole of the day for a reply from the solicitor. Walker had only just presented the missive to her a scant second ago as he brought in the tea tray and Miranda had been far too excited to leave the room before she broke the seal and hurriedly scanned the page. Now, she wished she'd been a deal more patient.

"It is quite evident that the gentleman's refusal to receive you has overset you, Miranda," Lady Heathrow began again. Both Katie and Lucy had wished to know what Mr. Fitch said and, despite her great disappointment, Miranda had told them, without divulging any of the particulars, or the reason she'd wanted to see the man, to Aunt Isobel.

"I expect I should have called on him in person," Miranda ventured.

Lady Heathrow ignored that comment. "If you girls are

facing any sort of difficulty at all," she said, "you must know that your uncle John and I are more than willing to help. It means a great deal to me to have found you after so many years. You may come to us with anything." She cast a last reassuring look at Miranda as she handed her a steaming cup of tea.

"Katie says Miranda is a worrywart," Lucy announced.

"What I said was," Katie spoke up, "is that she ofttimes oversets herself needlessly." She took a small sip of tea, then added, "I still say we've nothing to be overly concerned about, Miranda."

Miranda lifted her small chin, but no sparkle of conviction shone from her eyes. "Perhaps you have the right of it, Katie."

"All the same," Lady Heathrow remarked, "I insist that you come to me, or your uncle, if you girls have need of anything. Do I have your promise on that, Miranda?"

Fearful that if the subject were not dropped soon, she would burst into uncontrollable sobs, Miranda managed a tight nod and turned a smile on Lucy. "Do tell me again, sweetie, about all the wonderful things you saw in the shops today."

Lucy had come home from Bond Street this morning with two lovely new bonnets, a new gown, half a dozen pairs of kid gloves, assorted ribbons for her hair, and new pink satin slippers. Katie's gift was a bit less extravagant, a lovely new pelisse (which she sorely needed) and a matching bonnet with a dark-blue plume, all of which looked quite costly to Miranda.

"Oh, Miranda, you should have been with us!" Lucy replied, her blue eyes shining with glee. "Aunt Isobel has such exquisite taste! I fell top over tail in love with everything she pointed out to me!"

"I'd have selected something pretty for you, too, Miranda," Lady Heathrow said, "but I was hoping to persuade you to come with us on the morrow."

"We are to visit a modiste tomorrow!" Lucy announced, her blue eyes round with excitement.

"Hmmm," Miranda murmured. Despite her pain and frustration, she was pleased that both her sisters were enjoying themselves. At the moment, Katie and Elinor had their heads together over the latest issue of *La Belle Assemblée,* and Lucy had set her teacup aside to place one of her new bonnets atop her auburn curls.

"I cannot decide which of my new bonnets I like the best! What do you think, Aunt Isobel?"

Lady Heathrow laughed gaily. "I declare, Lucy is so like her mother, I get quite misty-eyed just looking at her. I find I can deny her nothing!"

Miranda could easily understand her aunt's sentiment. It *was* difficult to deny Lucy anything, which was one of the reasons Miranda had decided not to divulge to her sisters a single word of the heated debate she'd overheard that morning between her aunt and uncle. If Uncle John knew the real reason she and her sisters had come to Town, he would indeed throw a fit. Very likely he would throw them out. Uncle John would never believe that the girls had not come to Town to take up permanent residence right here beneath his roof.

Climbing into bed that night, Miranda felt near sick to her stomach with the weight of all their troubles pressed upon her. Katie still firmly believed that Divine Providence would see them safely through the muddle, but Miranda clung more to "the Lord helps those who help themselves" school of thought. Tomorrow she meant to call on Mr. Fitch herself no matter what Aunt Isobel said.

"Very well, dear, I can see that you are determined," Lady Heathrow said on a sigh. "But I do wish you would tell me what the trouble is. If the matter is as pressing as you say, I am certain your uncle John would know how to remedy it."

"And I am certain the situation will remedy itself once I am able to speak with Mr. Fitch," Miranda maintained.

"Still, I cannot like you going about the City alone, dear. Your uncle John would strenuously object to it."

"I am quite accustomed to going about on my own, Aunt Isobel. We are considerably more relaxed in regard to such matters in the country. Very few of the villagers have either a maid or a footman."

A sad smile crossed Lady Heathrow's face. "I expect things are a good bit different in the country, dear. Some day you must tell me more about Maryella's . . . that is, about your lives in Halifax." She blinked back the small droplet of moisture that had sprung to her eyes. "In the meantime, I insist that you avail yourself of the tilbury and allow Elinor's abigail, Betsy, to accompany you. Walker will see to a driver and a proper footman."

Miranda breathed a huge sigh of relief. "Thank you, Aunt Isobel."

Seated in the neat open carriage with the little maid Betsy beside her and a liveried footman standing atop the platform at the rear of the coach, Miranda might have enjoyed the lilting feel of tooling down the cobblestone streets of London if she weren't so anxious to have the disagreeable business with Mr. Fitch got behind her.

The afternoon was quite pleasant, however, despite the cloud of soot that hung perpetually over the city, which was quite unlike the fresh, country-scented air Miranda was accustomed to in Halifax. She tried to forget her troubles for the moment and take an interest in the sights Betsy was shyly pointing out to her: the impressive edifice of St. James's Palace, the street that led to Whitehall, and the many colorful shops and stalls lining the busy Strand.

Traveling farther down the wide thoroughfare that was every bit as congested as the narrower lanes they'd left behind them in the heart of Mayfair, Miranda longed for a glimpse of the famed Temple, but just as they drew near the intersection where it stood, the driver of her tilbury was forced to an abrupt halt as traffic snarled up ahead. Miranda craned her neck in an effort to get a clear view of what might be causing the obstruction, but it was no use. She could not see beyond the shiny flank of a large black stallion caught between her carriage and several others pressed in around them.

The high-spirited animal seemed quite impatient to be off and was skittering this way and that, tossing its thick mane about and swishing its long black tail back and forth.

As the tilbury began at last to inch forward, Miranda was brought alongside the rider's muscled thigh hugging the stallion's sleek side. She had a clear view of the gentleman's polished brown leather top-boot fitted snugly into the smooth leather stirrup. Because there was nowhere else to look, her eyes began to slowly travel up the gentleman's leg, clad in a pair of somewhat familiar-looking buckskin breeches. An odd tightness seemed to clutch at her throat as she took in the gentleman's strong forearm and very broad shoulder nicely molding the light woolen fabric of a maroon-colored riding coat. Next in her line of vision were the stiff crisp points of the gentleman's white collar and the corded muscles of his neck just barely visible above it.

The catch in Miranda's throat escalated to a definite shortness of breath when . . . *No!* it couldn't be! Dark curling locks peeked from beneath the gentleman's black beaver hat, pulled so low over his brow as to all but obscure his face. Suddenly, the gentleman turned full around and Miranda gasped aloud.

The look of surprise that simultaneously appeared on Lord Peterbloom's face at once relaxed into a dazzling smile when he spotted Miranda. She blinked at the brightness of his even white teeth next to the bronzed skin of his face.

"Well, good afternoon, Miss Miranda," the gentleman began, his tone quite warm, even friendly. "I had thought it was you when your carriage first pulled up, but I could not be certain till you lifted your chin and I got a glimpse of your pretty face beneath your—"

Miranda flinched when the stylishly dressed gentleman's gaze fixed on the tattered brim of her old Gypsy bonnet; her favorite bonnet, which was a good thing, since it was also her only bonnet.

"—bonnet," he concluded. The twitch of amusement that began to play at his full, sensuous lips sent a wave of irritation through Miranda. "Taking the air this afternoon, are you?" he asked.

"I have business to conduct in the City," Miranda replied crisply. For the veriest second she wished she had prevailed upon Katie to lend her her new bonnet for this small sojourn. Although why that thought crossed her mind, she could not say.

"Fine day for it," Peterbloom went on, "if one is not in too great a hurry, traffic being what it is." He glanced down at Miranda again, his expectant look telling her it was her turn to say something.

She sniffed. She had no desire to encourage further conversation with this gentleman, if, indeed, he could be called that. At length, however, she did risk another peek up at him from beneath the frayed brim of her bonnet. Surrounded as she was by a veritable arsenal of servants, and it being broad daylight, she supposed she was not unsafe with the Viscount Peterbloom. Still, when she noted that his dark eyes were fixed quite intently upon her, she felt her pulse quicken and was again filled with alarm.

Presently, the gentleman said, "I trust you and your sisters are enjoying your stay in Town?"

Miranda opened her mouth to assure him that that was, indeed, the case, when the animal beneath him commenced to dance sideways again. Lifting her chin, she watched with fascination as the gentleman's strong hands worked for a tighter grip on the ribbons and, with a firm tug, he finally pulled the animal to a standstill once more.

A few additional seconds elapsed before he said, "I recall Miss Lucy telling me that she'd not been to London before now. If you'd allow me, Miss Miranda, I should be happy to—"

"Absolutely not, Lord Peterbloom!" she sputtered, aghast, then realized she wasn't entirely sure what the gentleman had been about to ask—but whatever it was, the answer was no!

The forcefulness of her reply seemed to startle him. "Ah. Well, I . . . rather expect your aunt and uncle are quite enjoying the task of showing you young ladies about."

"Indeed, they are," Miranda replied firmly.

"Well, then," he said after another pause, "I wish you a pleasant stay in London, Miss Miranda." He touched the curly brim of his black beaver hat, then, with a tug to the ribbons that had held his mount in check, he directed the animal through a small hole that had opened up in the tangled traffic.

Miranda watched the horse and rider disappear from view. "And good riddance to you, Lord Peterbloom," she muttered beneath her breath.

Beside her, Betsy had been quietly taking in the proceedings. Now, she said, " 'E's quite a good-looking chap, ain't he, miss?

Miranda's lips pursed. "I expect he thinks so."

Betsy gazed in the direction in which the Viscount Peterbloom had vanished. " 'E didn't seem so full of hisself to me, miss. 'E seemed quite nice. Real polite like, too."

"Perhaps he did." Miranda sniffed primly. "But I have

it on good authority, Betsy, that the face certain gentleman show in public may not always be their true one."

Most astonishing! Lord Peterbloom exclaimed to himself as he urged his mount into a brisk canter. He had come within an inch of asking Miss Miranda if he might take *her* for a drive, or escort *her* to the opera, or somewhere, anywhere. He wasn't entirely sure what might have fallen from his lips before he was done, but apparently she was, for she'd refused him before he'd had the chance to complete the sentence. Which, he grinned crookedly, was equally as astonishing, since . . . well, since, not once in his thirty years of life had he heard the word No! fall from a young lady's lips in regard to anything he might ask of her. Anything! The phenomenon quite astonished him.

It was almost as astonishing as the fact that thoughts of the petite Miss Miranda had lingered so tenuously in his mind since the night he'd met her at the inn. She looked as pert and charming today in a pretty pink frock as she had yesterday morning when he'd bumped into her at her uncle's home in Mayfair. But that bonnet she wore was an absolute fright! He knew very little about women's fripperies and such, but he did know a well-worn bonnet when he saw one and Miss Miranda's looked fit only for the ragpicker's barrel. His lips twitched with amusement again as he thrust further thoughts of the spirited little miss from mind.

Reaching his destination—London's busy dockside—Peterbloom dropped to the ground, tethered his horse to a nearby rail and made his way through the teeming mass of humanity thronging London's busy quay.

A bit farther uptown, in the area known as Lincoln's Inn Fields, Miranda Fraser marched briskly up to the counter inside the imposing redbrick structure that housed the law offices of Fitch, Fitch, Abercrombie and Fitch.

"I should like to see Mr. Fitch," she said to the fresh-faced clerk who had glanced up from his work as she and Betsy advanced into the building.

"We've three Mr. Fitches, miss. Which Fitch would ye be wishing to see. Not that it matters a whit," the young clerk muttered, "they's all out of the office at the moment."

"Then I shall wait."

"Suit yeself, miss." The clerk turned back to his work, copying something from a bulky law book spread open before him on the desk.

Her head held high, Miranda took a seat in one of two high-backed chairs positioned just inside the doorway. Betsy slipped into the one next to her.

Fresh on Miranda's mind was her unfortunate encounter with the wicked Viscount Peterbloom. She had certainly not been wrong in her assessment of him; he, indeed, was dead set upon snaring Lucy. The very nerve of that man, thinking that she would actually grant him permission to . . . to, well, whatever it was he'd wanted to do with Lucy. The man was an unprincipled libertine and she would never, *ever,* allow him anywhere near her baby sister. Unbeknownst to Miranda, the tip of her boot had begun to tap impatiently against the planked wooden floor.

In seconds, the lone clerk glanced up. "Could be a long wait, miss. Perhaps ye'd do well to call another day . . . or request an appointment."

"I am here now, thank you, sir. I shall be here when Mr. Fitch returns."

The clerk shrugged thin shoulders and lowered his head again over his work.

However, when five of the clock dragged round and

the solicitor hadn't, Miranda reluctantly pulled herself to her feet.

"Come along, Betsy. We shall try again tomorrow."

Upon reaching Hanover Square, Miranda glanced beyond the pointed ears of the single horse trotting ahead of the little tilbury and noted the handsome equipage already drawn up to the curb before her aunt and uncle's town house. A wave of anxiety swept through her. Surely the caller was not the persistent Lord Peterbloom.

She relaxed the veriest mite when Walker informed her, as she and Betsy stepped inside, that the women of the household were taking tea in the ground-floor drawing room and that she was to join them. Miranda asked Betsy to take her bonnet and pelisse up to her bedchamber and proceeded at once to the designated withdrawing room. And was vastly relieved to find not a single gentleman lounging anywhere about.

But her relief was short-lived, for mere seconds after she'd joined the ladies, and Aunt Isobel had introduced her to her guest, a tall, elegantly attired woman named Lady Jersey, the conversation resumed.

Miranda nearly sputtered into her tea cup when she heard the woman say, "I daresay catching the Viscount Peterbloom's notice can only add to Lucy's consequence."

Miranda flung a horrified gaze at Katie, who as usual merely smiled serenely. Her stomach muscles tight, Miranda managed to hold her tongue. For the moment.

"I was just telling Sally about you girls' extraordinary encounter with the Viscount Peterbloom, Miranda," Lady Heathrow said. "And that the gentleman had called here only yesterday."

Lady Jersey nodded. "Most extraordinary indeed. Considering."

"Considering what?" Miranda asked, hoping against hope that the woman would relay some horrific scandal about the man that would once and for all render him totally unsuitable as a suitor for Lucy.

"He is the handsomest man I have ever laid eyes on!" Lucy cried before Lady Jersey had a chance to say a word.

"That is a view shared by half the women in London," she said now, a sly grin lifting one corner of her mouth.

"Do you know him quite well?" Lucy breathed.

Lady Jersey's lips continued to twitch. "As well, I expect, as half the women in London." She flung a pointed gaze at Lady Heathrow. "At least great numbers of them profess to." Her gray eyes crinkled with amusement while across from her Lady Heathrow coughed uncomfortably.

The exchange did not escape Miranda's notice. "It appears as if the Viscount Peterbloom has somewhat of a reputation," she said boldly.

Beside her Katie gasped. "Miranda!"

Lady Jersey cast a glance at Miranda, as if noticing her for the first time, despite the fact that the young lady had been presented to her only moments ago.

"Indeed, he does. Or, that is, he did."

"Did?" Miranda probed. She settled into her chair. "Do tell us more about the illustrious Lord Peterbloom, Lady Jersey."

"Miranda," Katie scolded again, her tone clearly telling her sister that to encourage such lewd talk was not the least bit seemly.

Lady Jersey glanced at her hostess as if seeking permission to speak openly on the subject.

"I suppose you may as well enlighten them, Sally," Lady Heathrow said on a sigh. "Though I fail to see the need to go into . . . great detail. I expect exaggerated accounts of the gentleman's . . . escapades will eventually reach their ears. With the young man back on the scene and Lucy out—"

"Out?" Miranda cried. Again, she nearly choked on her tea.

"Why, yes, dear. Sally and I have decided to bring Lucy out," Lady Heathrow said matter-of-factly.

"Indeed, we have." Lady Jersey turned an engaging smile upon Lucy. "With her smashing looks, I daresay we can expect at least an earl, or better."

Lady Heathrow's hands clapped together with glee. "Didn't I tell you she was the image of Maryella? Hearts will break, I am certain of it."

Miranda wondered irritably how quickly hearts would mend once the earl, or better, learned that Lucy's dowry consisted of two spinster sisters?

"I do not wish to marry an earl," Lucy said petulantly. "I told you, Sally, I am already top over tail in love with the Viscount Peterbloom." A sweet smile replaced the pout upon her pink lips. "You do not mind if I call you Sally, do you? I feel we are already bosom bows."

The elegant woman laughed. "You are the most engaging young lady I have met in an age, my dear. Indeed, you may call me Sally. I am honored to be your bosom bow."

Everyone but Miranda, who was still waiting to hear the colorful *on-dits* about Lord Peterbloom, laughed aloud. She was disappointed, however, when Lady Jersey next said, "Well, then, shall we get down to the business of presenting you, dear?"

After a good bit of discussion, the two older women decided that before applying for an official presentation to the Queen, it would better serve to have Lucy presented to all the "right" people at a number of important *ton* gatherings.

"The Queen is quite ill these days," Lady Jersey remarked, "so it is very likely that you might never be presented to her. I don't believe she held a single drawing last season."

"One." Lady Heathrow held up a finger. "Quite near

the end." She directed a warm smile on her own daughter.

"I was presented to Queen Charlotte," Elinor said quietly. Thus far, the shy young lady had said nothing at all.

"Ah, yes, so you were, Elinor," Lady Jersey muttered. "I had quite forgot that you were out, dear. Well, then, I shall have to also remember you when I request invitations for . . ." she flung a somewhat absent look at Katie and Miranda ". . . the other girls."

Miranda nearly blurted out that she, for one, had no intention of attending any *ton* gathering. While it was quite fortunate for them that Aunt Isobel and her friend wished to take Lucy under wing, she was as determined as ever to return home to Halifax and live quietly in the country. And—she glanced at her older sister, who with interest shining from her brown eyes was listening intently to all that was being said—she expected Katie felt the same as she.

At length it was decided that Lucy's official introduction into society would be at Almack's on Wednesday evening next. In the meantime, there was a musicale being held that very night that Lady Jersey thought would be advantageous to take Lucy to.

"The sooner word is out that an *exquisite* is on the scene, the better," she said confidently.

"I should dearly love to go to a party tonight!" Lucy cried. "Perhaps Lord Peterbloom will be there!"

"Oh, I shouldn't count on that, dear," Lady Jersey said. With a proprietary hand, she reached to brush an errant lock of auburn hair from Lucy's brow.

"But why ever not? You said yourself that half the ladies in London knew him. Would he have not received an invitation?"

Sally's lips began to twitch once more. "I did not mean *know* in that sense of the word, dear."

Across from them, Lady Heathrow squirmed uncomfortably in her chair. "The girls have been quite sheltered, Sally, I do not believe that they—"

"I do not understand what you mean." Lucy's blue eyes filled with tears. "I am simply dying to know all about him, Sally. You promised to tell me, you did!"

Lady Jersey looked to the girls' aunt. When Isobel, at last, nodded with resignation, Sally smiled.

Miranda took the liberty of refilling her teacup and settled back to, at last, learn all she could about the rakehell Peterbloom.

Seven

"Well," Lady Jersey began with relish, "it was once rumored that Peterbloom kept seven lightskirts, one for each day of the wee—"

"Sally," Lady Heathrow cut in hastily, "I doubt the girls are familiar with . . . that term."

"Ah." Lady Jersey nodded. "No matter. I expect the tale was highly embroidered upon anyhow. Let me see . . . another story circulated that he and two other chaps had actually wagered that Peterbloom could kiss fifty young ladies in a single night!"

"Oh!" Lucy's eyes sparkled with delight. "I daresay I would kiss him!"

"Lucy!" The scold fell from Miranda's lips.

"Well, I would, Miranda."

"I expect we have heard quite enough of this sordidness, Lady Jersey," Miranda said sharply. "Lucy is quite young, and that alone speaks for her experience in such matters."

"I have been kissed, Miranda!" Lucy cried.

"Lucy!" Katie sputtered, her brown eyes now wide with alarm.

"Well, I have and I quite enjoyed it!"

"There, there, girls." Lady Heathrow laughed. "I doubt any young man, no matter how dashing he is, could kiss fifty young ladies in a single night. Four or five perhaps, but not fifty. The *ton* takes a perverse pleasure in embellishing silly tales till they become quite outrageous. For my part, I rather expect many a young lady merely sought to enhance her own consequence by claiming to have been pursued by the dashing Lord Peterbloom, and that alone gave rise to the exaggerated number. In any event, if the Viscount Peterbloom had kissed fifty young ladies, or even half that number, it is certain that at least one charge of ruination would have stuck, with the result that the young man would have been forced to marry someone. To my recollection, not a single charge has ever been brought against him."

Lady Jersey laughed. "It is difficult to force a man to marry when he is nowhere to be found."

"That is quite true." Isobel smiled.

"But . . . where had he got to?" Lucy demanded.

Both the elder women shrugged elegant shoulders.

"Five years ago, Peterbloom simply vanished into thin air," Sally replied.

"He resurfaced in Parliament a few weeks ago," Lady Heathrow put in. "John said he takes his duties in the House quite seriously. John speaks very highly of him."

"As does my husband. Peterbloom was never ill thought of. Despite his roguish conduct as a young man, he was always a gentleman. Breeding seldom gives way."

Miranda's lips tightened. Perhaps it did and perhaps it did not. Nonetheless, she had heard quite enough. She was not willing to put Lucy's virtue on the line in order to test the theory.

"I do so wish Mama could have seen our Lucy tonight," Miranda said to Katie later that evening as the two girls sat alone in the small sitting room across the corridor from their suite after Lucy, Aunt Isobel, and Elinor had departed for the musicale in Lady Jersey's company.

"I daresay Elinor looked every bit as pretty as our Lucy," Katie added. "The blue sarcenet she was wearing set off her coloring quite nicely."

Miranda nodded. "Elinor looked very pretty."

"I feel as close to her now as I do to you and Lucy."

Miranda fell silent, an absent gaze taking in the opulence of the prettily appointed sitting room. Four delicate ebonized armchairs were drawn up before a gold leaf loo table and she and Katie were seated on a modern black-and-gold lacquered settee positioned before the hearth. "Elinor has had far more advantages than we, Katie, but I confess I do not envy her a bit."

"Nor do I. It is apparent that Aunt Isobel is devoted to her, but, I fear Uncle John . . ." Katie's voice trailed off.

"One wonders what he will say when he learns that Aunt Isobel means to bring Lucy out. I understand a young lady's debut can be quite costly."

"I expect Uncle John will be more than happy to finance Lucy's Season. We are, indeed, blessed to be part of such a wonderful family."

Miranda said nothing.

"I do hope Mama knows that all is well between us now, Katie went on. "She would be ever so pleased to know how dear Aunt Isobel and Elinor have become to us."

"I hope our Lucy will not take unfair advantage of Aunt Isobel's generosity. She seems intent on purchasing whatever trifle catches Lucy's fancy."

"Buying gifts for those she loves gives our aunt Isobel great pleasure, Miranda. Earlier today, she instructed me to tell you that if you were to spot something in a shop window that you'd especially like, you have only to sign your name and have the merchant send the reckoning to Uncle John. You really should treat yourself, Miranda. It would greatly please Aunt Isobel if you did."

One of Miranda's finely arched brows lifted. Perhaps it would please Aunt Isobel, but she seriously doubted Uncle John would share that sentiment. "I suppose it is possible that Uncle John does not know of Aunt Isobel's plan to bring Lucy out," she mused. "He is so seldom here."

"Our uncle does stay excessively busy with his duties in the House," Katie agreed. "But Aunt Isobel also maintains an active social calendar."

"Does she?"

"Indeed, Miranda. She divides her time between quite a number of charitable concerns in the City. You recall she attended a meeting of one of them the first night we were here. She has invited me to attend a meeting of the Society to Suppress Vice and Corruption tomorrow evening. And she is spearheading a new league to benefit runaway girls and orphans."

"We are orphans," Miranda said dryly.

"Aunt Isobel does not think of us as such. At any rate, she and Elinor both belong to a number of other leagues, one for the study of astrological concerns and another that studies flora and fauna. I expect you would find such a group fascinating, Miranda."

"Perhaps." Miranda nodded absently. She hoped Mrs. Willy-Harris was remembering to water the new seedlings she had set out just before they left for London. "One wonders that Aunt Isobel will have the time to bring Lucy out," she said thoughtfully.

"From what I gather"—Katie smiled—"launching a young lady into society in London takes precedence over all other matters."

"Still—" Miranda chewed on her lip, "I confess I am not convinced that this is the wisest course for our Lucy just now. I want nothing more than for Lucy to be happily wed . . . but, at sixteen, she is still quite young, you know.

One wonders how she will fare pitted against other young ladies who, I expect, are far cleverer than she."

"Aunt Isobel says that with a sponsor as powerful as Lady Jersey, Lucy's success is guaranteed. Aunt Isobel referred to Sally as a lioness of the *ton*. I cannot help but think Mama would be thrilled if she knew Lucy is to have a London Season. Papa would be pleased, as well."

"Papa would not like our Lucy to wed a man the likes of Viscount Peterbloom!" Miranda blurted out, her tone suddenly quite agitated.

Katie cast her sister a quizzical look. "I daresay you are judging the gentleman far too harshly, Miranda. His kindness toward us at the inn was unsurpassed. You forget, he was the only gentleman to step forward and offer aid," she reminded her overset sister.

"Nonetheless, I cannot discount all that Lady Jersey said about him. Where there is smoke, there is fire. I refuse to believe that he is not after our Lucy, Katie." It was on the tip of Miranda's tongue to tell Katie of her seeing Lord Peterbloom that afternoon on her way to Mr. Fitch's office, but she decided against it. Hopefully she had succeeded in discouraging the gentleman, and they would never see his handsome face again. At least, she fervently hoped that to be the case.

"Lady Jersey mentioned our Lucy snagging an earl, or better," Katie said. "Perhaps she has someone in mind."

"I only pray that she does," Miranda said forcefully.

"Do you, Miranda?"

"Do I what?"

"Do you pray, Sister?"

"Well, of course, I do, Katie. I have not forgot all that Papa taught us."

"I confess I worry for you on that head, Miranda."

"Well, then you may put your mind at ease."

"It is just that I . . . I should so very like to see our Lucy happily wed."

"As do I. But I assure you she would not be happy wed to that rakehell!"

"Miranda!" Katie looked shocked. "Must you persist in slandering that nice young man?"

Miranda sniffed and thrust her chin up a notch. "Where there's smoke, there's fire," she muttered again.

"I truly do not believe we have a thing to concern ourselves with on that head."

"Hummph!" Miranda sputtered. "I doubt you would find him attending a meeting for the Society to Suppress Vice and Corruption!"

Katie again looked aghast. "You are indeed judging him unfairly, Miranda. One would think you harbored a personal grudge against the gentleman. And that, of course, cannot be true. Both our Aunt Isobel and Lady Jersey agreed that there was very little truth to those frightful *on-dits.* I expect the tales regarding his . . . escapades as a young man were quite highly exaggerated. He may have been a bit of a wild card in his youth, but that does not mean he would conduct himself in such a fashion today. So far as I am concerned, Lord Peterbloom has already proved his character to us. And I did not find him the least bit lacking"

Miranda clamped her lips tightly shut. She wondered what her sisters or her aunt or even Lady Jersey would say if they knew *she* had been one of those fifty innocent young ladies the Viscount Peterbloom had shamelessly plundered that night? It had been the height of the season when she and Katie were last in Town; there had been two other gentlemen with Peterbloom that night, and he had stolen a kiss from her. So, there it was. She knew of few leopards whose spots changed with age. Actually, she knew no leopards at all, but that did not signify. The analogy stood.

When a sudden image of the handsome gentleman sitting astride his horse this afternoon sprang to mind, her anger increased. Lord Peterbloom, was, indeed, a shameless libertine, otherwise he would not be so intent upon spoiling their Lucy.

She thrust thoughts of the evil man aside and changed the subject. Sort of. "I wonder who amongst the village lads has been trifling with our Lucy?" she asked Katie.

"I expect it was Theodore O'Malley." Katie grinned. "She is quite fond of him, you know."

"But Teddy is just a boy," Miranda protested. *And she had been just a girl when the Viscount Peterbloom had . . . Oh!* Miranda's nostrils flared again with rage.

"Lucy is quite mature for her age, Miranda. If you did not keep your nose buried in a book or a flowerpot, you might have noticed that our Lucy has quite grown up."

At Katie's mention of the penny novels Miranda liked to read, and which she took great pains to conceal from her sisters, Miranda's eyes cut round. "My . . . books?"

Katie laughed. "Yes, Miranda. Those tattered little Minerva novels you borrow from Mrs. Willy-Harris and that you attempt to carry concealed in your apron pocket."

"You know about them?" Miranda looked sheepish.

"Even Papa knew about them. And," Katie's brown eyes twinkled mischievously, "I confess, even I have read one or two on occasion."

"You, Katie?" Miranda felt a gurgle of laughter bubble up in her throat and she had to admit that it felt quite good. She had had very little to laugh about the past several days.

"Some of the stories are quite entertaining," Katie said. "I admit I have dreamt of . . . falling in love."

"Have you, Katie?" The fire in Miranda's green eyes softened. "I confess I have wondered on occasion what love would feel like, as well."

"You will meet a gentleman someday, Miranda. You are but one and twenty, there is still plenty of time for you. As for me . . ." Her voice trailed off. "I fear I am destined to spend the rest of my days on the shelf. Who would have an old maid like me?" Her smile grew a trifle sad.

Miranda's chin shot up defiantly. "Any number of gentlemen would be proud to have you for a bride, Katie." She fell silent, then said, "I wish I were more like you."

Katie was listening raptly.

"You are so very good and kind, Katie. Would that I could be as gentle as you are."

"You are good and kind, Miranda. While it is true that you are far more spirited and lively than I, you have a warm heart, and you are every bit as pretty as Lucy. I fear Lucy can often be quite . . . thoughtless."

Miranda said nothing. It was true, Lucy was thoughtless on occasion, but not a one of her sisters was cursed with *her* greatest fault.

Katie was watching her sister closely. "Yes, Miranda, you do possess a temper." Her gaze was gentle as she seemed to read Miranda's very thoughts. Katie's astuteness had astonished Miranda on more than one occasion. "I only pray your impulsiveness will not land you in deep trouble one day, Sister."

"I do try to curb my temper, Katie. Truly, I do."

A faraway look crept into Katie's eyes. "You will meet a gentleman one day who will love you just as you are, Miranda." Her brown head tilted to one side. "I have the strangest feeling, Sister, that our lives are somehow inexplicably linked with the Viscount Peterbloom's. We met him that night at the inn, when we could have met any number of other gentlemen. And it was *he* who came to our aid when we needed help." She gazed up at Miranda, who had suddenly jumped to her feet and whose cheeks were suddenly growing quite pink. "Do you not find that extraordinary, Miranda?"

Unable to think of a thing to say, Miranda simply bid

her sister a hasty good night and retreated across the corridor to the safety of her own bedchamber.

In the wee hours of the morning, Miranda awoke with a start. In her dreams, the most splendidly handsome man in the world was leaning over her bed, a gentle smile on his lips as he watched her sleep. When she tried to blink the vivid image away, the gentleman refused to vanish, instead, his sculptured features softened into a dazzling smile and the warm, loving look emanating from his dark-brown eyes was . . . enough to bring tears to hers.

Eight

His mind focused upon the work he'd set for himself this morning, the Viscount Peterbloom picked his way through the intricately laid-out garden behind his home and entered the potting shed adjacent to the greenhouse. The day was bright and sunny, at least it appeared to be this far from the city, and Peterbloom was especially looking forward to spending the entire morning at his workbench.

He'd returned from another trip to the wharf late last evening with quite a large sampling of exotic seeds and a variety of new plantings that a trader he was acquainted with had collected for him during the sea dog's latest voyage. Peterbloom had met the crusty old gentleman five years ago when he, himself, left Town in order to travel the world and contemplate the sordid direction his own life had taken.

Peterbloom felt quite relaxed this morning. His ailing mother was again resting comfortably, following a brief visit from Dr. Keating, who was one of the few people from Peterbloom's salad days he still associated with. Keating was a childhood friend, who during Peterbloom's years of rather debauched living, had known that beneath the jaded surface there still beat the heart of a worthwhile human being.

From the top shelf just inside the potting-shed door,

Peterbloom selected a few items: a small knife, a piece of twine, and an amber bottle that contained his own secret formula of granulated nutrients, guaranteed to awaken the precious life within dormant seeds and cause them to grow with vigor. He then entered the greenhouse and set to work.

An hour later, Peterbloom had nestled more than a dozen seeds into warm beds of rich, dark soil, and separated and planted a handful of seemingly lifeless seedlings into compact clay pots. He placed all the new plants on a sunny ledge in the greenhouse, then turned his attention to a delicate operation he was especially looking forward to—grafting a stem from a gall-oak tree the trader had brought with him from India to the sturdy English breed growing in his own garden. By hybridizing the two, Peterbloom hoped to create a strong plant that would yield a health-giving sap, useful in a number of healing herbal tisanes. He'd know in a matter of days if the graft was successful, and in a fortnight or two, he'd transplant the healthy plant into a larger pot and move it from the incubation shelf to the garden where he hoped the tree would thrive and grow.

Peterbloom enjoyed the peaceful serenity that surrounded him in his greenhouse. The soothing sounds of birds chirping in the garden and the occasional hum of a bee flitting by added greatly to the tranquil ambiance. By noon, however, he began to feel a bit peckish, and deciding it was also time to look in on his mother, he began to clear away the work space before him, absently gathering the brownish twigs and leaves he just snipped from an assortment of mature plants into a small pile. As he was brushing the strawlike clippings onto the floor, he became aware of something tugging for attention at the back of his mind.

Unable to put a finger on precisely what it was at first, it suddenly occurred to him that the brownish haylike snippings sifting through his fingers reminded him of the tattered Gypsy bonnet Miss Miranda Fraser had been wearing the other afternoon when he'd chanced upon her tilbury in the Strand. His lips twitched again with amusement.

What was it about the spirited little country mouse that so intrigued him?

She was not the flashy sort of young lady who years back would have captured his notice—although her petite stature quite appealed to him, as did her snapping green eyes and short, dark curls. However, the attraction meant nothing. These days, he wasted no time at all ruminating on the charms of the fairer sex, that is, unless one counted the occasional indulgence of a gentleman's normal urges, which, since Peterbloom had abandoned what had years ago amounted to nothing short of a revolting lifestyle, he now managed to satisfy in quite a discreet manner.

No longer a dedicated rakehell whose life constantly teetered on the brink of disaster, Peterbloom was now a reformed man, whose half-decade of traveling about the world had spawned within him a new appreciation for life and all living things. He took great pride now in his sensitivity to the various nuances of nature and to that delicate balance between life and death inherent within all human beings. He read constantly, eager to discuss new ideas on medicines and herbal remedies and cures with his lifelong friend, Dr. Reginald Keating.

In fact, he was looking forward to spending this very evening in Keating's company. The two planned to attend a formal dinner given in order to raise money for a charitable concern that Peterbloom firmly believed in—the completion of the new surgeon's hospital begun some months back on the site of an abandoned building near Mayfair.

Though Peterbloom's passion for plants now bordered on obsession, he enjoyed his work immensely. He'd recently begun the tedious process of cataloging each and every plant he'd cultivated over the past several years. On good days, when she felt up to it, his mother helped. Although Lady Peterbloom was unable to visit the cluttered but cheerful greenhouse, Peterbloom frequently carried the frail old lady to the little gazebo in the garden where the pair of them sat together for hours at a time, Peterbloom poring over his journals, his mother, at times, transcribing her son's hastily scribbled notes into a well-ordered notebook. Lady Peterbloom maintained that her son's work with healing herbs would one day benefit all mankind.

Peterbloom smiled to himself now as he made his way back to the house. As a young man, his mother used to be at him constantly to mend his wicked ways and do his duty, which meant, marry a proper young lady and produce an heir. She rarely spoke to him in that vein now. Peterbloom suspected she was simply grateful that five years ago, when he had seemingly dedicated his life to serious raking, he hadn't got himself killed by some amour's jealous husband. More than once he had had to exit in haste when a gentleman who'd not been expected to return home for hours had suddenly done so. Those days were behind him now. Peterbloom was vastly content with his well-ordered life and had no plans to change it.

Luncheon was just over at the Heathrow town house in Mayfair and Lady Heathrow had whisked Lucy and Elinor off to the hairdresser's to have their hair professionally dressed. Katie and Miranda were enjoying a coze in the small upstairs sitting room.

"I do wish you'd accompany us to Almack's tonight, Miranda," Katie said. "Lady Jersey secured a voucher for you, as well, and it would mean so very much to Lucy if you were there." Katie's brown eyes were alight with anticipation. "This could very well be our only opportunity to visit the famous Assembly rooms. It would give us something to tell our friends about when we return home to Halifax," she added with a laugh.

Miranda smiled as she listened to her sister's gentle plea. She had ceased wondering how Aunt Isobel had persuaded Uncle John to finance Lucy's come-out, though she was certain he was aware of it. Aunt Isobel had mentioned that he would be accompanying them to Almack's tonight. Miranda attributed the change in her uncle's attitude to her aunt's new-found courage, a direct result of the girl's sudden appearance in Town. Aunt Isobel was determined to mend the rift that had torn her from her sister's side those many years ago.

Katie was watching her sister intently. "I know how disappointed you are, Miranda, over not yet getting to see Mr. Fitch, but so long as the gentleman is not even in London, there is nothing to be done about the matter until he returns."

A sigh of frustration escaped Miranda. "I admit waiting the whole of this week for him to return to his office has quite lowered my spirits."

"Do you yet know . . . which Mr. Fitch is ours?"

A smile softened Miranda's lips. "I've narrowed the field to two. While Betsy and I were sitting in the foyer yesterday, I overheard another gentleman refer to the *late* Mr. Fitch. I took that to mean that at least one of them would not be returning any time soon."

Katie grinned. "Well, I shall take it to mean that you should accompany Lucy and me to Almack's tonight. The outing will do you good, Sister.

Miranda absently fingered the frayed edging on the sleeve of her well-worn blue stuff gown. "I would adore going with you, Katie, but, as you well know, I've nothing appropriate to wear."

"Nonsense." Katie sprang to her feet, a smile of delight

now on her lips. "You shall wear one of my new gowns. We are very nearly the same size. Come. We shall decide this very minute which one will suit. And, if it needs a bit of altering, we have all afternoon in which to do it."

"Miranda, I am *so* pleased you decided to join us," Lady Heathrow said as the party of five women settled themselves inside the elegant, high-sprung Heathrow coach that evening. "I wish I could have ordered something special for you to wear, but you look quite charming in Katie's ice-green sarcenet. Does she not look pretty, John?"

Beneath bushy gray brows, Lord Heathrow's eyes cut round. "I have decided to spend the evening at my club tonight, madam," he announced grumpily.

"But you will return to collect us before eleven," Lady Heathrow admonished. "You recall the doors to the Assembly rooms are closed promptly at eleven, John, and no one is allowed to enter."

Lord Heathrow nodded irritably, and with an impatient wave of his hand, signaled the driver to be off after the ladies had alighted on the flagway in King Street. Lady Heathrow ushered her charges inside, where Miranda and her sisters became instantly enthralled by the many splendors within.

"I have never seen so many candles," Miranda breathed, gazing about with awe. "And all of them lit."

"It is as bright as heaven must be," Katie murmured.

"It *is* heaven!" Lucy exclaimed happily.

Miranda cast a wary glance at her younger sister. Lucy looked beautiful tonight in a sheer white dimity gown with a lilac ribbon tied beneath her full breasts. Garlands of embroidered white roses decorated the long skirt and the low-cut bodice of the rather simple gown, which Lady Jersey had insisted a girl of Lucy's tender years was expected to wear. Despite that, the bodice of the dress had been altered a bit, which to Miranda's mind was quite unnecessary, for it now revealed a good deal more of Lucy's charms than Miranda thought prudent. But Lady Jersey maintained that Lucy's bosom was far too magnificent to conceal entirely.

"We must use every weapon in our arsenal," Sally said.

The scandalous cut of Lucy's gown was one more reason Miranda had agreed to come along tonight. Someone had to protect Lucy's virtue, and although she did not expect they would be accosted here by the notorious Lord Peterbloom, Miranda did not feel entirely secure anywhere they went in Town. After all, who'd have thought anything untoward could have happened to her while ensconced in the safe confines of her uncle Oliver's garden?

Trailing behind Aunt Isobel through the arched doorway that gave onto the ballroom, Miranda gave a nervous little tug to the bodice of the pretty satin gown she had on. She was not accustomed to wearing anything quite so revealing herself, although she admitted she felt quite grand tonight as the whisper-soft folds of the long, elegant skirt brushed against her legs. A pair of elbow-length white kid gloves and green satin slippers completed the ensemble. Katie had on a champagne-colored silk gown trimmed with gold thread and Elinor looked sweet in a blue silk gown with tufts of silver lace on the sleeves and hem.

Inside the brilliantly lit Assembly room, the women were joined at once by Lady Jersey and a host of other Important Patronesses, and from that moment on, the evening became a blur of welcoming smiles and polite conversation as the lioness Lady Jersey presented Lucy to the *ton.* As the hours dragged by, Miranda, Katie, and Elinor seemed to slip further and further to the rear of the noisy throng of women clustered about Lady Heathrow, Lady Jersey, and a beaming Lucy.

"Lucy is already a huge success," Elinor remarked to her cousins.

Miranda detected not the least trace of envy in Elinor's tone as the three of them—Katie, wearing a proud look on her face—continued to watch Lucy, who appeared to be quite enjoying herself in the limelight.

Some moments later, Miranda mused, "Does it not seem a bit odd to you that the other women, who are also seeking husbands for their daughters, should so quickly welcome another young lady into the fold, especially one so lovely as our Lucy?"

Elinor smiled. "To slight her, Miranda, would be to run the risk of having their own daughters cut. That is why having a sponsor as powerful as Lady Jersey is so very important. Lucy will be invited to all the balls now."

"I see," Miranda murmured. To say truth, she hoped Lucy did snag an earl or better, for it would, indeed, bring all their troubles to an end.

"From the look of it," Katie said, "Lucy will soon have a goodly number of suitors to choose from."

Miranda nodded in agreement. A number of eligible gentlemen had already made their way to Lucy's side. Although, the second they left, the gentleman's title, holdings, and income were ticked off by one or another of the patronesses in quite a matter-of-fact manner.

"Only a baronet, but he has twenty thousand a year."

"The Duke of Fronton. A good catch, indeed, if one can get past his unfortunate looks."

"He may be an earl, but he hasn't a feather to fly with. I wouldn't if I were you, dear."

Miranda's long gaze swept the sea of unknown faces gathered in the spacious ballroom. That a certain dark-haired gentleman whose dazzling smile had an odd way of setting her heart aflutter was *not* here, lifted her spirits considerably. Perhaps Lady Jersey did have the right of it where the infamous Lord Peterbloom was concerned.

"Lord Peterbloom did not make a habit of showing his

face on the Marriage Mart five years ago, Lucy dear. It is highly unlikely you will ever see him at Almack's."

Though Lucy had expressed supreme disappointment over that, Miranda had smiled broadly when she'd heard the pronouncement.

As the hour of eleven neared and the Viscount Peterbloom was nowhere to be seen, she began to relax a bit more. When Elinor suggested that she and Katie retire to the row of chairs lining the wall in order to wait out the remainder of the evening, Miranda cast one last anxious gaze at Lucy before following her cousin to the sidelines. Not a single one of the girls, she mused, including Lucy, who'd been kept far too busy meeting the *ton,* had been asked to dance. Miranda had enjoyed watching those on the dance floor, but, as she and her sisters had not had the advantage of dance lessons, not a one of them knew how anyway.

As she and Katie slipped onto a straight-backed bench along the wall, Miranda noted Elinor's attention diverted by some sort of disturbance near the arched doorway of the ballroom. Miranda glanced in that direction and was astonished to see at least two dozen women suddenly run shrieking and tittering toward the foyer. Miranda strained to see over the heads of the crowd but was unable to catch even a glimpse of what the trouble might be.

"What has happened?" Katie murmured, leaning closer to Miranda's ear, her eyes, as well, trained that way.

Suddenly, at the top of the room the orchestra struck up a fanfare and nearly everyone in the ballroom broke into riotous applause.

"Why, look!" Katie cried, springing to her feet, a gloved finger pointing as the crush of people at the door spontaneously separated into a clear aisle down the center. "It is very like the parting of the Red Sea."

Miranda's brows drew together as she, too, rose to her

feet to catch a glimpse of the phenomena. "But why . . . who?"

"Oh, my!" Elinor excitedly exclaimed. "It is Father and . . . and the Viscount Peterbloom!"

Miranda's knees buckled beneath her. With an alarmed gasp, she reached for the wooden arm of the bench in order to support herself.

Her worst nightmare was about to come true!

Nine

In a very few seconds, an indignant Lord Heathrow came stalking toward the tight knot of women gathered about his wife. "Devil take it!" he grumbled, twitching at his shirt cuffs with first one gloved hand and then the other. "One would think there were no other gentlemen present here tonight!"

Miranda, with Katie and Elinor close on her heels, scurried toward Lord and Lady Heathrow, Miranda intent upon reaching Lucy's side before *he* did.

"My," Katie marveled, "Lord Peterbloom is as popular as . . . as surely the Prince must be."

"More popular," Elinor said simply. "The Prince is very often booed."

Miranda was tempted.

"Did you see him?" Lucy cried, excitedly squeezing Miranda's arm. "Lord Peterbloom has come! Uncle John said he'd bumped into him at his club tonight, and when Uncle John said he was coming to collect us at Almack's, Lord Peterbloom asked if he might come along. Isn't it thrilling?"

Miranda didn't think so, but she was far too overset now to speak her mind on the subject.

"He has come especially to see me," Lucy insisted. "I just know it! Lady Jersey said it was fortunate he wasn't wearing trousers."

At that, both Miranda and Katie gasped aloud.

Lucy giggled. "He would be turned away at the door if he had not been formally attired. Doesn't he look dashing in his black coat and white satin knee breeches?"

Miranda's lips pursed. How the *ton* kept all their silly rules straight was beyond her.

"It appears Lord Peterbloom is *quite* well liked, Lucy dear," Katie ventured, her gaze still fixed on the gentleman as he and the press of cloying women clustered about him slowly made their way across the glittering ballroom. "Perhaps he did not come *especially* to see you, sweetheart."

"He did, Katie!" Lucy stamped her foot. "I know he did!"

"Lucy, dear," Miranda began, trying, despite the white-hot anger pulsing within her, to maintain a calm tone with her younger sister. "Katie may very well have the right of it. You mustn't be too terribly disappointed if the gentleman—"

"Good evening, ladies."

Before a single one of the Fraser girls had a chance to address Lord Peterbloom, the group of fawning women that had been clustered about Lady Jersey now turned their attention to the devilishly attractive viscount. Literally shoved from Lucy's side by the more insistent of his admirers, Miranda felt near sick to her stomach by the outrageous display.

Presently, the ladies quieted down and Lady Jersey, who was standing closest to the gentleman, said, "I daresay I speak for all of us when I say I never thought to see your handsome face here, Peterbloom." She tapped his sleeve flirtatiously with her folded-up fan. "Does this mean we will commence to see you . . . elsewhere this Season?" Her eyes twinkled merrily as she lifted an artfully curved hand, presumably for the gentleman to kiss.

Peterbloom clasped Sally's elegantly gloved fingertips,

but merely nodded politely. "A delight to see you again, Lady Jersey."

Suddenly, pandemonium broke loose once again as every woman in the group began to wave her gloved fingertips beneath the Viscount Peterbloom's nose. Miranda's eyes rolled skyward as she willingly allowed herself to be pushed even further to the fringe of the cloying crowd.

At length, the hubbub subsided and Miranda heard Lady Jersey's voice again. "I have decided to allow you to be the first to stand up with my lovely new find, Miss Lucy Fraser. But only one dance, mind you. This is her first evening out and I positively forbid you to monopolize her."

A wave of murmuring and indrawn breaths were heard from the other women. Peterbloom darted a cool glance at the beaming debutante, who throughout the confusion had steadfastly held her ground beside him. "I would consider it an honor to stand up with Miss Lucy," he said politely.

A squeal of delight escaped Lucy's pink lips. "Oh, sir!" she cried, and latched at once on to the arm he extended.

Having caught only a glimpse of the above action from her tenuous position on the edge of the crowd, Miranda now watched the viscount, who stood a good head and shoulders taller than all of the women and even the few gentlemen gathered there, aim a gaze at the very spot where she and Katie stood, a few yards behind Lady Jersey. Apparently Katie took the look to mean that the gentleman was seeking their permission as well to dance with Lucy. With a reassuring smile on her face, Katie quickly nodded assent.

Miranda wished she had the courage to deny it, but fearing a scene from Lucy, she held her tongue and with a pounding heart merely watched the pair—Lucy, with her flaming auburn hair piled atop her head and the tall, handsome gentleman—as they progressed toward the polished dance floor. Which, because the entire assembly's attention had lately been diverted, was deplorably thin of company.

As the attractive pair reached the edge of the barren dance floor, it suddenly occurred to Miranda that there really was no need at all for her to say a word. She watched as a panic-stricken look crossed her sister's face and Lucy turned to address her escort. Though quite tall herself, Lucy had to stand on tiptoe in order to whisper into the viscount's ear. That gentleman nodded, then with Lucy still on his arm, he turned and headed straight back toward Lady Jersey and whispered something into her ear.

Lady Jersey blinked as if stunned, then flung an appalled gaze at Aunt Isobel, who, apparently having no idea what was amiss, merely shrugged silk-covered shoulders. However, the smug smile that had settled on Miranda's lips disappeared with astonishing rapidity when Lucy and Lord Peterbloom set off again, this time headed for the refreshment table at the bottom of the room.

Faith! She'd hoped Lucy's inability to dance would bring an end to the wastrel's attentions upon her sister.

Miranda watched with growing dismay as Lucy and her elegant escort drifted further and further from sight.

Lord Peterbloom was near speechless by the unprecedented notice his appearance at Almack's was causing tonight. Had he any inkling such a disturbance would have ensued the minute he set foot into the place, he never would have agreed to accompany Lord Heathrow here.

Following the benefit he'd attended tonight with Dr. Keating, he'd decided to stop off at his club for a brandy. Sipping the drink, he'd strolled into the gaming room and spotted Lord Heathrow seated before a green baize table.

Heathrow, it appeared, was enjoying extraordinary good luck at cards tonight. In the few minutes Peterbloom stood by, he watched the gentleman scoop up several piles of crisp pound notes. After another round, Heathrow even accepted a marker from one Lord Ashton—known as Ash to his friends—a notorious gambler who was deep in his cups tonight.

"Thish is m' newest acquisition, Heathrow, mighty proud of it, too," Ashton had said. "All I got left to wager t'night, but mark 'm words, I be wantin' it back! Just as soon as I win thish next round."

"You do that, Ash," Heathrow bellowed. "But you'd best make haste before I dispose of this worthless piece of soil!"

The company of men had guffawed loudly as it was well known about Town that Lord Heathrow was far too tight-fisted to sit on anything that could be turned into ready cash.

When the card game had concluded, Lord Heathrow invited Peterbloom to join him for another drink and the two men had quickly fallen into a discussion regarding the finer points contained in the agricultural report that Peterbloom had compiled for the parliamentary committee to review. Heathrow mentioned that Lord Jersey, as well as a number of the other committee members, also wished to discuss it with him.

"I'm on my way to Almack's now, son. M' wife's presenting one of her nieces. If you'd care to join me, perhaps we could take the matter up with the gentlemen before the committee officially convenes tomorrow."

Peterbloom had eagerly agreed, it not occurring to him that his sudden appearance at the famed Assembly rooms would cause the least bit of notice.

Upon reaching the refreshment table now, Peterbloom silently procured two glasses of watery lemonade and presented one to the smiling young lady who stood beside him.

"I trust this will quench your thirst, Miss Lucy," he murmured politely.

"I adore lemonade, sir. This looks quite delicious!"

A dark brow quirked as Peterbloom brought the insipid brew to his lips and swallowed a cursory sip. Delicious was not a word he'd use to describe the King Street brew. He turned a disinterested gaze toward the dance floor, which now held a sprinkling of couples going through the intricate motions of a French quadrille. Fuzzy memories of the countless routs and soirées he'd attended many years back sifted listlessly through his mind.

"I do apologize for not knowing how to dance, my lord Peterbloom," Lucy said, her tone quite sincere.

"No harm done, Miss Lucy. It was good of you to inform me of that fact before we stepped onto the dance floor." He grinned crookedly and, beside him, Lucy giggled nervously.

"I expect I'd have made quite a cake of myself," she said.

"I daresay you are far too pretty for that ever to be a concern, my dear." Peterbloom regarded her coolly.

She beamed. "So are you, sir," she breathed.

"Excuse me?"

"Pretty. You are . . . very pretty, sir."

Peterbloom's lips twitched. "I do not believe gentlemen are generally described thusly, Miss Lucy."

"I am sorry, sir, but . . . well . . . my sisters and I all think you are the most handsome man we have ever laid eyes on."

Peterbloom digested that. "Your . . . sisters?"

Lucy nodded vigorously.

Peterbloom flicked a gaze over one shoulder, his midnight-black eyes casting about for the petite figure of Miss Miranda Fraser, whom he'd caught only a quick glimpse of when Lady Jersey had foisted her protegée upon him.

"And what of your sisters, Miss Lucy? Does your aunt and Lady Jersey mean to present them, as well?"

Lucy shook her head. "Katie is far too old to make her debut, and Miranda—" At that moment, Lucy spotted someone on the dance floor to whom she had been previously introduced. She giggled and waved excitedly at the rather astonished young lady.

Peterbloom's ears had perked up at the mention of Miss Miranda's name. "You were saying . . . ?"

"Oh!" Lucy gushed. "I feel so very *grand* here with you tonight, Lord Peterbloom. To have a London Season has been my dearest wish!"

The sight of the girl's blue eyes glittering as brightly as sapphires in her flushed face softened the set smile on Peterbloom's lips. "And you look very grand tonight, Miss Lucy," he said. "But you were about to tell me about your sisters," he prodded.

"I am so very lucky!" Lucy went on. "Everyone has been excessively kind to me. You most of all sir." She gazed up again into his eyes. "And Sally is my bosom bow. She is acquainted with *everyone*, and everyone simply adores her!"

"And . . . your . . . sisters, Miss Lucy? Are they also . . . Sally's bosom bows?"

"No." Lucy giggled. "Especially not Miranda. She is such a cross-patch!"

"A cross-patch?" Another gaze flitted toward the sidelines. He noted that Miss Miranda had moved closer to where he and her younger sister stood, and that she was now watching them intently. She looked quite charming tonight in a pale, ice-green satin gown, although . . . the hard look in her eyes and the decided frown upon her face did rather spoil the effect. "A cross-patch, eh?" he murmured again.

Lucy nodded again. "Miranda wants only to go home

to Halifax. If she'd had her way, we'd have left Town the very day we arrived!"

"Is that so?" Peterbloom directed another long gaze at the young lady under discussion. The two made eye contact this time. Peterbloom was about to acknowledge her with a polite nod, but before he could do so, she thrust her pert nose in the air and jerked her head away.

By jove! He elicited the strangest reactions from that young lady!

Thinking further on it, he realized the oddity had begun the night he'd met her at the inn. She'd seemed loath to speak to him that night and excessively eager to remove herself and her sisters from his sight. To be sure, he'd never had such an adverse effect on a young lady before. Most females treated him along the same lines as Miss Lucy and the dozens of others here tonight who seemed eager to . . . ahem, renew old acquaintances. He'd never encountered such a resistant woman before! What could have caused Miss Miranda to take such a strong disliking to him, he wondered?

"Katie doesn't expect ever to marry," Lucy was prattling on beside him. "And Miranda's never had a beau in her life. If you ask me, I doubt she ever will."

His curiosity fully aroused now, Peterbloom asked, "Why ever not? I daresay Miss Miranda is every bit as charming as any young lady here."

Lucy stared at him as if he'd gone daft. Then she shrugged bare shoulders, the action causing her ample breasts to rise and fall seductively. Of their own accord, Peterbloom's eyes drifted downward. Some years back, he'd have found Miss Lucy quite charming, but now . . . His gaze reverted again to the chit's older sister. *What was it about the petite Miss Miranda that drew him so?*

"Katie says Miranda is far too disagreeable," Lucy said airily. "I shouldn't think a gentleman would like that in a lady."

"And what does Miss Miranda find to be so very disagreeable?" Peterbloom asked, every fiber of his being now aching for the least bit of information he could glean regarding the intriguing Miss Miranda.

"Oh, she doesn't like London. She says the air is too sooty and the streets too snarled with traffic. She's never once been shopping with us, but she goes out nearly every day. Personally, I hope she never finds Mr. Fitch in. That way, we shall never have to leave."

"Mr. Fitch?"

"Oh, silly me." Lucy giggled. She took another drink from her nearly empty glass of lemonade. "You haven't the least notion what I am talking about, have you? I declare, I am so atremor to actually be here at Almack's, speaking with you, I seem unable to keep my wits about me beyond a single second."

Peterbloom shifted impatiently from one foot to the other. It might take a bit of doing, but he was determined to unravel the mystery before he returned Miss Lucy to her sponsor.

"If you like," Lucy said, gazing coyly at him from beneath long, dark lashes, "I shall begin at the outset and tell you the whole of it."

Peterbloom brightened visibly. "I would like that above all things, Miss Lucy."

"Just look at them now, John!" Lady Heathrow exclaimed, all but pointing a gloved finger at her niece and the handsome gentleman with whom she was conversing. "Do you not see how Peterbloom is looking at her?"

"If I weren't seeing it with my own eyes, I wouldn't believe it," Lady Jersey remarked dryly before Lord Heathrow had a chance to respond. "As it is, I can scarcely fathom the infamous Lord Peterbloom smitten by a mere schoolgirl."

"I fear we may have already lost our shiny new diamond," Lady Heathrow lamented, although her tone sounded none too sad. "He is hanging on to her every word. A gentleman listening that intently to a young lady can only mean one thing. He is top over tail in love."

Beside her, Lord Heathrow snorted his disgust. "I wouldn't engage the parson right away, Isobel. No doubt Peterbloom finds your niece excessively attractive, but I'll wager he don't mean to saddle himself with the skitterwit for all eternity."

Miranda turned a sharp gaze on her uncle. *If the Viscount Peterbloom did not mean to marry Lucy, precisely what did he intend doing with her?*

The Viscount Peterbloom could not recall hearing anything quite so arresting as the tale spun in the past quarter hour by the fetching Miss Lucy. When she came to the part about the girls' home in Halifax being sold to an unknown London gentleman who meant to turn the cottage into his hunting lodge, he nearly choked on his lemonade. Actually, he did notice a speck of lemon pulp spew forth from his mouth and disappear somewhere in the tangled ringlets of Miss Lucy's hair, but he hadn't the inclination to concern himself with that now. Far more pressing, at the moment, was . . . how to retrieve the marker Lord Ashton had signed over to Heathrow earlier that evening that, unless Peterbloom missed his guess, contained the deed to the very property in Halifax where the Fraser girls' home was situated. He clearly recalled Ash mentioning something about a renovation and a new hunting box.

Moreover, according to Miss Lucy, the girls' aunt and uncle knew nothing of their troubles, which explained why Heathrow had said nothing at the gaming table regarding the fortunate turn of luck that literally dropped the deed to the property in his lap.

Peterbloom could not contain the sly grin that lifted one corner of his mouth. The scheme forming in his mind was a tad bit devilish, but what better way to ensure that, in time, Miss Miranda Fraser would find him equally as attractive as he found her?

"I expect I've kept you to myself quite long enough, Miss Lucy," Peterbloom said at length. "Although, may I say, I have enjoyed our coze immensely?"

Lucy's blue eyes sparkled happily. "Not nearly so much as I, sir. Not nearly so."

Peterbloom cleared his throat. "Well, then . . . shall we?" He extended an arm, which she latched quite firmly on to.

Once across the room, Peterbloom returned Miss Lucy to her sponsor, and after exchanging the proper pleasantries with the other women there, he purposely ignored Miss Miranda and turned to address Lord Heathrow.

"Might I have a private word with you, sir?"

Heathrow flung a startled look at his wife, then on a resigned breath, said, "Very well, son. Just hope you know what you're getting into."

"Beg pardon, sir?"

The two men were barely out of earshot before Lucy began to squeal with delight.

"Oh, Sally, do you think he loves me as much as I love him? Do you? Is he offering for me this very insta—"

"Do be still, child." Lady Jersey's tone was mildly censorious, although her eyes had, as well, registered surprise when Lord Peterbloom requested the private audience with Heathrow. "At this juncture, we cannot be certain of a thing." She tapped her chin thoughtfully with her folded-up fan. "I daresay we shall know soon enough what the gentlemen are discussing."

Soon enough was not soon enough for Miranda. Having experienced a sickening wave of terror as she overheard the above conversation, she was determined not to waste a single second in uncovering for herself the true nature of the gentlemen's tête-à-tête. Unnoticed by the other women in the party, she ducked behind an alabaster pillar, then scurried after the men into the foyer.

Reaching it, she hid behind a potted palm and commenced to peek between two feathery branches at the pair of gentlemen standing only a few feet from her.

"I admit you had me a trifle worried there," Lord Heathrow was saying on a laugh. He reached into his waistcoat pocket and handed something across to the viscount. "Here you are. Though what you want with this worthless piece of chattel is beyond me."

Not knowing for certain what the gentlemen were referring to as a "worthless piece of chattel," Miranda bristled only slightly and continued to listen.

"Suffice to say, I've plans of my own that do not include marriage or settling down in the country," the viscount said, also laughing. "At least not at present."

Miranda's eyes widened. *What had he just said?*

"What shall I tell Ash when he comes round demanding this back?"

Peterbloom grinned slyly. "You may send anyone, *anyone,* who inquires into this matter straight to me, sir."

"Very well, son. Will do."

Miranda chewed on her lower lip as she watched Lord Peterbloom stride toward the street. So as not to be caught eavesdropping once again by her uncle, she whirled about and hurried back into the Assembly room. *Had she been dead wrong about the viscount?* Had they *all* been dead wrong about him? So far as she could see, not a single reference to Lucy had been made by either of the men. Lord Peterbloom had been quite clear when he said he had no intention of marrying anyone at present. Apart from the fact that Lucy would be disappointed beyond measure over what had *not* transpired between the gentlemen just now, Miranda realized she hadn't felt this elated since she and her sisters had arrived in Town.

Rejoining the party of women inside the ballroom, she thanked the good Lord for small favors. Perhaps Katie did have the right of it. Perhaps she had been oversetting herself needlessly. All would, indeed, turn out well. Just as soon as she was able to speak personally with Mr. Fitch.

Ten

For the first time in a long time that night, Miranda slept like a babe. How blessedly glorious it felt to put her worries about the Viscount Peterbloom behind her and fix all her attention on her prime reason for coming to London. Of course, with Mr. Fitch out of the city for the whole of this week, there was still nothing to be done toward settling the matter of their home, but all the same, having her mind finally at ease where Lord Peterbloom was concerned felt like a giant leap forward.

By luncheon of the following day, the silver salver in the foyer of the Heathrow town house was brim full of cards—many with the corners turned down. Included among them were invitations to a vast number of balls, musical evenings, and important society functions. Lady Heathrow spent the better part of the midday meal exclaiming over Lucy's splendid success the night before at Almack's.

"The only blemish I can detect in an otherwise perfect evening," the older woman said, "is the discovery that you young ladies have not had the benefit of dance lessons. But we shall remedy that straightaway. I engaged a music master this morning, and a dance instructor will be here in—" she consulted the pretty gold watch she wore pinned to the bodice of her gown—"precisely one hour."

"Oh, my," Katie murmured, "have we sufficient time to finish our meal, dress and . . . get there?"

Seated beside her, Elinor giggled shyly. "Our teachers come to us," she said, grinning at her lookalike cousin.

"Oh. Of course. Silly me."

Miranda suddenly thought back to the conversation she'd overheard between her aunt and uncle in which Uncle John had said it would take a battery of tutors to bring the girls up to the mark. Since Uncle John was not at table today, she could only guess what denigrating remark he might have made if he'd known his predictions were coming true. She glanced across the table at Lucy, who, thus far, had expressed no enthusiasm whatsoever over the proposed dance lessons. In fact, Lucy had seemed unusually quiet all morning.

"Are you feeling unwell today, Lucy dear?" she asked.

Lucy barely glanced up from the plate from which she had not eaten a bite.

"Sweetie, what is it? You've barely said a word all day."

Lucy shrugged and continued to listlessly toy with the delicious delicacies on her plate.

Presently, Lady Heathrow said, "Is something amiss, Lucy dear? If you are not feeling well, I shall have Walker send for a physician at once."

They all watched as Lucy's lips pressed together tightly, but her eyes remained downcast.

"Lucy, do tell us what is amiss?" Katie insisted.

Katie turned to address the girl's aunt. "Last night may have been a bit overmuch for her, Aunt Isobel. Not a one of us is accustomed to staying up so very late, or to such a . . . great deal of excitement. Perhaps we should forgo the dance lessons today and let Lucy rest—"

Just then, Lucy sprang from her chair and, with a little cry, scampered from the room.

"Oh, dear," Lady Heathrow exclaimed.

"I'll go and see to her," Katie said. A servant rushed

forward to pull Katie's chair out and she hurried after her sister.

A possible reason for Lucy's dejected state occurred to Miranda. "Aunt Isobel, did you or . . . Uncle John divulge to Lucy the nature of the private conversation between our uncle and the Viscount Peterbloom last evening?"

"Why, no. That is, I mentioned nothing about it to Lucy. John informed me this morning that the discussion concerned a simple business matter. Since it did not involve . . . what we thought it did, I saw no reason to speak of it to Lucy." She aimed a glance in the direction the young ladies had vanished. "Do you suppose . . . ?"

Miranda nodded "If you will excuse me, please?"

"Of course, dear."

Miranda darted up the stairs to Lucy's bedchamber where she felt certain she'd find both her sisters. Hurrying down the corridor toward the suite, she could already hear Lucy's plaintive sobs. Gaining the room, she found Katie standing beside the bed, upon which Lucy had flung herself.

"She is inconsolable," Katie lamented. "She was certain the Viscount Peterbloom meant to offer for her last evening, and since Uncle John said nothing about it—"

"I know," Miranda said, her irritation with the heartless libertine returning once again in full force. She slipped onto the bed beside Lucy. "Sweetie, do stop crying. The horrid man is not worth the trouble."

"Oh!" Lucy lifted a tearstained face to glare at her sister. "Don't talk about him that way, Miranda! He is an *exquisite!"*

Miranda's lips pursed. Where had Lucy heard that term, she wondered.

"I shall die if I cannot have him!" Lucy wailed.

Miranda and Katie exchanged helpless looks, Miranda becoming painfully aware of the familiar churning sensation returning again to her stomach. There was only one way she could think of to placate her overset younger sister, though she detested giving voice to the thought.

Still, she drew a deep breath and said, "I am certain you will have another chance to win him over, sweetie. Aunt Isobel means for us to attend quite a number of balls and soirées in the next few weeks. Lord Peterbloom will most assuredly be at some of them. It is quite early in the Season, you know. Perhaps he thinks it wise that you meet other gentlemen, so that you might be . . . certain of him." A wave of revulsion washed over her when she voiced that sentiment, but, nonetheless, she pushed on. "You saw for yourself what a splendid reception he received last evening at Almack's, and how, once there, he ignored all the other young ladies and advanced straight to you. After fetching you lemonade, he left."

Lucy's sobs eased a bit. With a sniff, she sat up. "I—I hadn't thought of that, Miranda." She brushed aside her tears and grinned sheepishly. "I was so certain he loved me as I love him. Perhaps I was expecting him to declare himself far too early. He will come round, won't he?"

Miranda nodded tightly as she reached to tuck an errant lock of her sister's hair back into place.

"I am certain he cares for you, Lucy dear," Katie put in. "When Sally noted how very intently he was listening to you last evening, she said it could only mean one thing. That he was top over tail in love. He is quite devoted to you."

The roiling in Miranda's stomach became a hard fist of anxiety. "Even if he does not come round," she added optimistically, "it is quite clear that you will soon have plenty of other suitors to choose from."

Lucy ignored that comment. "I have decided I should very much like to learn to waltz," she said, springing up from the bed. "The young ladies I spoke with last evening said it was quite romantic to have a gentleman put his arms about one's waist. I should dearly love to waltz with Lord Peterbloom!"

The relieved feeling that had swept over Miranda last night now vanished entirely.

Still, she quite enjoyed the dance lesson, despite the fact that both she and Katie laughingly declared it unlikely they'd have a chance to show off their new skills.

Before the caper merchant took his leave of them, Lucy insisted that he demonstrate the scandalous new dance that everyone was talking about—the waltz.

"It is, indeed, all the rage," Elinor said. "Not everyone is allowed, you know."

Watching the demonstration, Miranda could very well imagine that not all young ladies would have their mama's permission to dance in such a brazen fashion! She wondered if she ought to forbid Lucy to perform it with Lord Peterbloom?

At table that evening, Lady Heathrow announced that they were all to attend a Venetian breakfast the following day.

"The *ton* throws a party just to eat breakfast?" Lucy asked incredulously, her blue eyes alight with excitement.

"No, dear," Lady Heathrow said on a laugh. "It is simply called that, because, well, I do not know why it is called that. It begins at three of the clock in the afternoon. Does seem a bit silly to call it a 'breakfast,' I suppose." She laughed again.

"Are we not allowed to break our fast before we go?" Lucy queried, her tone quite serious.

"Indeed we are. You may eat both breakfast and luncheon, Lucy dear. I expect the fete should more aptly be called a Venetian *tea*."

* * *

The girls had another dance lesson the following morning so as to give the women plenty of time to prepare for the breakfast and to drive the considerable distance it would take to get to Lord and Lady Malmesbury's by three of the clock.

Although Miranda did not expect to look nearly so fashionable as the others in their party, she donned her best gown, a lilac-sprigged muslin she'd worn several times already. However, when the five women gathered belowstairs in the foyer, Lady Heathrow pulled a face when she caught sight of the frayed straw bonnet atop Miranda's dark curls.

"Oh, my, Miranda. I fear I've been frightfully remiss in tricking you out. Elinor, do send Betsy abovestairs to fetch one of your bonnets for Miranda. Make haste, girls, our carriage is at the curb now."

An hour later, the Heathrow coach wheeled into the wide circular drive before the lovely country home of Lord and Lady Malmesbury located a few miles beyond London on the new Oxford road. Already, several groups of fashionably turned-out folk were strolling across the shady lawn toward a bevy of colorful barges lined up along the shore of a sparkling little lake.

Gazing across the expanse of greensward and the pretty water, Miranda spotted a striped tent affair with bright red flags at all four corners that were gaily whipping back and forth in the breeze. On the green velvet lawn surrounding the open-air tent, several different types of outdoor games were in progress. She recognized shuttlecock and battledore, and even an archery range, where a number of young ladies, assisted by liveried footmen, were taking turns with the oversize bows and arrows.

As the Heathrow party set out for the barges, Lucy

caught up to Miranda. "Do you think *he* will be here, Miranda?" she whispered into her sister's ear.

It was the first mention Lucy had made of the gentleman since her outburst a few days back. Because Lucy had not spoken of the viscount since, Miranda had silently hoped her sister had forgotten all about the attractive man. She had certainly endeavored to do the same herself, and except for the occasional dream she continued to have about the wretch, she had very nearly succeeded.

She schooled her features to remain impassive now. "Oh, I shouldn't think so, Lucy dear, it being daytime. Uncle John had a committee meeting to attend this afternoon. I shouldn't be surprised if Lord Peterbloom did, as well."

"Oh." Lucy smiled bravely. She looked quite lovely this afternoon in a gown of frothy blue tulle that brought out the blue of her eyes. The dress had large puffy sleeves and a wide flounce round the hem. When a breeze wafted by, the skirt of Lucy's gown fairly floated round her long, slim legs. Tilting her chin up, Lucy unfurled the pretty matching blue parasol she carried and skipped on ahead of Miranda toward the shoreline.

Miranda was pleased to see that, at once, two splendidly turned-out young men stepped forward, each intent upon helping Lucy into the flat-bottomed boat of her choice. Miranda sighed. Surely with all the attention her pretty younger sister was likely to draw in the next few weeks, she'd meet another gentleman who'd be a far more suitable candidate for her hand than the odious Viscount Peterbloom.

Once they'd all gained the opposite side of the lake, the Heathrow women drifted apart, Lady Heathrow seeking out the company of Lady Malmesbury, who was conversing with others of their friends, and Katie, with Elinor at her side, opting for a stroll along the water's edge. Lucy was swept away with her gentlemen friends and several young ladies who were headed toward the archery range. Left to her own devices, Miranda was drawn to a field carpeted with bluebells just beyond the refreshment tent.

For half an hour or more, she amused herself admiring the pretty wildflowers. Beyond the bluebells, she discovered a splashy bed of scarlet pimpernel and pale lemon charlock, and adjacent to it, a field of cornflowers and cow parsley. She'd hadn't seen such a wide variety of flowers since coming to London. She suddenly felt quite homesick for Halifax.

As she was bending over to examine the delicate purple blooms growing on a long stem of foxglove, the deep sound of a gentleman's voice coming from behind her made her jump.

"I shouldn't think Lady Malmesbury would mind if you plucked one or two."

Miranda whirled about and spotted *him* lounging against a nearby tree, a half-grin on his face as he stood watching her. *Had he been here all along or had he been following her?* Her alarm grew when she realized she'd wandered a good deal farther afield than she'd intended. Not a single other party guest was anywhere in sight!

"I . . . I had no idea that I was not alone, sir," she said, trying desperately to still the rapid pounding of her heart.

Lord Peterbloom's gaze on her did not waver as she watched him push up from the tree and move a few steps closer to her. Hardly realizing she was doing so, Miranda advanced the same number of steps backward.

"I—I really should be returning to the party," she murmured.

He grinned, his dark eyes crinkling at the corners. "You're not likely to meet up with them going that direction." He jabbed a thumb over one shoulder. "Most everyone is now enjoying a delicious breakfast inside the tent. Your sisters became alarmed when they discovered you were not amongst them. I gallantly offered to go and search for you."

"Hmmm." The sound was more a high-pitched squeak really. Still, Miranda managed to tilt her chin up bravely, but the smile she'd willed to her face felt a trifle shaky. "As you can plainly see, sir, I am not lost. I was just"—she glanced down at the sea of buttercups at her feet—"admiring the flowers." *Why did he persist in looking at her that way and why did she feel so very . . . captivated by it?*

Lord Peterbloom continued to advance toward her, his long legs moving one slow, deliberate step after another. "Lady Malmesbury has quite a lovely garden," he said in a pleasant tone. "She cultivates a good many herbs. Several physicians—" he directed a long gaze beyond Miranda's right shoulder—"gather herbs here and grind them into medicines. Many have extraordinary healing properties, you know."

Despite her fright at being alone with the infuriating gentleman, Miranda did find his comments arresting. She longed to question him further, herbs being an area of especial interest to her. She stole a tentative glance toward the herb garden.

"Just there," he said, "beyond the potting shed. There's quite a large bed of feverfew that should be in bloom now; and on that slope next to the sycamore is a patch of wild willowherb." His head turned until his piercing dark orbs again locked with Miranda's. "Shall I show you?"

She swallowed tightly. The gentleman looked inordinately handsome this afternoon in a pair of biscuit-colored pantaloons and a forest-green coat over a waistcoat of pale jonquil linen. His dark-brown hair was in tousled disarray, and even from this distance, she could detect about him a pleasant aroma of musk and woodsy lime. The overall effect of his presence upon her sent her pulse racing.

"I . . . I—"

"Thought so," he concluded lazily. His dark head at a

tilt, he strode closer to her, and when next he flashed that dazzling smile of his, Miranda felt her knees turn to jelly. Drawing up beside her, he did not even break stride as he scooped up her small gloved hand in his and draped it possessively over his arm.

Miranda feared she might swoon on the spot when she felt the pressure of his strong fingers curl over her hand. Beneath her fingers, she became acutely aware of the corded muscles of his forearm through the fine fabric of his coat.

Suddenly, she realized that the gentleman had been talking the entire time they'd been walking, but she'd been too distracted by his nearness to hear a single word he'd said. She worked feverishly to ignore the powerful effect his presence was having on her and focus her thoughts instead on what he was saying. Something about nightshade, or navew, or was it filipendula? She couldn't be certain.

"Hmmm," she murmured when a response seemed appropriate, and, "Ah" a bit later.

Presently, the gentleman ceased walking and talking. Instead, he turned and gazed deeply into Miranda's eyes. "You appear to be finding my talk of plants and herbs quite unentertaining, Miss Miranda."

Although his gaze upon her lips seemed fiercely intent, Miranda suddenly realized that she did not feel the least bit fearful. As always—of late, that is—he was behaving like a perfect gentleman.

Miranda found she had to drag her eyes from the dark pools of his in order to formulate a reply. "On the contrary, sir." How she wished to tell him she was desperately interested in growing things, and that she found his talk, and yes, *him,* or, at least, the odd effect he was having upon her, vastly intriguing, but . . .

To her chagrin, the viscount's only response was a deep-throated chuckle.

"Spoken like a young lady who is far too polite to tell a gentleman he is as boring as paste." Lord Peterbloom's dark eyes continued to search hers. At length, he inhaled a deep breath and said, "Perhaps a glass of rataffia and a slice of lemon cake would be more to your liking, my dear."

The seductively low tone of his voice sent an unwelcome ripple of delight coursing through Miranda. Without a word, she let the tall, elegant man escort her back through the fields of colorful wildflowers to the blue-and-white striped tent where refreshments were being served. Very soon afterward, the Viscount Peterbloom took his leave.

He decided the afternoon had been well spent, despite the discovery that Miss Miranda Fraser did not share his absorbing interest in horticulture.

Since Peterbloom's impromptu visit to Almack's the other evening, he'd been virtually flooded with invitations to all the best homes in London. And, to his surprise, he had decided to accept a few of them. Not because he had decided it was time to set his cap at anyone. No. Peterbloom believed himself quite impervious to love. After all, had he been susceptible to that emotion, it would, no doubt, have assailed him five years back when he was virtually surrounded by the *crème de la crème* of England's eligible young ladies.

No, the odd pull he felt toward Miss Miranda Fraser was merely an aberration of some sort. But it, or she, had captured his interest and, truth to tell, he was rather enjoying the diversion. No lady had ever led *him* on a chase before. Another oddity stemming directly from this little intrigue was that he was beginning to feel more like his former self. Jaunty, carefree, with a certain swagger to his step. He hadn't realized what a solemn, almost brooding young man he'd become. He had quite enjoyed stepping out this afternoon and was looking forward to other such evenings.

For now, it did not occur to him that the smile he so wished to coax to Miss Miranda's sweet pink lips would take flight the very second that young lady became aware of the Important Document now in his possession.

Eleven

On Sunday morning, Lady Heathrow and Elinor decided to accompany Miranda and Katie to morning church services held at St. Luke's Cathedral, in Chelsea. Because Lucy was still abed when the women gathered belowstairs to eat breakfast and discuss their plans for the day, they decided that, taking into account what had happened to Lucy the previous evening, it was best to let the child sleep.

"Poor dear, I expect she is exhausted," Katie said to Miranda as the two of them returned abovestairs to fetch their bonnets and gloves. Katie peered into the dressing glass to settle a new lilac silk Huntley atop her light-brown curls. "It must have been quite late when Lord Peterbloom and Lady Jersey saw Lucy home last evening."

"We should not have allowed Lucy to attend the soirée," Miranda remarked firmly, as she, too, drew on her gloves. "I cannot like it when she goes off to society functions with only Lady Jersey as chaperone. Last night's disaster merely proves my point."

"I quite agree with you on that head, Miranda. But we must not forget that our Heavenly Father was also watching over our dear sister last evening."

"I suppose that is true, Katie. And I am exceedingly grateful that He saw fit to let nothing beyond a broken carriage wheel befall the Jerseys."

"It was also quite fortuitous that the Viscount Peterbloom was nearby when it happened. Considering Lord Jersey's helpless state, I shudder to think what might have occurred otherwise."

Miranda strongly concurred with her sister on that point. She and Katie had only moments ago learned of last night's mishap, Aunt Isobel having decided not to awake them so very late last night in order to tell them. As the story went, only moments after Lady Jersey and Lucy—accompanied by a foxed Lord Jersey, who fell to snoring the minute he entered the carriage—had set out from the ball to return home in the wee hours of the morning, they were frightened to death when suddenly one corner of the coach plummeted to the cobblestone street below. Seconds later, the Viscount Peterbloom appeared on the scene and insisted upon personally seeing the ladies home in his own equipage.

"It appears we are once again in Lord Peterbloom's debt," Katie said, turning a serene smile upon her sister. "The viscount is becoming a true friend to us. He is indeed a gentleman."

Miranda said nothing. Since her last encounter with the top-lofty lord in Lady Malmesbury's garden, she had given that gentleman's true character a great deal of thought. She had concluded that while he might *appear* to be a gentleman on the surface, in truth, he was not. That while he might have, indeed, endeavored to make everyone *think* he had abandoned his roguish ways, the truth was, he was still a rogue. The polite demeanor he wore was only a sham, intended to fool unsuspecting young ladies and their mamas. Deep down, Lord Peterbloom was still the same reprehensible rake who had ravaged her five years ago in her uncle Oliver's garden. This wicked aspect of his character, Miranda believed, he called to the fore when it suited his purposes, for instance, when he found himself alone with a green girl, an innocent, who would be easily fooled by his attractive facade and the polite smile of indifference he wore.

The other afternoon in Lady Malmesbury's garden, he had been on his best behavior with Miranda. Firstly, she reasoned, his sort could, no doubt, sense when a young lady was . . . well, not unwise in the ways of the world. They somehow knew when a young lady had experienced . . . passion. As he had seen to it that she had when he shamelessly stole a kiss from her. Feeling an unwelcome surge of warmth flood her cheeks at the thought, she cursed the rogue again. It angered her that her cheeks colored with great regularity these days whenever she so much as thought about the insufferable wretch! Indeed, the despicable man had ruined her for good and she could not, would not, let him ruin Lucy.

Oddly enough, at services that morning, the parson's sermon was on forgiveness. Despite the roil of anger churning in Miranda's stomach, she listened reverently to the parson's words. And when he'd concluded, she bowed her head in prayer and sincerely tried to summon the least smidgeon of Christian charity toward the Viscount Peterbloom. But it was no use. Therefore, she settled by asking to be forgiven for her own persistent outrage against him. Although, from what she'd been taught by her papa, she knew her plea would do no good until she'd abandoned her hatred of the man entirely. At this point, however, that was asking a tad too much.

When the service concluded, she followed her aunt and cousin and Katie down the aisle of the impressive spired cathedral and into the cobbled courtyard. It was a typical London day, overcast, with only tiny patches of blue visible through the cloud of soot that perpetually hung about London's shoulders like a gray shroud. Miranda likened the cloak of fog to the heavy weight of responsibility she felt in regard to protecting her sister from Lord Peterbloom.

Katie seemed not to notice the oppressive atmosphere. "The reverend's words were quite inspiring this morning," she said, a bright smile lifting her lips.

"I daresay we should endeavor to attend services more often, Elinor dear," Lady Heathrow said. "Perhaps next Sunday, we shall persuade your father to join us."

Katie linked an arm companionably through Elinor's. "I feel inclined to bless everyone I see." She laughed merrily.

Miranda walked silently along beside the others. She wished only to be back home in Halifax. Services at the little church in the glen always left her with a glorious feeling of peace and goodwill. She wondered how Katie had managed to capture such a feeling here.

"The reverend's words quite reminded me of Papa," Katie went on. "Did you not notice the similarity, Miranda?" She gazed around Elinor at her sister's solemn face.

"Indeed," Miranda murmured with little feeling. "And I, too, feel quite inclined to forgive everyone I see," she said, her tone laced with a good bit of sarcasm.

"How very charitable of you, Miranda!" Lady Heathrow smiled at her niece.

Miranda's aunt had no sooner spoken those words when Miranda glanced up and spotted *him!* Coming straight at them. The reverend's words flashed like lightning through her mind. What a hypocrite she was. She worked to school her features into some show of charity.

Lord Peterbloom paused when he came face-to-face with the party of women. "A pleasure to see you lovely ladies this morning." The dazzling smile on his face encompassed all of them.

Lady Heathrow laughed gaily. "It is a pleasure to see you, Lord Peterbloom"

Miranda's lips were a straight line of disgust as, quite against her will, her eyes began to travel over his impeccable form. Light-gray trousers hugged the hard muscles of his legs and the beautiful claret coat he wore fit his powerful shoulders to perfection. Against her will, she felt her breath catch in her throat as her chin tilted upward to search the gentleman's sharply chiseled features. Although the curly brimmed black beaver hat he wore was shading his deep-set dark eyes, it seemed only to add definition to the attractive arch of his thick, dark brows and the sensuous planes and angles of his deeply tanned face. Lord Peterbloom was, indeed, a breathtakingly handsome man.

At that moment, he turned to gaze full at Miranda. She flinched. "The parson delivered a fine sermon today, did he not?" the viscount asked pleasantly.

When Miranda made no reply, Lady Heathrow said, "The girls and I were just remarking upon that very thing."

Miranda cursed the man for causing her such discomfort, while beside her, Katie said, "Allow me to express our heartfelt gratitude to you, sir, for coming to the aid of our sister and Lady Jersey last evening."

He nodded. "Was my pleasure, Miss Fraser. Although I cannot help noticing that Miss Lucy is not amongst you. I trust she is not suffering ill effects from last night's mishap?"

"Oh, indeed not," Lady Heathrow said. "She was understandably shaken from the ordeal, so we decided it best to let her rest this morning. I am quite certain we shall find she has recovered nicely. We are, indeed, grateful for your kind attention, Lord Peterbloom."

"A pleasure," he murmured again. Then, perhaps because Miranda had still said nothing, he directed another look at her.

This time, her chin shot up and she aimed a disinterested gaze across the courtyard.

Apparently undaunted by her reaction to him, or lack

thereof, the viscount said, "I was disappointed to not see the rest of you at the Wexbridges' rout last evening."

"We elected not to attend the party," Lady Heathrow put in. "But we will be at the Chalmers' tomorrow evening, or is their ball on Tuesday?" She laughed merrily. "I declare, we've received so many invitations of late, I can scarce keep up with them. At any rate, I seem to recall I have a Society meeting tomorrow evening, but we shall be at the Chalmers' whenever the fête is. In the meanwhile, Lady Jersey and I are diligently at work on our plans for Lucy's come-out ball. It will be held in Lady Jersey's lovely ballroom. You will be sure to attend, will you not, Lord Peterbloom?"

Miranda could not resist stealing another peek at the gentleman and caught him staring at her once more. On his handsome face was a look of such smugness, she had to fight a powerful urge to slap him silly.

But all he said was, "I would be honored to attend Miss Lucy's come-out ball." Her lips tightened when, still looking at her, he asked, "By the by, how are the dance lessons progressing? Miss Lucy informed me last evening that she was finding the waltz quite to her liking."

Miranda's eyes widened with horror. The reprobate was all but announcing his intent to ruin Lucy! If she'd been carrying a parasol, she would indeed, have beaten the evil intent right out of his heart!

"All the girls are proving to be very apt pupils," Lady Heathrow responded brightly.

"Ah." Lord Peterbloom nodded politely. "Then I shall look forward to standing up with each of you at the Chalmers' ball on Tuesday." Another of his dazzling smiles charmed three of the women. "Good day, ladies."

Miranda managed to murmur some pleasantry or other as the tall gentleman stepped past them. Once he was out of earshot, however, she sputtered, "Why, the very brazenness of that creature! To speak of pleasure-seeking and dancing when we are but a few feet from the Lord's House! It is unconscionable!"

It was a few seconds before any one of Miranda's companions recovered sufficiently from her outburst to speak. Presently, Lady Heathrow said, "Why, I thought the gentleman quite polite, Miranda. It was I who first brought up the ball, you know. I do believe he wished merely to inquire after Lucy's health."

Miranda sniffed piously. "I still say his remarks were exceedingly sinful."

A few seconds later, Elinor said, "Perhaps you could find it in your heart to forgive him, Miranda.

Miranda felt a prick of guilt at that, but when the other ladies burst out laughing, she could not help sheepishly joining in.

As expected, Lucy was thrilled to learn that following services that morning, the Viscount Peterbloom had inquired after her. They were all enjoying a late luncheon, during which Lady Heathrow was relaying the details of the incident to Lucy.

"He not only asked after your health, but he agreed to attend your come-out ball."

"Oh!" Lucy squealed with delight. "Do you think he will lead me out?"

"I think that not the least bit unlikely," her aunt replied, a wide smile on her face. "I daresay it is becoming more and more apparent to me, and, I expect, to everyone"—she laughed—"that the gentleman is quite taken with you."

Lucy sighed dreamily. "And I with him." She turned to Miranda, who, as usual, was having great difficulty keeping silent. "You were quite right, Miranda, when you said that Lord Peterbloom wished me to be sure of my feelings for him before he declared himself to me. Last evening, at the rout," she began conspiratorially, "I was continually surrounded, as I generally am these days, by a score of other admirers, and although the viscount never once asked to stand up with me, I felt his eyes on me the entire time. Then, in the carriage, he said that it pleased him to see me happy and enjoying myself. And then he cautioned me against attaching myself too soon to anyone. What do you think of that?" she concluded with high satisfaction.

Miranda could think of nothing plausible to say to it, but Katie said, "I think that wise counsel, indeed."

Miranda did manage a brisk nod before she added, "In the meantime, perhaps another gentleman will catch your fancy, sweetie."

Lucy looked horrified. "My heart is set on marrying Lord Peterbloom, Miranda!"

Miranda awoke the following morning more determined than ever to protect her younger sister from the evil viscount. Today, she had an *appointment* to see Mr. Fitch, and dressing for the interview, she felt supremely confident that it would turn out well. She further decided it would be in Lucy's best interests if her sister were to be removed altogether from London. Lucy has acquired quite enough Town Bronze. It was high time they all went home to Halifax.

"Mr. Fitch will see you now, miss," the young clerk in the solicitor's office said only minutes after Miranda and Elinor's abigail, Betsy, arrived.

"Thank you, sir." Before Miranda followed the clerk down the corridor, she turned to address Betsy, who had earlier complained of a stomachache. Now, Miranda suggested the little abigail might rather wait for her in the carriage as the air inside the dank office was quite chilly.

"Thank you, miss."

Her chin elevated, Miranda nodded at the clerk, her look telling him she was ready to proceed.

When she stepped into Mr. Fitch's office, she noticed that gentleman made only a cursory effort to rise to his feet.

"Good afternoon, Miss Fraser. What might I do for you today?" A lackluster gesture indicated a straight-backed chair opposite his desk.

Miranda eased her small frame into it and at once drew apart the ribbons of her reticule. "I have brought the legal document, sir, that grants my sisters and myself permission to occupy our home in Halifax." She withdrew the folded-up piece of parchment and reached to hand it across to him.

Seated now behind his desk, the man made no move to take the paper from her. "You have wasted your time in coming to London, young lady. As I explained to you a few weeks back, no legal entailments to the property in Halifax exist. Whatever previous agreements, written or otherwise, that were made between your father and—"

"My great-grandfather!" Miranda fairly shouted, eager to impress upon the man what a very long-standing agreement it was.

Mr. Fitch nodded calmly. "Whichever of your ancestors was involved does not signify, Miss Fraser. By law, the agreement is null and void now that the property has changed hands." The man's tone grew impatient. "Therefore, if you will please excuse me, I have a great deal of work to do."

"No!" Miranda sprang to her feet, her green eyes blazing. "I did not come all this way to be turned aside as if I am . . . nothing! My sisters and I have a legal right to occupy our home, and this proves it!" Her hands verily shook as she spread the frail piece of parchment onto the gentleman's desk. "There"—a shaky finger tapped the spot on the page that in legal parlance spelled out the terms of the grant—"it quite plainly states 'for as long as he,' meaning my great-grandfather Fraser, 'or any of his ancestors shall live.' " She glared at the man. "That means me, Mr. Fitch! And, both of my sisters."

When he said nothing, Miranda added, "It says so, Mr. Fitch, it does!" It angered her when she suddenly felt her chin begin to tremble. She had not cried over their predicament thus far and she did not intend to do so now. *Why would the man not see reason?*

She felt a modicum of satisfaction when, at length, Mr. Fitch said, "You may take a seat, young lady."

Miranda leveled an expectant gaze at him.

"I understand that you and your sisters are not without relatives in Town," he began.

Miranda nodded. "That is correct. We are staying with my aunt and uncle, Lord and Lady Heathrow."

"Lord Heathrow is quite well known in political circles, and I understand Lady Heathrow is involved with a number of charitable concerns."

Miranda nodded again, uncertain what significance this had on the matter at hand.

"Well, then," the solicitor went on, "I see no reason for you or your sisters to fret over having to remove from your little cottage in the country. No doubt, with your aunt and uncle's help, the three of you will soon find husbands and there'll be an end to it."

Miranda's eyes widened. "We are not a one of us casting about for a husband, Mr. Fitch! I have determined never to marry, and my older sister is of the same mind. We wish only to return home to Halifax and take up our lives where we left off. And there is an end to it, Mr. Fitch."

When the cold-hearted man merely snorted, Miranda's anger grew.

"You are forgetting one very important thing, Miss Fraser. You and your sisters no longer have a home in Halifax. Now, I must insist that you excuse me, for I—"

"No!" Miranda gasped, springing to her feet again. True, the fortnight the new owner had granted them to vacate the premises had elapsed, but surely with them gone, the gentleman had not— *"No!"* she cried again.

"It is a day after the fair for this nonsense, Miss Fraser. I rather expect Lord Ashton has already begun the renovation process. You've no choice now but to—"

"No!" Miranda cried once more, well aware that she had interrupted the solicitor again but unable to stop herself. "I demand that you give me leave to speak directly with the new owner, Mr. Fitch. I demand to know where this Lord Ashton resides. I demand it!"

On his feet, as well, Mr. Fitch exhaled an exasperated breath. "Very well, Miss Fraser. But I assure you, to speak to Lord Ashton will be to no purpose." He reached for a pen, and after dipping the tip into the inkwell on his desk, he scratched a few words onto a slip of paper. Miranda held her breath as she watched him meticulously dust the wet ink with powder, then, finally, hand the scrap across to her.

Flinging a last glare of contempt at the hateful man, Miranda mumbled a curt "Thank you" and flounced into the corridor.

A quick glance at the two empty chairs just inside the doorway of the office told her that Betsy was, indeed, waiting for her in the carriage. Nearing the heavy front door, Miranda reached for the latch to open it, when suddenly it swooshed open from the outside with such force that she was flung clean against the firm chest of the gentleman making his way inside.

"Beg pardon, miss," the Viscount Peterbloom said, one hand reaching to steady the young lady who had toppled headlong into his arms. "By jove, is that you, Miss Miranda?"

Her bonneted head jerked up. "You!" Already white-faced with anger over her disastrous interview with Mr. Fitch, Miranda tried to brush past the infuriating gentleman, but during the collision, one long, pink ribbon of her reticule had managed to wrap itself around a shiny brass button on the front of his navy-blue superfine coat. The resulting tangle was now preventing her escape.

"Unhand me!" Miranda cried indignantly, as yet unaware it was the ribbon of her reticule that held her captive and not the persistent viscount.

"Allow me to . . ." Peterbloom's voice trailed off as he bent his head to undo the mischief. Taking a step backward from the threshold onto the flagway behind him, the action caused Miranda, who was still fiercely gripping her end of the purse, to again topple against him.

Peterbloom reached to steady her. "Are you quite all right, my dear?" he asked, then, without waiting for a reply, he slid one strong arm across her back and placed the other at the bend of her knees and scooped her clean up into his arms. "I see your tilbury just across the way. I shall have you safely there in an instant."

"Put me down this minute!" Miranda cried, already acutely aware of the feel of her soft breasts pressed against the firm wall of his chest as he carried her aloft in his arms. "I am perfectly capable of taking myself to my carriage!"

Peterbloom's dark head shook. "On the contrary. You appeared quite near to swooning just now, Miss Miranda. Wouldn't do to have you faint dead away on the street."

"I was not about to faint! I have never fainted in my life!"

"Nonetheless, the collision was entirely my fault. It is my duty to see you safely to your coach."

When the tall gentleman stepped from the flagway onto

the cobblestone street, the action caused Miranda's old straw bonnet to tumble down her back. "I am losing my bonnet!" she cried. One hand reached to clutch at the frayed pink ribbon that now hung loosely about her neck, the bonnet itself swinging to and fro at her back.

"Leave it be," Peterbloom said gruffly. "I daresay I can't imagine why you persist in wearing that frightful old thing. You were wearing quite a pretty one yesterday at services, and last week, too, when I saw you at Lady Malmesbury's party."

Miranda's eyes narrowed. "I fail to see where that is any of your concern, but if you must know, both of those bonnets belong to my cousin Elinor. This one is mine."

A dark brow cocked. "Well, I shouldn't wish to claim it if I were you." He skillfully dodged a carriage that was bowling down the street at a frightful pace, and after a few steps more, set Miranda down on her feet inside the small open carriage. "There you are, my dear. Safe and sound, just as I promised."

Miranda glared at the arrogant man as she swatted at the wrinkles crumpling her skirt, then began to adjust the long sleeves of the tiny spencer jacket she wore. "To have been escorted to my carriage in such a fashion, my lord, was hardly necessary," she said firmly.

Peterbloom's lips twitched. "I thought it quite necessary. And quite pleasant," he added rakishly.

Miranda stared aghast at the man. "You forget yourself, sir!" She busied herself retying the well-worn ribbons of her bonnet beneath her chin.

The viscount next directed an amused gaze at her hat. "Might I suggest you borrow a leaf from Miss Lucy's book and go shopping for a new bonnet, my dear? London is full of millinery shops. I daresay something on the order of the pretty blue confection Miss Lucy had on at Lady Malmesbury's last week would look quite fetching on you." He continued to stare at Miranda's headgear. "That old straw thing might serve for weeding the garden, but it hardly seems appropriate for an afternoon in the City."

"Oh!" Her mouth agape, Miranda glared daggers at the bold creature.

Peterbloom's eyes were still twinkling with merriment as he sketched a polite bow. "Good day, Miss Miranda."

She continued to watch the infuriating gentleman as long strides carried him back across the busy street to the solicitor's office again. To wonder at his business there did not enter her head. What had transpired between the two of them just now was too firmly fixed in it. Indeed, she had not misjudged the Viscount Peterbloom. He was the same unprincipled rotter she had thought him to be all along. The sooner she removed herself and her sisters from London, the better!

Twelve

As the small coach wheeled down the street, Miranda very nearly forgot her joy over at last uncovering the name of the gentleman who now owned Fraser Cottage. Instead, all she could think about was *him. How dare he address her in so forward a fashion! Buy a new bonnet, indeed!* One hand strayed absently to finger the admittedly well-worn Gypsy hat that sat atop her dark curls. For some reason, she felt angry enough to do precisely as he'd suggested. Even Aunt Isobel had pulled a face this morning when she spotted the floppy old straw hat yet again.

Glancing about at the shops the carriage was now rolling past, Miranda noted a fashionable millinery establishment just across the way, its windows chock full of gaily decorated headgear.

"Stop the coach, please!" Miranda called to the driver.

A footman scurried to let down the steps and Miranda scrambled to the ground. "No need to accompany me," she said to the wide-eyed abigail, "I shall only be a moment."

Miranda marched across the street and into the tiny shop. Moments later, she reappeared, wearing a lovely high-crowned Coburg with a bright red plume that curled fetchingly round her cheek. In one gloved hand, she carried a paisley-papered band box that contained her tattered old Gypsy hat.

"La!" exclaimed Betsy, a look of surprise on her face. "I 'spect his lordship would approve of that one, miss. It's quite lovely!"

Gaining his lordship's approval was not Miranda's intent. Furthermore, she meant now to go straight home and prevail upon Aunt Isobel and Katie to accompany her to Lord Ashton's home this very afternoon. If all went as she planned, she and her sisters could be on their way back to Halifax tomorrow and she would never be obliged to lay eyes on the uppity Lord Peterbloom again.

Traffic in the City being what it was, however, the return trip to Hanover Square took considerably longer than Miranda wished. She put the time to good use, regaining her composure. It would never do to let her irritation with the arrogant Lord Peterbloom overset her to the degree she could not present an altogether convincing case to Lord Ashton.

Approaching the Heathrow town house, Miranda was so intent upon her mission that she failed to note the handsome equipage already drawn up before the curb. Hurrying into the house, she merely nodded briskly when Walker informed her that the ladies were in the drawing room. As she advanced into that chamber, Miranda came to an abrupt halt when she caught sight of who was lounging before the hearth, one long leg crossed nonchalantly over the other. *Peterbloom!* She was about to turn and flee from the room when Lady Heathrow addressed her.

"Miranda, dear, do come and join us for a cup of tea. We've another gentleman caller this afternoon." She turned to the viscount. "Goodness me—" she laughed, "I don't mean to prose on about it, but you are the fourth or fifth young man to call upon Lucy today. Her popularity has increased to such an extent there is no keeping up with it."

"Indeed," Lord Peterbloom murmured, but his piercing dark eyes were not fastened on Lucy.

Suddenly, Lucy blurted out, "Look, everyone! Miranda's got a new bonnet!"

Miranda wished only to sink into a hole in the floor. For a farthing, she'd have flung the brand-new bonnet into the fire and run all the way home to Halifax, hatless. Instead, her heart hammering wildly in her ears, she thrust her chin up and managed to bravely address her aunt.

"I've a pressing business matter to discuss with you, Aunt Isobel."

"But Miranda dear, would you not like a cup of tea—?"

"Please, Aunt Isobel. I really must . . . *please!*"

"Very well, dear." A small set smile appeared on Lady Heathrow's face. "Katie, if you will be good enough to . . ." Lady Heathrow's voice trailed off as she reluctantly set her teacup aside and rose to her feet.

Before she joined Miranda, however, Lord Peterbloom said, "I daresay it is time I took my leave." He moved to deposit the delicate teacup in his hand onto the small rosewood tea table near Katie.

"Must you go so soon, sir?" Lucy cried, from where she sat on the sofa. She looked so stricken, Miranda feared her sister might throw herself at the attractive gentleman's feet in order to bodily prevent his escape.

Peterbloom did pause, a gaze flitting from Lucy to Katie. "Perhaps I could persuade you charming young ladies to take a turn about the park with me this afternoon?" He aimed a look straight at Miranda. "Would give you a chance to show off your pretty new bonnet, Miss Miranda." The merry twinkle in his dark eyes only irritated her further.

Glaring at him, she felt white-hot anger pulse through her veins for the second time that day. "Thank you, no, sir. As it happens, I haven't the time . . . nor the inclination, to go promenading about the park with you."

"Miranda!" Lady Heathrow sputtered.

"Didn't I tell you she was a cross-patch?" Lucy said to

Peterbloom. "But"—her lips lifted coquettishly—"I should very much like to take a drive in the park with you, sir. I understand it is the fashionable thing to do at this hour. You will come with us, won't you, Katie? Elinor?"

Elinor, who'd said nothing thus far, looked a question at her mother, who quickly nodded assent. "What a perfectly splendid idea, Lord Peterbloom." Lady Heathrow turned to address Miranda. "You really should go along, dear. You do look quite charming in your pretty new bonnet."

"My thoughts exactly," Lord Peterbloom said roundly. The rakish grin on his face made Miranda wish he would sink into a hole in the floor.

At length, everyone, save Miranda and Lady Heathrow, quitted the room. After the older woman had pressed a cup of tea upon her niece, Miranda, as best she could, considering her agitated state, outlined her troubles to her aunt. She left nothing out, including the fact that it was *all* their money that had been stolen from them that night at the inn and that unless Lord Ashton honored their grant and they returned home to Halifax straightaway, they had nowhere else to turn.

"Oh, dear," Lady Heathrow said. "I can clearly understand your persistence in speaking with Mr. Fitch now. But I can't think what *I* can do to help sway the gentleman."

"It was not my purpose to burden you with our troubles, Aunt Isobel, I merely wished you to accompany me, and Katie, in approaching Lord Ashton. I . . . had hoped we might make the call today," she added anxiously.

"Oh, no, I shouldn't think that would be possible, dear. It is far too late now. Perhaps tomorrow would serve. I am acquainted with Lady Ashton," she added.

Miranda brightened. "Then you'll come?"

"I . . . don't know, dear." Lady Heathrow hesitated. "Now that I think on it, the problem does seem more of a . . . gentleman thing. Business and all that. Perhaps we should seek John's counsel. John will surely know what to do in a case such as this."

Miranda's brows pulled together in a worried frown. "I shouldn't wish to trouble him, Aunt Isobel. Uncle John is quite busy." She turned an imploring look on her aunt. "I feel certain that once Lord Ashton is made aware of the entailment, the matter will iron out smoothly. I came to you simply because I . . . felt it the proper thing to do. I shouldn't wish to appear offputting to Lord Ashton by not being all that is proper, or . . ." She paused.

"Of course, not, dear."

"And since you are already acquainted with Lady Ashton, she and her husband would not hesitate to receive us if you were along."

Lady Heathrow seemed torn. "I suppose a simple morning call would be . . . oh, I don't know, Miranda. I really should consult John. If he should object . . . well, there is the matter of Lucy's come-out to consider. I—I shouldn't want to . . . John can be quite . . ." Her voice trailed off again, her hesitant tone conveying far more than her words ever could.

Miranda felt hot tears stinging the back sides of her eyes. Nothing today had gone as she'd planned. Encountering the infuriating Lord Peterbloom hadn't helped matters any. She hated the fact that Lucy was even now in the rakehell's company, but, with Katie and Elinor along to chaperone, perhaps Lucy was safe. She managed to shove the unpleasantness from mind and fix her attention instead on the vexation at hand. "I simply *must* speak with Lord Ashton as soon as possible, Aunt Isobel. Perhaps if you sent a note of introduction along with Katie and me, we could call on Lord and Lady Ashton ourselves." She paused. "My sisters and I love our home dearly, Aunt Isobel, and not a one of us wishes to leave it."

Lady Heathrow reached to pat Miranda's hand. "Indeed, I do understand, my dear. But I really must consult with John first. If he agrees to it, then I shall send a letter of introduction first thing tomorrow. Will that suffice?"

Miranda's chin began to tremble. She did not wish Uncle John to know what dire straights they were in. He would surely accuse her of trying to manipulate her aunt and uncle into extending an offer for them to take up permanent residence here. Miranda tried to gulp down the frustration building within her.

"I believe Lord Ashton to be a fair man," Lady Heathrow said, "although, I daresay he is somewhat a . . ."

"A what?" Miranda cried. She had no energy left to deal with yet another difficult man!

Lady Heathrow shook her head sadly. "It doesn't signify. I merely recall that Lord Ashton is quite a . . . gambler. But all gentlemen gamble." She smiled reassuringly. "I will speak with John tonight. It will all turn out well in the end, you'll see."

"That is what Katie keeps telling me," Miranda said glumly.

"Well, Katie is right. She has also told me a few things about you," Lady Heathrow said brightly. "About how very much you love your pretty garden at home and the lovely flowers you tend. I should like you to accompany me tonight to a meeting of my Horticulture Society, The Ladies of the Leaf. We've been promised a surprise guest speaker, an expert on hybridization. I am certain you will enjoy the outing. Say you will come."

Miranda smiled through the mist of tears that were blurring her vision. "I do miss my garden. Ever so. I had just set out a score of new plantings before we left to come up to London. I fear they must all be dead by now. We had not planned to be away so . . . very long."

Lady Heathrow smiled sadly. "Well, we shall simply have to get you some new plants, won't we? I'm told the gentleman who is set to speak tonight is bringing a sample of a splendid new strain of tea rose he has specially developed in his own greenhouse. The shade of the miniature rose is said to be amethyst!"

"Oh-h." Miranda sucked in her breath. "It sounds perfectly splendid. I should very much like to see it."

"Then it's settled. Perhaps the gentleman will consent to part with the rose. Since I've not yet presented you with a special gift, Miranda, it would give me great pleasure to purchase something lovely for your garden. A memento of your visit to London. Would you like that, dear?"

A mingling of joy and sadness welled up in Miranda's breast. Aunt Isobel was being so very kind. Her lower lip trembled as she murmured, "Indeed, I would, Aunt Isobel."

The surprise guest speaker that night at the Ladies of the Leaf Society meeting was quite astonished himself to spot Miss Miranda Fraser sitting primly in the front row of the seats arranged before the dais in the elegant meeting room of London's Egyptian Hall.

From his aspect before the podium, Lord Peterbloom had a clear view throughout his lengthy speech of the pert little miss in the pretty new bonnet with the bright red plume. Though, in the beginning, she appeared to not pay close attention to his talk, before he'd got halfway through it, she was listening as raptly as any of the other women there.

Aware that he had now gained Miss Miranda Fraser's undivided attention, Peterbloom relaxed a bit and began to insert more and more interesting footnotes into the material he'd prepared. At length, he held up the prized tea rose he'd brought along for the ladies to view, going into great detail to explain the cross-hybridization process he'd conducted between a classic white rose and a pale damask one.

"That plant was then grafted back again with a darker

shade of damask rose, which is a native of France, but we shan't hold that against it," he added, with a laugh. The dazzling smile he directed at the audience was met in kind by every last woman there, who tittered amongst themselves at the small joke he'd made.

Fingering a shiny leaf of the potted plant, Peterbloom added, "I believe a bit of dog-rose must have crept in somewhere with the original white rose I first grafted, which may account for the deep green of these leaves. But against the pale amethyst petals, it makes for a pleasing contrast, don't you agree?"

"Oh, indeed!" came the murmured reply from the audience.

Peterbloom went on to eloquently deliver a receipt for a syrup that could be made from the velvety petals of the damask rose that after boiling and adding several drachms of treacle could be used as an excellent purge for children.

"It is also quite healthful for adults," he added. "A small amount taken every night is found to keep the bowels soluble and open."

Watching the women in his audience nodding with interest, Peterbloom blithely continued. "I have also brought along a copy of a receipt that uses the dried petals of the common red rose, which combined with the oil of vitriol and a fine powdered sugar, makes an excellent tincture that is useful for certain . . ." He paused, then realizing that perhaps he'd gone a bit too far to turn back, concluded in a somewhat small voice, "Women's complaints." A slight pink flush crept to his own cheeks.

But the women in his audience did not notice. The attractive gentleman had presented his excellent talk in so warm and personable a manner that not a one of them took offense at anything he said. The brilliant smiles he'd directed to all of them had the effect of making each and every lady present feel that he had singled her out.

When it came to charming women, the Viscount Peterbloom was a master.

"What a perfectly enjoyable and enlightening talk Lord Peterbloom presented," Lady Heathrow enthused to Miranda as the applause began to die away and ladies from all corners of the hall began to stream toward the podium to speak personally with the handsome gentleman.

In spite of herself, Miranda also wore a pleasant smile on her face. "Indeed, it was most enlightening. I had no idea the viscount was such a knowledgeable man."

"Well, I daresay his absence from Town these past years has been fully explained now."

Miranda directed another admiring gaze at the dark-haired gentleman, surrounded at the moment by at least two dozen beaming women, and more on the way. "He must have been everywhere in the world to have gleaned so much knowledge."

Lady Heathrow advanced a few steps toward the front of the room.

"Wh-where are you going?" Miranda asked, suddenly aware of a certain breathlessness overtaking her.

"Why, to speak to him, of course. We really must give the gentleman our regards, Miranda." Lady Heathrow reached to grasp Miranda's gloved hand. "Do come along, dear. I mean to ask the viscount if I might purchase the lovely amethyst rose as a gift for you."

Miranda stood frozen in place, the crippling anxiety she always felt in the viscount's presence escalating to such a degree she felt as unable to move as Lot's wife.

Lady Heathrow flung a gaze at the platform. As there were still far too many women clustered about Lord Peterbloom to make their speaking to him possible, she turned back to Miranda. In a hushed tone, she said, "One cannot help but notice that you do not seem to share your sisters' high regard for Lord Peterbloom, Miranda. I wonder if it is because you are unable to forget that horrid tale about him that Lady Jersey relayed to you girls at the outset?"

Miranda's response was a frightened rise and fall of her small shoulders.

"He was quite a young man then, Miranda," her aunt went on. "I have heard nothing untoward about the gentleman since. Although, I own, I was reluctant to believe it at first, it is quite evident to me now that he is a changed man. His mother, Lady Peterbloom, is very well respected in London society, as was his father, though that gentleman is no longer with us, and I understand his mother is ailing these days. The family is very well connected, Miranda. I see no harm in you girls befriending him."

She glanced again at the personable young man, whom apparently all the women tonight found quite agreeable. "The very fact that Peterbloom is hanging after Lucy has increased her consequence considerably," Lady Heathrow added. "Both an earl and the younger son of a duke called today. What I am trying to say, Miranda, is that perhaps you should endeavor to be a bit more . . . charitable toward the young man. You are a sweet girl, my dear, but, I fear, none but myself and your sisters, and Elinor, is aware of it. You quite offended Lady Jersey, you know, and I shouldn't like to see the same thing happen with Lord Peterbloom."

Miranda felt deeply the truth of her aunt's words. She had not meant to offend Lady Jersey and she did not wish to harm Lucy's chances for happiness. Standing with her back toward Lord Peterbloom and his circle of ardent admirers, she said, "I am indeed sorry, Aunt Isobel. I never meant to offend Lady Jersey. I have just been so *very* worried about our home and—"

"Well, good evening, young man!" Lady Heathrow said, addressing someone over the top of Miranda's head. "What a splendid talk you presented to us tonight and indeed, what a surprise, a *nice* surprise, I might add, to discover that *you* were the Society's well-kept secret!" Lady Heathrow's gay laugh all but obscured Peterbloom's pleasant greeting.

Her heart pounding in her ears, Miranda turned slowly about. She fervently hoped the smile on her lips appeared genuine to him.

It did, and Peterbloom was quite pleased to see it. Since making Miss Miranda Fraser's acquaintance, he'd been privy to precious few of those from that young lady.

"I hope my talk of herbs and plants did not bore you to tears, Miss Miranda," he said. He gazed intently into her wide, sea-green eyes. She looked especially charming tonight in a simple dove-gray gown with black braid lining the scooped neck and marching in rows down the long sleeves and round the hem. The bright red plume on her lovely new bonnet made for a delightful contrast. "I recall your decided disinterest in flowers when we spoke that afternoon in Lady Malmesbury's garden."

"*Dis*interest?" Lady Heathrow sputtered. "Why, Miranda has a keen interest in horticulture!"

Peterbloom's eyes widened. "Say, what?"

Miranda smiled nervously. "It is true, sir, I do. I cannot think why I . . ." She appeared flustered, her long lashes fluttering, her green eyes downcast.

"Miranda has been quite overset these last weeks," Lady Heathrow offered by way of explanation. "I am quite certain she did not mean to impart the impression that she . . . Oh, dear, I suddenly realize that since I was not with you in Lady Malmesbury's garden, I haven't the least notion what you two were talking about." She laughed gaily. "Well, I shall leave you to sort it out whilst I go and speak to the other ladies. Ta!" She gave Miranda's hand an affectionate pat before she flitted away.

"So, you possess a *keen* interest in horticulture, do

you?" Peterbloom's lips twitched with amusement. "And do you have a particular area of interest?"

Miranda smiled up into the gentleman's midnight-brown eyes. "I have no . . . particular area of interest, my lord. I enjoy growing all flowers and planting and cultivating new varieties of them. I have never tried to develop a whole new specie, such as you have done. I daresay I quite . . . envy your success," she added, in quite a sincere tone.

"I find the hours fly by when I am in my greenhouse."

Miranda's smile widened. "My sisters often remark that they cannot fathom how I can pass such a great deal of time with only my plants for company, but I find the work very . . ."

After a pause, he supplied, "Peaceful?"

"Why, that is . . . precisely the word I meant to use," she said, gazing again with wonder into his eyes.

"Then why did you not say it?" he asked, locking gazes with her. He found her quite enchanting.

After another pause, she said, "Because I feared you might . . . laugh at me."

Peterbloom searched the depths of her soulful eyes. "I would never laugh at you, my dear."

Those soulful eyes snapped. "You laughed at me only today, sir!"

A somewhat sheepish grin softened the chiseled lines of Peterbloom's countenance. "Touché." He bent a nod her way. "I did, indeed, make sport of your bonnet this very afternoon, Miss Miranda. Although I can clearly understand now why you must have favored it. The wide brim must have come in quite handy for shielding your face from the sun when you were weeding your garden."

Miranda nodded tartly. "It did, indeed."

"Well then, I hope you did not toss it away," he said.

"Rest assured, I did not, sir. Once I return again to

the country, I shall resume wearing it. At once." She grinned up at him.

Peterbloom laughed aloud, despite the sharp pang of guilt he felt when the young lady mentioned her home in Halifax. After his interview that afternoon with Mr. Fitch, he knew it was now only a matter of time before Miss Miranda came knocking at his door demanding to present her petition to him.

"If you will accept my apology, sir," she was saying, "I have been quite preoccupied these last weeks with a . . . a distressing business matter."

Peterbloom shifted uncomfortably. He'd been rather looking forward to the fireworks that would erupt when Miss Miranda learned that he now possessed the deed to the property in Halifax. But, after the delightful conversation he'd had with her tonight, a part of him now deeply regretted setting the dastardly scheme in motion.

On impulse, he said, "I wonder if you would allow me to . . ." A gloved hand indicated that he'd like the young lady to accompany him to the platform where he'd delivered his speech. Once they were standing there, Peterbloom said, "I should like you to have the amethyst rose, Miss Miranda."

It was a small gesture but it assuaged a modicum of the guilt he felt. It also delighted him to watch her sea-green eyes grow round with happiness.

"Oh, no, sir, I couldn't!"

"I insist. It would please me to know that my lovely rose is growing in . . . Where did you say you hailed from?" he asked innocently.

She gazed up at him, her heart-shaped face guileless with trust. "Halifax. My sisters and I have a lovely old manor home called Fraser Cottage located on the outskirts of the village. It is situated in the most beautiful part of England," she said longingly. She turned an admiring gaze on the plant with the single lavender bloom that the gentleman was holding out to her. "I am quite anxious to return to my home in the country. I miss my garden frightfully, and my home."

Peterbloom felt a sharp pang of guilt when the sweet trill of her voice nearly broke. Had the deed to her home been in his pocket that very moment, he'd have gladly given it to her right then. As it was, he had only the rose to present to her now.

The rest, he knew, would come later.

Thirteen

More astonishing than discovering that the Viscount Peterbloom was the surprise speaker at Aunt Isobel's meeting was the revelation that he was so very well versed on the subject he'd addressed. Miranda supposed she'd have learned that about him if she'd been paying closer attention to the conversation she'd shared with the gentleman that afternoon at Lady Malmesbury's breakfast. But, discovering it now, coupled with the afterglow of their pleasant talk last evening and the lovely gift he'd given her put Miranda in an excellent frame to completely reverse her opinion of the man. Aunt Isobel did have the right of it, she decided. Lord Peterbloom was, indeed, a changed man.

The smile on Miranda's lips lingered as she joined her sisters at the breakfast table that next morning, and persisted even whilst she listened to the gentleman's virtues being extolled by Lucy, who'd quite enjoyed her drive through the park in the viscount's company the previous afternoon.

Katie noticed Miranda's change of face, and remarked upon it. "I daresay, Miranda, you are being exceptionally charitable where Lord Peterbloom is concerned this morning. I expect his gift to you last evening must have lifted your spirits considerably."

"The gentleman's gift was most generous," Miranda

agreed pleasantly, "but the truth of the matter is, in all fairness, I find I cannot fault a man who dedicates such a great deal of his time to the well-being of others." She asked Katie to please pass the dish of marmalade, and while spreading a glop of it onto a hot buttered scone, she added, "In addition to explaining the delicate hybridization process he'd performed on the roses, Lord Peterbloom told us last evening that he is working closely with a physician here in London, by the name of Doctor Keating. The pair of them are conducting controlled experiments in the combining of various herbs and powders to test the healing properties on those of Dr. Keating's patients whom traditional medicines have failed to cure. I find that quite extraordinary, do you not, Katie?"

"Indeed, I do," Katie marveled.

"And," Miranda went on, "the viscount brought along several receipts for purges and tonics that he has already found to be especially helpful in the treatment of various ailments. I intend to make copies of them for our use."

"Oh-h," Katie intoned, whilst Lucy exclaimed, "There, you see, Miranda. I was right about the Viscount Peterbloom. He is a wonderful man! Not a one of my other suitors compares. They are every last one of them quite ordinary."

Cousin Elinor had been listening intently to the girl's discussion. Now she said, "I think your Mr. Dunworthy is quite nice."

Lucy pulled a face. "Dunworthy is far too plain for me. And only a poet. I do not understand half what he says."

"Nor do I." Elinor shrugged. "But the half I do understand is quite nice."

They all laughed at that, then Lucy announced, "If the viscount does not offer for me soon, I fear I shall have to apprise him myself of my deep feelings for him. I am quite set on marrying him."

Miranda experienced a sharp pang at that, not unlike

a knife being plunged into her heart. But, unable to determine a logical reason for the odd reaction, she decided it was but a final scrap of her old anger with the viscount and consequently meant nothing. She had, indeed, forgiven the gentleman his past transgressions and entertained naught but charitable thoughts for him now. If Lucy loved him and he her, she would not stand in the way of their happiness. She would not wish the same sort of unfortunate rift to develop between herself and any of her sisters that had sprung up, and lasted a lifetime, between her mother and Aunt Isobel.

Mama and Papa had fallen in love with one another on sight. She had always expected the same thing to happen to Lucy. Perhaps now it had. With the Viscount Peterbloom. Lucy was certainly beautiful enough for a man to be swept away after just one look at her, and well, so was Lord Peterbloom. Suddenly, Miranda recalled her first look at the heartbreakingly handsome man that night in Uncle Oliver's garden. Lord Peterbloom had been quite attractive then, though not nearly so dashing as he was today. She squirmed in her chair when, of their own volition, her thoughts fixed again on those few delicious moments five years ago when his sensuous mouth had been pressed to hers.

"You are smiling quite oddly, Miranda." The lighthearted trill of Lucy's voice jarred Miranda to her senses. "Whatever can you be thinking about?"

"N-nothing," Miranda stammered. It would never do to tell Lucy of that experience. *Never!* She nervously thrust the admittedly pleasant memory aside as Aunt Isobel stepped into the room.

Miranda had last night told Katie about her interview with Mr. Fitch and of the talk she'd later shared with their aunt. A bit ago, Aunt Isobel had excused herself from the breakfast table to go and speak with the girl's uncle John before he left for the day. Miranda was quite eager now to hear the results of that conversation. But catching sight of the troubled look upon her aunt's face, Miranda's stomach tightened with fresh fear.

"If I might have a private word with you, Miranda?" Lady Heathrow said.

Miranda flung an anxious gaze at Katie as she sprang to her feet and hastened after her aunt, who was leading the way back down the corridor to the book room.

Once there, Lady Heathrow closed the door and turned a grave look on Miranda.

"I told John all about the trouble that has befallen you dear girls, and he went at once to see what can be done about it"

"Went?" Miranda's eyes widened. *Uncle John intervening on their behalf?* "He is calling on Lord Ashton? But without taking the document along to show him, how will Uncle John convince the gentleman that our claim is—"

Lady Heathrow shook her head sadly. "John is not calling on Lord Ashton. He went to see Lord Peterbloom."

"Lord Peterbloom!" Miranda sputtered. "But why? He knows nothing of . . ."

"Do sit down, dear."

In short order, Lady Heathrow told Miranda of the strange set of circumstances that now placed the deed to their home in the Viscount Peterbloom's unsuspecting hands.

"Oh-h-h." Miranda's heart sank. "I can scarce believe that Uncle John actually had the deed to our home in his possession and was unaware of its significance." She bit her lower lip to halt the flow of painful tears that swam in her eyes.

"I do so wish you had confided in us at the outset, Miranda dear. Though I expect I understand your reticence in doing so. At least where John is concerned." She reached to lay a comforting hand on Miranda's arm. "You must believe me, dear, when I say how simply horrid my husband feels about your troubles now. Which is why he left straightaway to call on Lord Peterbloom. I am certain that when he explains the situation to the viscount, he will not hesitate to return Lord Ashton's marker to John."

Suddenly, Miranda recalled her collision with Lord Peterbloom yesterday afternoon on the flagway in front of Mr. Fitch's office. Had the viscount's business at the solicitor's somehow involved their home? "Oh, Aunt Isobel, do you really think he will return it?"

Lady Heathrow nodded. "I not only think it, Miranda, I am certain of it. After all, what could the property possibly mean to the viscount? I understand Peterbloom has quite a lovely country estate of his own; and his home here is situated on the outskirts of the city. The property in Halifax can mean nothing to him." She paused, then settled a wise look on Miranda. "How very fortunate that you took my advice last evening and behaved in quite a civil fashion toward the gentleman."

"Oh, Aunt Isobel." An enormous breath of relief escaped Miranda. "Thank you, ever so, for taking me to task over my uncharitable attitude. It is precisely what my dear mama would have done." She turned a shaky smile on her aunt, then, unable to quell the urge, she flung herself into her aunt's arms and let the vast reservoir of unshed tears that had been gathering within her breast these last weeks course down her cheeks. *How very dearly she missed her mother and their home, and how vastly sorry she was to have held the Viscount Peterbloom's ugly deed against him.*

At length, she drew back and accepted the scrap of linen her aunt handed her with which to dry her eyes. "I am ever so grateful to you, Aunt Isobel. You have been so very kind to us. I only wish Mama could know of your . . . that she could know that all of us are now . . ." Unable to complete the heartfelt sentiment, Miranda held the lacy handkerchief to her nose and gently blew into it.

Beside her, Lady Heathrow blinked back her own tears.

"I am quite certain Maryella knows we are together, Miranda."

The two shared a small moment of remembrance, then Lady Heathrow said, "Come. Let us go and have a nice cup of tea while we wait for John to return with the good news."

Miranda could hardly believe the bizarre twist of fate that had once again entangled their lives with that of the Viscount Peterbloom. Katie likewise found it astonishing. The two girls were seated alone in the small sitting room abovestairs still awaiting word from Lord Heathrow.

"Our Heavenly Father is, indeed, looking out for us, Miranda. Who better to have possession of the property than Lord Peterbloom? Especially if he and Lucy are to wed."

The odd pang again gripped Miranda's middle. She managed to ignore it and said, "I wonder if he will return the deed to Uncle John or simply honor our claim to occupy the cottage?"

"Either way, we are safe."

Miranda nodded thoughtfully. Suddenly, she wondered if she had witnessed the very transaction last week at Almack's when she'd spied on her uncle John and the viscount? Uncle John and Lord Peterbloom had referred to the property as "a worthless piece of chattel." Then Uncle John had handed the viscount something and that gentleman had said . . . *What?* That his plans "did not include marriage or settling down in the country." So, what did he want with the land, Miranda wondered. Perhaps he meant to use it for growing plants and herbs for his experiments. If so, she had no objection to that. In fact . . . she rather liked the idea. Even if he and Lucy did not ultimately marry, the setting out of plants and cultivating them would bring him to Halifax for at least part of each year. She could not say for certain why that seemed so very agreeable to her now. But, at first thought, she could find nothing objectionable to the idea.

"Perhaps he means to live in the big house on the hill," she mused aloud.

Katie smiled serenely. "Lucy would like that above all things. Although"—she looked thoughtful—"I cannot think it a good idea just now to mention that possibility to her."

"Whyever not?"

Katie shrugged. "Lucy quite likes the City. I don't know how she'd feel if the man she married merely took her straight back to Halifax."

Miranda nodded. "I suppose you are right." She mulled their situation over a bit longer, then said, "But surely Lucy would come to miss our home and wish to return for a visit. You miss it, do you not, Katie?"

"Oh, indeed, I do, Sister. Nothing will ever replace our lovely cottage in my heart. We've so many wonderful memories there, with Mama and Papa. I shall never forget it, but—"

"We shall not be obliged to forget it!" Miranda cried. "If the viscount returns the marker to Uncle John today, you and I may return home at any time. I expect Lucy will want to linger here a spell, at least until the Season has run its course, but you and I—"

Katie was shaking her head. "No, Miranda. I would not leave London as long as Lucy is here. Mama would want one of us to look after her."

Miranda sighed. Of course, Katie was right again. But Miranda did *so* miss the country and she was *so* very weary of trying to hold onto what was dear to them. Perhaps, when Uncle John returned this morning, the good news he brought would enable her to feel differently about staying in Town. Who knows, she might even be able to relax and enjoy part of their trip. The fact that she finally felt in charity with Lord Peterbloom meant that anything was possible, didn't it?

Less than a half hour later, Miranda was more overset than she'd ever been before. "That cannot be!" she cried.

"I am afraid it is, dear," Lady Heathrow said. Lord Heathrow had just returned from the call he'd made at the viscount's home, and after relaying the outcome of the interview to his wife, left it up to her to tell the girls the news. "John said the viscount seemed quite unmoved and merely stated that he'd been informed by Ashton's solicitor that the property was unentailed. Moreover Peterbloom told John that he had no intention of selling it, that he had plans of his own for the house and the estate."

"Oh-h-h!" Miranda cried afresh. "How could he?"

Sitting beside her on the sofa in the small sitting room where she and her sister had been awaiting word from Uncle John that morning, Katie slipped an arm about Miranda's small shoulders. "It is not so bad as all that," she murmured.

"How can you say that, Katie?" Miranda sprang to her feet and began to wave her arms about. "What are we to do now?"

"Your sister is right, Miranda dear. Things are never as bad as they seem," Lady Heathrow began gently. "For instance, John has invited the three of you to stay right here, for as long as you like."

Katie's gentle "thank you" to her aunt's generous offer was drowned out by a fresh cry of alarm from Miranda.

"But what does *he* mean to do with Fraser Cottage?" she demanded. "Lord Ashton meant to convert it into his hunting lodge!"

"Well, I cannot think of a thing worse than that," Katie said emphatically. "Did Lord Peterbloom give Uncle John any indication what he means to do with the cottage?"

"Indeed, he did." Lady Heathrow nodded. "Something about a . . . laboratory, or was it a conservatory? At any rate, it has something to do with his work."

"Oh-h-h," Miranda groaned, forgetting all the kind and charitable thoughts she'd entertained only that morning for the viscount. She now thought him selfish and insensitive and unprincipled. He obviously took no thought for anyone but himself. Why, only last evening she'd told him how very much she missed her home. And the conniving thief had actually asked her where she hailed from, when he knew the answer all along. He was the most evil man she'd ever met. "We must speak with him, Katie!" She whirled to face her older sister. "We must. *You* could convince him to change his mind, I know it. I am so very angry now, I fear I would kill him!"

Katie looked shocked. "Oh, Miranda, you must ask our dear Lord's forgiveness for entertaining such a sinful thought!"

"Of course I would not kill him. I simply meant I wished to."

"It is one and the same," Katie maintained, then she fell silent, thoughtfully tapping her chin. "A man is far more likely to be swayed by his wife . . . than by her sisters," she finally said.

Lady Heathrow nodded gravely. "The viscount does appear to be smitten with Lucy. Perhaps the best course, Miranda, is to bide your time. I expect Lord Peterbloom will come up to scratch any day now."

"All things work together for good," Katie gently reminded her sister. "I am confident Divine Providence will see us through this trial the same as always."

Lady Heathrow turned a smile on Katie. "You are wise beyond your years, Katie dear. Moreover, as long as Lord Peterbloom remains in London, you girls have nothing to fear. He cannot be in two places at once. If he intends altering the cottage in any way, he will surely alert you to his plans." She paused. "I will allow that I find it a trifle surprising that he did not accept your uncle John's offer. I understand it was quite generous. But"—she shrugged—"there is no figuring why gentlemen behave as they do. I am certain the viscount has his reasons, however obscure they may seem to us. In the meantime"—she smiled at her nieces—"a great deal of good has already come from this."

Katie was listening raptly; Miranda now also looked up.

"John has not only extended the invitation to you girls to remain here with us, but he has given me leave to bring Lucy out in grand style," she announced brightly.

"I thought he had already agreed to that," Miranda muttered morosely.

"Well—" Lady Heathrow looked a trifle guilty, "I confess I had not told John about all of the plans I had already set in motion. Now"—she laughed gaily—"there is no need to keep anything hidden from him. Everything has worked out splendidly, I think. Lucy will have a brilliant career, and who knows, we may even snag husbands for the pair of you!"

Katie looked pleased, but Miranda merely rolled her eyes. She was certain of only one thing: the infuriating viscount was tenaciously hanging on to their home and there was not a thing in the world she could do about it.

Lying abed that night, Miranda was still stewing over the bumblebroth she and her sisters had landed in. She tossed and turned for an interminable length, her thoughts still brimming with rage at the deceitful man. Finally, she decided that, once again, the Viscount Peterbloom had revealed his true colors. Furthermore, Lucy, or, for that matter any proper young lady, could never be happy married to such a man. Lord Peterbloom was a most unsuitable suitor and it was up to her to see that a match between her sister and the scoundrel never took place.

Fourteen

Peterbloom had not expected the call from Lord Heathrow that morning on behalf of the Fraser sisters. Although he was prepared to answer to it, having already decided that in order to further his acquaintance with Miss Miranda Fraser, it was necessary that he contrive to keep the young lady in Town. What better way to prevent her leaving London than to refuse to renew the grant that gave the young ladies the right to occupy the cottage in Halifax that Peterbloom now owned?

Lord Heathrow did not take offense at Peterbloom's position, because, quite honestly, he, too, questioned the legality of the centuries-old claim.

"It's neither here nor there to me, Peterbloom," the older gentleman had said. "Merely promised m' wife I'd look into the matter. If ye've plans of ye' own for the property, there's an end to it. Although"—the stout man laughed—"it now appears I'll be obliged to keep the chits beneath my roof for an undetermined length. For that reason alone, I would not have given up Ashton's marker quite so easily."

Peterbloom shrugged. "We neither of us knew then, did we?"

Heathrow shook his head. "I don't recall Ash even mentioning the location of his land, though even if he had, it wouldn't have meant a thing to me." He laughed again. "I expect finding husbands for the girls will give m' wife something to occupy herself with this Season."

Before he'd taken his leave, Lord Heathrow then engaged Peterbloom in a brisk discussion of the new Enclosure Bill now on the floor of the House. Peterbloom felt that many of the small landholders would be unable to pay their share of the cost of enclosure legislation, as many could not afford now to hedge or drain their land. Still, the prospect of allowing perfectly good land to lie fallow each year was both unnecessary and wasteful.

The discussion ended on an amiable note whereupon Peterbloom bid the older gentleman good day and returned again to his own work. He expected his good friend Dr. Keating to call before the day was out and the two men planned to gather together an assortment of herbal powders and tonics which Keating meant to take to the hospital that evening with him. He'd invited Peterbloom to join him on his rounds that night in order to begin a journal that would document in great detail the progress of the patients receiving the new treatment.

At the Heathrow town house that afternoon, Lady Jersey and two other Almack patronesses, the beautiful Lady Cowper and the Countess Lieven, along with a niece of hers, Miss Elizabeth Phillips and a friend of the girl's, Anne Bingham up from Bristol, arrived soon after luncheon. On the agenda today was finalizing the elaborate plans for the extravaganza that was to formally launch Miss Lucy Fraser into society.

All three of the Fraser girls and Elinor were also present as the meeting got under way. Miranda hadn't particularly wished to be included in the planning session, but upon Katie's urging, had, at last, agreed to join the others.

Seated on a rolled-arm sofa next to the young ladies, Elizabeth and Anne, both prettily turned out in the first stare of fashion, complete with tiny velvet spencer jackets and white kid gloves, Miranda felt almost as fashionable as they, wearing one of her very best gowns, a sheer white dimity with dainty puffed sleeves that were trimmed in a double row of blond lace. Had she been at home, she'd never have donned the delicate dimity in the middle of the week, choosing instead to save it for a special occasion or at the very least, for Sunday services. But in London, Miranda'd noticed that women dressed every day as if they were attending a fancy-dress ball. Lucy looked quite lovely this afternoon in a pretty lemon-yellow sprigged muslin that brought out the golden highlights in her auburn hair. She'd draped her new paisley shawl casually about her elbows.

An hour into what was becoming quite clear to Miranda would be an *overlong* meeting, what with Lady Jersey's detailed analysis of each and every aspect of the huge undertaking, Miranda noted that she was not the only one who'd begun to suffer from the sheer tedium of it. When Elizabeth and Anne at last asked permission to take a stroll about the Square, and Lucy begged to join them, Miranda, recalling her aunt's admonition to be a bit more gracious toward Lady Jersey and her friends, at once offered to accompany the girls as chaperone.

"How very kind of you, dear," said the Countess Lieven, directing a pleasant smile at Miranda. "Though I do hope you have a timepiece. I should like Elizabeth and Anne back within the hour. We are expected at the Princess Esterhazy's this afternoon for tea. See that you are not late, girls," she called as the four young ladies scampered happily from the room.

Advancing onto the flagway in front of the elegant brick town house, Miranda was again reminded of her and Katie's first visit to London.

"Katie and I used to take long walks every afternoon whilst Papa and Uncle Oliver were occupied elsewhere," she told Lucy.

"Did Papa allow you to visit the shops on your own?" Lucy asked curiously.

"We visited a few but not nearly so many as you and Katie have with Aunt Isobel and Cousin Elinor."

The girls hurried across the street to the pretty park in the center of the square and commenced to leisurely stroll about the shady perimeter of it. Coming again to the corner where they'd entered the park, they recrossed the street and traversed the stone flagway all around. The aspect in Hanover Square was quite pleasant this afternoon, the outdoor air felt brisk without being too cool, and there was only a slight breeze to ruffle the dainty edges of the girls' gowns as they walked.

Presently, Anne, a petite blonde with a pale complexion and light-blue eyes, said, "While I am in London this time, I should like to purchase a complete new set of hair ribbons. I especially want a lovely rose to match the new slippers I purchased last week. We've not nearly so many clever shops in Bristol as there are in London."

"Anne only just arrived yesterday," Elizabeth told Miranda and Lucy.

"Are you to stay for the Season?" Lucy asked.

"Oh, indeed." Anne nodded vigorously. "That is the primary reason I came."

"We are not so very far from Piccadilly Circus, you know," Elizabeth remarked, gazing up the street that led away from the square. "Perhaps we might stroll in that direction. There are quite a number of fashionable millinery shops at this end of Piccadilly Circus." She glanced at Miranda, the elder of them and, as such, the chaperone. "It shan't take a great deal of time," she added brightly. "I am certain my aunt would give us leave to go."

"Please, Miranda, may we?" Lucy begged.

"Well, if you are certain it isn't too terribly far," Miranda replied. "You do know the way? I fear I should become quite lost on my own," she added, with a laugh.

"We could take the carriage if you'd prefer," Elizabeth offered. She cast a gaze across the square at the shiny black vehicle parked at the curb.

"Oh, I much prefer to walk," put in Anne. "Besides, if we shan't actually be leaving Mayfair, we cannot possibly lose our way, can we?"

"You are quite right," Elizabeth agreed.

"Well, then," Miranda said. Beside her, Lucy clapped her hands together with glee.

Miranda smiled at her pretty younger sister as the little group set off for Piccadilly Circus, their gentle voices and feminine laughter rippling like music on the scented air wafting after them. Listening to the younger girls talk, Miranda realized she was rather enjoying the outing. She'd seen precious little of London since she'd been in Town and this was the first time she'd ventured out for a stroll.

In what seemed like no time, the girls emerged onto the busy thoroughfare of Piccadilly Circus. Here, the wide cobbled street was alive with the bustle of horses, carriages, and carts clattering thither and yon. The flagway along both sides of the street was crowded with a throng of well-dressed and some lesser, well-dressed, folk.

"We mustn't venture too far afield," Miranda said as she anxiously took in the scene. Across the way, she recognized St. James's Street, which she knew led to the Palace and Pall Mall. Beyond that, however, nothing looked familiar to her.

Elizabeth took the lead, and a few moments later, the four of them entered a small millinery shop where, after a good deal of browsing, Anne shook her head, indicating she saw nothing there that she liked.

On the flagway again, the girls had advanced only a few paces when Lucy cried, "Look! Linen Draper and Silk Merchant to the Royal Family." She read aloud the sign that was posted above the heavy front door of the shop.

"May *we* also shop there?" Anne asked, nearly as wide-eyed as Lucy over the wonder.

Elizabeth laughed. "Of course we may."

Miranda wasn't at all certain that they'd be welcomed into this particular shop, not a one of them being royal . . . well, perhaps Elizabeth was, being the niece of a countess. But, since she was also a longtime resident of the city, perhaps she did, indeed, know whether or not commoners were allowed inside.

Her fears were soon put to rest when the young ladies were at once greeted, and quite cordially, by the shop clerk, a young man dressed in an extraordinary fashion in a puce satin waistcoat with brightly colored birds embroidered all over it. His face was painted to resemble a French doll and he smelled like a perfumery. With exaggerated court manners, he ascertained precisely what the girls were seeking and set about showing them quite a large selection of costly ribbands and expensive laces.

"Hmmm," Anne sighed, after fingering nearly every sample laid out on the silver tray before her. "I don't see anything I like. Perhaps we should look elsewhere."

"But I am certain if milady wishes to—" the foppish clerk began.

"We shall be leaving now," Elizabeth announced importantly. She breezed past Miranda, who'd been standing a bit apart gazing longingly at bolt after bolt of the most elegant watered silk and figured muslins she'd ever seen.

"Burlington's is just up the street," the young lady added, perhaps a trifle too loudly.

"I am certain milady will not find anything there that . . ." The dandy's words trailed into oblivion as the four young ladies exited the shop.

A few paces later, Anne squealed, "Was he not the silliest fribble you have ever seen?" Her loud burst of laughter was joined by merry giggles from both Elizabeth and Lucy.

"Girls . . ." Miranda began, her tone a gentle scold, then, with a shrug, she decided against reprimanding them. Lucy knew better than to make fun of other people, but in the company of other young ladies her own age, Miranda expected her sister was merely chiming in so as not to appear different.

As they drew near Albany House, the entrance flanked by two identical pairs of shops, Miranda heard Lucy announce to her new friends, "One of my suitors, Mr. Dunworthy, resides here."

"Oh-h!" Elizabeth enthused. "I understand the flats are quite impressive. My brother wished to take up residence here when the building was first opened to gentlemen lodgers, but there was quite a lengthy waiting list and he ended up marrying before he was accepted."

"Have you ever been inside a gentleman's apartment?" Anne asked Lucy.

Overhearing this particular exchange, Miranda did interrupt sharply. "Indeed, she has not! Discussing a gentleman's place of residence is hardly a seemly topic of conversation for proper young ladies. I insist you cease speaking of it at once," she added firmly.

Looking duly reprimanded, the three younger girls fell silent for a spell. Upon approaching Hatchard's, a book and print seller's shop, Elizabeth quietly asked if they might step inside.

"I have been wishing to acquire a copy of Mary Meeke's newest novel," she said. "Shall we see if the book is in?"

When Miranda nodded assent to this suggestion, the girls filed in. A half hour later, after both Elizabeth and Anne had made purchases, Anne professed a frightful hunger for a pastry and a cup of tea before they headed back to Hanover Square.

"I know a wonderful little bakery shop just around the corner on Sackville Street," Elizabeth suggested.

Although, Miranda, too, was beginning to feel a bit peckish, she had no money with which to purchase anything for herself or Lucy. Besides, she suspected it was time they were heading back to Hanover Square.

"I do not think we should stop again," she said. "Your aunt was most adamant about—"

"Oh, we've plenty of time yet," Elizabeth protested. "I'll wager my aunt and Lady Jersey have not even looked up. You've no idea how Lady Jersey can go on and on and—"

"On and on," Lucy chimed in, her blue eyes twinkling merrily.

The three girls dissolved again into giggles.

"Please may we go, Miranda," Lucy begged. "I confess I haven't the strength to walk back without something to eat first."

"But Lucy, I did not bring my . . ." Miranda turned palms upward to indicate that she hadn't brought along her reticule and, therefore, had no money. Not that she had any anyhow.

"It shall be my treat," Elizabeth interjected brightly. "Anne is my guest, and I've plenty of money with me."

"Please, Miranda."

Miranda glanced up at the sky. Already the shadows were beginning to lengthen. "I cannot think it advisable. The countess wishes Elizabeth and Anne to—"

"Doesn't signify!" Elizabeth thrust her chin up, her dark eyes sparkling mischievously. "It we are late, I shall simply blame it on Anne." She took off running, tossing over her shoulder, "Anne is a hungry piglet!"

"I am not a piglet!" Anne called back hotly. She darted off to catch up with her friend.

"Miranda, I am near to famished," Lucy cried before she, too, hurried off on the heels of her new friends.

Miranda sighed heavily. She had no real authority over the girls, and what she used to have over Lucy had diminished considerably of late. She hastened her step and eventually drew nearer to the three giggling teenagers. She didn't mind in the least lagging a few steps behind them. The younger girls' incessant chatter and bubbly laughter were growing a bit tiresome, actually.

After it seemed they'd walked a great length, Miranda began to wonder if perhaps Elizabeth did, indeed, know the way to the pastry shop.

"Elizabeth," she called, "are we quite near? I haven't a clue where we are and I shouldn't want us to become lost."

"Just a bit farther," the dark-haired girl flung over her shoulder.

Several blocks later, Miranda's concern grew. Either Elizabeth had become so caught up in talking with her friends that she'd failed to note where they were going, or she'd completely forgotten the direction of the shop. What was worse, ominous clouds were gathering overhead and not a single one of them had anything with which to protect themselves from a shower. Elizabeth and Anne were both wearing lightweight spencers, and Lucy had her shawl, but Miranda was not wearing any sort of outer garment at all. She glanced down at the now very dusty hem of her finest dimity gown and grimaced.

"Elizabeth, we really ought to return to Hanover Square. I fear it is coming on to rain and not a one of us has a bonny."

"Is it?" the dark-haired girl asked. She paused to gaze about as if only just now realizing where they'd got to. "Dear me . . ." she muttered. "We truly should have reached the bakery shop by now." She darted a look across the street. Her brow furrowed as she gazed up and down. "What do you suppose has become of it?"

"Perhaps it is shut down," Anne suggested. "In Bristol, one very often finds a perfectly good shop shut up tight."

Lucy cast an alarmed look at Miranda. "You do know the way back to Aunt Isobel's, do you not, Miranda?"

"No," Miranda said truthfully, "I do not." She cast a worried gaze at Elizabeth.

That young lady was chewing on her lower lip. "Oh, dear."

"Miranda!" Lucy cried.

Miranda flung an anxious look up and down the busy cobblestone street. Jammed one against another like soldiers standing at attention, tall narrow buildings lined both sides of the thoroughfare as far as the eye could see. Miranda recalled they'd crossed street after street on their way here, but not a single name or signpost stuck in her memory. She had no idea where they were.

"Oh, dear, we *are* lost, aren't we?" Anne cried with dismay. Her blue eyes filled with tears and she began to sniff, and then to sob.

Elizabeth slipped an arm across her friend's shoulders. "Miranda knows the way back, Annie. She is older and wiser than we. She will show us the way."

Miranda gasped, then, straightening her shoulders, she attempted to gulp down the fear that was gripping her middle. It would not do to let the younger girls know how very frightened *she* was! She tried for a light tone. "We shall simply retrace our steps back to Piccadilly Circus, and from there . . . it is a simple enough task to find our way back to Hanover Square." She turned a brave smile on Lucy. "Come along, sweetie. We shall be at Aunt Isobel's in time for tea."

The small group that set out walking this time was far more solemn than they had been on the way here. When in only minutes, the heavens opened up and it began to pour, Anne's sobs increased to the degree that it was difficult to tell which was coursing down her cheeks the fastest, her salty tears or cold wet raindrops.

"We shall drown!" she cried. "In Bristol, there was a girl once who—"

"Oh, do be still, Anne. I am sick to death of hearing about Bristol! We shouldn't be in this fix if you had purchased the pink ribband we saw at the Queen's draper."

Teary-eyed Anne turned a hurt look on her friend, but said nothing. Miranda, too, wondered how Elizabeth had arrived at that particular conclusion, when it was *she* who'd insisted they visit the pastry shop *she* knew of.

Apparently the same thing crossed Anne's mind. "But it was you who wished to walk to Piccadilly Circus in the first place, and the pastry shop was *your* idea!"

Elizabeth glared at her companion, but when she opened her mouth to protest, Miranda said firmly, "Let's not quarrel, girls. If we hurry we shan't become too terribly wet." She ducked her head so as not to be totally blinded by the rain. Nonetheless, she feared her pretty new bonnet was already ruined. From the corner of one eye, she could see its bright red plume hanging limp and soggy, the tip dripping pinkish-colored spots onto the flattened wet sleeves of her best dimity gown.

"But where could they have got to?" Lady Heathrow cried, her tone shrill with alarm.

"With both our husbands and the count out looking for them, they are bound to turn up soon," Lady Jersey said.

"We should never have let them set out on foot. Miranda knows nothing of the city. Lucy is perhaps more familiar with Mayfair than Miranda. Did not any one of the coach drivers see which way the girls went?"

The countess Lieven shook her head. "I expect the drivers and footmen were every last one dozing, or not paying the least bit of attention. I cannot imagine why Elizabeth would wander off without telling us where they were headed! It is not like her to be so thoughtless."

"Nor is it like Miranda," Katie murmured.

She, her aunt and cousin Elinor, Lady Jersey, and the countess Lieven were all gathered before the fire in the foremost drawing room of the Heathrow town house awaiting word of the girls from the search party.

It seemed they'd waited an eternity when a scant second after the tall case clock in the foyer had chimed eight bells a sudden commotion coming from that direction caused all the women in the room to jump.

"They're here!" cried Lady Heathrow. She sprang to her feet and scurried into the hall. Catching sight of the four rain-soaked young ladies, she ran toward them, completely ignoring the two tall gentlemen who had also entered the marble-tiled foyer, water coursing from their clothing and puddling at their feet.

"Oh, my stars!" Lady Heathrow cried, flinging her arms about a shivering Miranda, then reaching to also enfold Lucy into her embrace.

The Countess Leiven had enveloped Elizabeth and Anne in her arms. "Come and sit by the fire, girls. You must be chilled to the bone."

Lady Heathrow briskly addressed Elinor. "Take the girls abovestairs, Elinor. Walker will bring up dry clothing while I send a footman for a doctor."

"That will not be necessary, madam." One of the gentlemen stepped forward into the light.

Lady Heathrow turned a gaze on the gentleman who'd spoken.

"Lord Peterbloom!" she exclaimed as Miranda, huddled beneath a coat several sizes too large for her, said, "The Viscount Peterbloom and his companion, Doctor Keating, found us only moments ago, Aunt Isobel. We had . . . wandered into—"

Suddenly, Miranda's teeth began to chatter and a violent shudder precluded further comment from her.

"Best get the young lady abovestairs at once and into dry clothing," Dr. Keating said with authority. A large man, though not as tall nor as powerfully built as the viscount, he was carrying a black medical bag in one hand. "I will be glad to examine all the young ladies and prescribe whatever medicines are needed for their complete recoveries."

"Oh, my." Lady Heathrow turned a worried look on Miranda.

Katie slipped an arm about her sister's shoulders. "I'll take Miranda to my room. Elinor, please see to Lucy and the other two."

Advancing up the stairwell, Miranda heard the deep timbre of Lord Peterbloom's voice explaining to the concerned women belowstairs how he and Dr. Keating had come upon the four of them huddled in the doorway of the new Surgeon's Hospital just beyond Mayfair.

"Whatever were you doing at the hospital?" Katie asked incredulously as she and Miranda gained the landing.

Miranda shivered. "We became quite turned around in the rain," she replied, beginning to feel a bit of her strength returning now that she was safely indoors . . . and away from Lord Peterbloom's piercing gaze.

She'd been too stunned to speak when he, of all people, had come striding down the hallway and through the wide double doors of the only building on the narrow street that the girls had decided looked inviting and . . . well, lit up. Though they had not yet worked up the courage to enter the austere-looking edifice, they'd been close to it when Lord Peterbloom and his friend had emerged and found them taking refuge from the deluge in the small covered enclosure in front.

"We did not know it was a hospital," Miranda added.

"It was the only building with lights on and an overhang. We hadn't the least notion where we were."

Katie bustled into the bedchamber on the heels of a housemaid who'd been sent to build up the fire and lay out dry clothing. "We were worried to pieces about you. Uncle John and Lord Jersey and the count are even now out searching for you."

Still clutching the large wet overcoat tightly about her shoulders, Miranda backed up to the blazing fire.

Across the room, Katie snatched up a cloth with which to rub her sister's bedraggled hair dry and carried it to Miranda. "How serendipitous that once again it was the Viscount Peterbloom who came to your rescue," she said firmly.

"I suppose." Miranda's lips trembled as Katie dropped the towel and absently reached to remove the many-caped coat that engulfed Miranda.

"I take it this is the viscount's coat?"

Miranda nodded thinly.

"How very gallant of him to give it to you." She draped it over the back of a chair to dry, then turned again to her sister, who stood stock-still before her, both arms crossed over her chest.

Catching sight of Miranda's odd posture, Katie looked perplexed. "What is it?" she asked.

Miranda gave a little cry. "Look at me." Slowly, she uncrossed her arms.

When Katie's eyes fluttered downward, she gasped aloud.

"I am practically naked!" Miranda cried. "The rain soaked completely through my gown. *This* is how Lord Peterbloom found me!"

"Oh, dear me." Katie reached to draw her sister into her arms to comfort her. "Perhaps he did not notice."

Miranda wrenched away and began to undo the fasteners of her wringing wet gown. "He noticed. The instant he saw me, he removed his coat and flung it about me! At the time, I did not know why he'd singled me out, but in the coach, the coat came partway open and I saw the horrified look on Lucy's face."

Katie's smile was sad. "Well, it was kind of him not to say anything, Miranda. I did not notice the other girls . . ."

"All wearing wraps. Both Elizabeth and Anne had on dark-colored spencers and Lucy had her shawl. I was the only one so . . . shamelessly exposed." She sniffed indignantly. "I suppose we should be thankful that Lucy brought along her shawl. With a rain-soaked bodice, *she'd* have caused quite a stir."

Katie grinned. "Perhaps you might have been rescued a bit sooner."

"Katie!" Miranda stared with horror at her sister.

A half hour later, after Dr. Keating, ably assisted by a gentle Katie, had examined the ears and throats of each of the young ladies, he pronounced them every one fit and merely prescribed large bowls of warm broth and several days rest.

Katie returned the viscount's damp coat to him and thanked both gentlemen profusely for once again coming to the girls' rescue.

"You seem to be on hand whenever we are in need, sir. How shall we ever thank you?"

The viscount bent a polite nod. "Glad to be of service, Miss Fraser."

After both Lady Heathrow and the Countess Lieven had expressed their deep gratitude, the gentlemen climbed into Peterbloom's closed carriage and drove away.

"An extraordinary young lady," the doctor remarked, settling his medical bag on the floor at his feet.

"Indeed," Peterbloom murmured, his tone somber, almost brooding.

"I can easily understand your preoccupation of late, Peterbloom. She is warm and caring and possesses the most serene nature I've ever beheld in a woman."

Peterbloom glanced up. In all the years he'd known Keating, he'd never once heard Reginald prose on so about a woman. A dark brow lifted. Since "serene" was not a word anyone in their right mind would use to describe Miranda, he presumed it was Katie who'd so favorably impressed his good friend, the doctor.

"I assume you are referring to the elder sister, Katie?"

Keating quirked a brow. "Weren't you?"

Peterbloom snorted, though when he spoke, his tone was placid. "Miss Fraser is all that is kind. However, it is . . . the little one, Miss Miranda, whom I find . . . intriguing." He paused. "There is something . . . extraordinary about her. I admit I am quite at a loss to explain the attraction."

Keating grinned at his longtime friend. "Perchance you have fallen in love, old man."

Peterbloom's dark eyes flashed. "I merely said I found the young lady intriguing, I did not say I loved her, nor do I intend ever to marry. Least of all, her!"

Dr. Keating's lips twitched. "Indeed."

Peterbloom cleared his throat and turned to gaze out the rain-splattered window at his side. London was a dastardly place to be on a night such as this. "Although someone needs to marry her," he muttered irritably, "if for no other reason than to look after her. Dashed foolish of those girls to go parading all over town on foot. And her without a proper wrap."

"Quite fortunate they turned up on the hospital doorstep," Keating agreed. "I shudder to think what might have happened to four unprotected females on a night such as this."

And Miranda with that wet gown plastered to her bodice. Aware of a sudden tightening in his loins, Peterbloom squirmed uncomfortably on the coach bench. The little minx did, indeed, need a man to look after her.

Peterbloom inhaled sharply.

Had he been alone with that young lady in the coach tonight . . . in *that* condition, he was not certain he could have refrained from . . .

The scowl on his face deepened as he shifted on the bench again.

Dr. Keating had been watching his friend intently. "I'll be demmed, Peterbloom," he said, "you are in love."

Peterbloom huffed. "Demmed foolish of those girls to go . . ." His fingers began to drum on the polished wooden armrest at his side.

Keating threw his head back and laughed aloud. "Head over ears, old man. Head over ears!"

Fifteen

Lady Heathrow insisted that both Miranda and Lucy remain in their bedchambers for the next several days, not as punishment but in order that they might recoup sufficiently from their ordeal so as to be fit for Lucy's come-out ball. She instructed the girls' maids not to awaken them each morning but allow the girls to sleep until they woke of their own accord. She sent books, magazines, and pen and paper up to them so they might be entertained with quiet pursuits.

Miranda was delighted with the half dozen new Minerva novels her aunt brought her, and for the next several days, both she and Katie spent long pleasurable hours reading. Lucy, not given much to intellectual pursuits, began the Herculean task of writing letters (which Uncle John was good enough to frank for her) to all her friends in Halifax.

"I simply must tell everyone about London and my new gowns and my come-out ball," she exclaimed.

Lucy also told her friends, her *girl*friends, about meeting the nonpareil Lord Peterbloom on the way to Town, and about her *tendre* with the magnificent gentleman. Not long after, the post began to deliver return letters to Lucy from Halifax, one from her favorite beau in the village, Theodore O'Malley.

"Teddy is not terribly happy that I am set to wed another," she told her sisters, a hint of genuine regret coloring her tone.

"If you did not think he would be, you should not have told him," Katie said.

"I didn't tell him. I expect Prunella did. She wants Teddy for herself, I know she does. But it doesn't signify. It doesn't, does it?" Lucy cried petulantly.

"No, I expect it does not," Katie replied evenly.

Miranda said nothing during the exchange, but she took note of it. Was it possible Lucy still harbored feelings for Teddy O'Malley?

For the entire week after the girls' drenching, Lady Heathrow also had their meals sent up on trays until Miranda balked, declaring that she felt quite fit enough to leave her bedchamber and dine belowstairs with the family. After all, both she and Lucy had been encouraged to come down every afternoon when Dr. Keating and Lord Peterbloom came to call. The calls were understandably short, with most of the light banter during them centered around Lucy's upcoming ball.

Everyone of consequence among London's upper ten thousand had been invited to the gala debut, which the planning committee had finally decided should be held in the Count and Countess of Lieven's ballroom, as theirs was far more spacious than Lady Jersey's. For those guests who did not wish to dance, dice and card games would be set up in one of the anterooms, with light refreshments—champagne, rataffia, lemonade, and an assortment of hot and cold delicacies—laid out in another. Still another chamber would serve as a smoking room for gentlemen, complete with billiard tables and a well-stocked cellarette.

In addition, there were three or four smaller, but well appointed, withdrawing rooms at the opposite end of the ballroom that would be suitable for light conversation or general mingling amongst the hundreds of guests that were expected to attend. Tucked in a far corner was the ladies' necessary room, where a maid would be on hand to repair a torn hem or flounce, repin a tape, or tuck an errant curl back into place should it have come loose whilst dancing. Miranda assumed that in the chamber set aside for gentlemen's needs, that a footman would be present to assist them with . . . whatever.

In all honesty, she was as atremor with anticipation to see the countess's lovely home as she was to attend the ball itself. In her twenty-one years of living, she'd never imagined being invited to such a place, or attending such a gala affair. She only hoped that neither she nor her sisters, most especially Lucy, embarrassed themselves or Aunt Isobel with some unfortunate lapse in decorum, however unintentional the lapse might be.

She was thankful that once Lucy again felt up to it, her deportment lessons were resumed, the hired tutors instructing her in such basics as how to execute the proper curtsy and what sort of thing she should and should not speak of when conversing with a lord or lady of rank. Miranda rather expected this sort of last minute tutelage was generally not the norm, that a proper *tonish* education would have already smoothed out whatever rough edges might be lurking about in a young lady's makeup. Except that in Lucy's case, no such education had ever taken place, and by both her aunt and sponsor, it had been deemed vitally necessary.

"I am afraid Lucy's 'rustic charm' is becoming every bit as legendary as her beauty," Miranda heard Lady Jersey lament one afternoon.

"My niece has not had all the advantages," Lady Heathrow replied briskly. "But that is easily remedied," she insisted, and in the singular fashion of one who has great wealth at her disposal, set about doing precisely that.

Aunt Isobel also insisted on new ball gowns for everyone. As it turned out, Lucy's—required to be in keeping with what was considered seemly for a young lady not yet out—was less elaborate than apparently Lucy had hoped.

"I look positively insipid in white!"

"Nonsense," Lady Jersey declared, "you look . . . virginal."

Overhearing that remark, Miranda had gasped aloud but managed to hold her tongue. For once, she quite agreed with Lady Jersey. For once, the bodice of Lucy's gown was cut in a style that actually covered her. Miranda thought the delicate white muslin with the pale pink sash quite proper for a girl not yet seventeen.

Her ball gown, on the other hand, featured a shockingly low-cut square neckline with a wide flounce that fluttered fetchingly when she moved from side to side. The ruffled flounce, she noted, intently scrutinizing her reflection in the cheval glass as a team of skilled seamstresses buzzed about her, gave the delightful illusion of fullness in a place where nature had neglected to supply Miranda with a great deal of it. She loved the dress and felt quite stylish wearing it. The exquisite peach-colored silk was quite on a par with any of the costly fabrics she'd beheld in the exclusive shop in Piccadilly Circus designated as Linen Draper to the Queen. Tiny peach satin rosebuds with pale green satin leaves and silver-threaded stems decorated the edge of the pretty puffed sleeves and seemed to have been tossed in a helter-skelter fashion on the delicate folds of the pencil-slim skirt. With peach kid gloves and silver satin slippers to match, it was the most elegant ensemble Miranda had ever seen, let alone owned.

Katie's new gown was equally as lovely. Made of ice-blue silk, the rich color emphasized her lovely dark eyes and honey-brown hair. She and Miranda were both set to have their hair professionally dressed on the day of the ball with specially fashioned headdresses that featured sparkling jewels and a feathery plume. Miranda had never worn a headdress before.

On the day the fashionable French modiste had first been invited to the Heathrow town house, arriving with an impressive entourage of seamstresses and footmen, who had spread out bolt after bolt of beautiful fabric at the ladies' feet, Aunt Isobel had also ordered up several additional new gowns for Miranda, one a replica of her favorite puff-sleeved dimity that'd been ruined by the rain. She also now had several new bonnets, new slippers and gloves, a half-cape and cloak, and two new pelisses.

"I am beginning to understand how easily it has been for Lucy to forget her austere upbringing and fall in with Aunt Isobel's wishes," Miranda told Katie on that last afternoon before the ball. "I confess it has been quite easy for me to become swept along."

When Katie made no immediate reply, Miranda turned a concerned gaze upon her. Katie had seemed prodigiously withdrawn of late. Miranda smiled sadly. No doubt, her sister had finally begun to miss their home as sorely as did she. But there was nothing to be done for it now, not till Lucy was out and they discovered which way the wind blew in regard to Lord Peterbloom's affections.

At length, a melancholy sign escaped Katie's lips. "I wonder if Aunt Isobel has invited that nice Doctor Keating to the ball? He has been so very kind to you and Lucy."

"That he has," Miranda agreed pleasantly, relieved that Katie's thoughts had returned again to the ball. Yet, her own lips thinned when she added, "Although I did not think it necessary that he and Lord Peterbloom call to personally check on us the past ten days in a row."

Katie smiled warmly. "The gentlemen were merely being thoughtful, Miranda. One of you might have caught a chill. Lord Peterbloom knows how very much Lucy's ball means to her. It would have been disastrous had she fallen sick and been unable to attend."

Miranda's eyes rolled skyward. "How many times have the three of us been caught in a sudden downpour on our way home from the village and suffered no ill effects from it?"

Katie turned a frown on her younger sister and then, quite uncharacteristically, cried, "Miranda, you are being incorrigible! It is quite obvious to all of us that the Viscount Peterbloom is as taken with Lucy as she is with him. You had best accept the fact that he will one day become our brother-in-law!"

Stunned speechless, Miranda stared at her older sister aghast. *Katie never raised her voice!*

"Only this morning," Katie continued in an impatient tone, "Aunt Isobel declared she has no objections to the match, and Lady Jersey champions the viscount most strenuously. Only you persist in your dislike of him. Why is that?"

Miranda sniffed piously. "Suffice it to say that you do not know all there is to know about the man."

"Well, perhaps I do not," Katie retorted, "but what I do know is above reproach."

In keeping with her sister's ill humor, Miranda did nothing to quell her own rising emotions. "Including the fact that for no good reason he has turned us from our home?" she snapped.

"That has not been decided for a certainty. Once he and Lucy are wed . . ." Katie's lips pursed as she apparently worked to rein in her temper. "We have discussed this matter at length, Miranda. If we are invited to live in the big house, it will be very nearly the same as continuing to reside in Fraser Cottage."

"It will not be the same at all," Miranda maintained stubbornly. "Furthermore, I do not believe he has the least intention of marrying Lucy. He simply wishes to . . . I believe that he means to . . . well, before it is over, I expect that he will . . ."

"Will *what,* Miranda?"

She thrust her chin up. "I don't know." Thus far, she

was one hundred percent certain that nothing untoward had happened between her sister and the viscount, but that did not mean if the opportunity presented itself, he would not turn into the unprincipled bounder she personally knew him to be.

"I believe the viscount means to state his intentions toward Lucy the night of the ball," Katie said in her usual well-modulated tone. "It would be the perfect setting. He has been quite attentive of late. He has been attentive to *both* of you," she added. "Every time he called last week, he brought flowers and sweets to you, as well as to Lucy."

Miranda's lips thinned. The viscount's small gifts meant nothing to her. He was obviously trying to win her over the same as he'd already won Aunt Isobel and Katie over. He might *state* his intentions to marry Lucy, but Miranda did not for one minute believe that he meant to do so. The man's intentions were anything but honorable. For instance, a real gentleman would not have behaved in so rakish a fashion after he'd carried her aloft to her carriage. For that matter, a real gentleman would never have scooped a young lady into his arms and carried her in the first place, especially when the young lady was not needful of being scooped or carried. Which clearly proved that Lord Peterbloom was the type of man who hid lascivious motives behind a cleverly concealed sham of chivalry.

The viscount may have called upon her and Lucy every day since he'd rescued them from the storm under the pretext of inquiring after their health, but Miranda had not failed to note the multitude of piercing looks he'd settled upon her—as if he were seeing right through her clothing again to her skin. Most days, she'd been too mortified to look the man directly in the eye, but every time she did glance up, he'd be staring straight at her. It was most unsettling. And clearly proved again that with a mind as evil as his, there was no saying what sort of ruination he had in mind for Lucy.

Miranda knew for a fact that Lord Peterbloom had no intention of marrying or settling down in the country. Had not those been the very words he'd uttered that night at Almack's to Uncle John? Indeed, they had been. So, what was his plan? To offer for Lucy, force his attentions upon her, and then walk away, leaving her a fallen woman, or so deeply scandalized no proper gentleman would have her?

Not if Miranda had anything to say about it, he wouldn't. She vowed to stay alert at every turn, on the night of the ball, prepared to take immediate action, to do *whatever* might be necessary in order to prevent the undue tarnishing of Lucy's reputation. Lucy was as innocent as a newborn babe. Well, almost as innocent. She had admitted to being kissed once, but all the same, Miranda expected the kiss had been quite innocent. She did not know a single lad in Halifax with the seduction prowess of the rakehell Peterbloom. He was a vile, contemptible man and she would not let him compromise her sister as he had compromised her.

On the evening of the ball, Miranda arrived looking quite splendid in her new finery, her dark curls professionally coiffed, her cheeks prettily flushed with excitement, her green eyes alert for any sign of impropriety from the wicked Viscount Peterbloom.

He and Dr. Keating arrived at the Lievens' promptly at nine of the clock, but were obliged to endure a lengthy wait before being formally announced and admitted into the crowded ballroom. They spent the next half hour politely smiling and nodding their way through the receiving line. Afterward, Peterbloom graciously did the pretty for Miss Lucy, leading her out for the traditional first set, a quadrille. A few steps into the dance, the handsome couple were rewarded with riotous applause from the cheering throng of onlookers, whereupon Peterbloom relinquished his pretty partner to a new one, one of the many gentlemen who were eagerly awaiting a turn to stand up with the newest darling of the *ton.*

Now, Peterbloom stood on the fringe of the dance floor, watching the intricate patterns being made by those of the guests who were still stepping and turning through the set. So far this evening, he'd gotten only a quick glimpse of the one young lady present here tonight who he particularly wished to see.

Miss Miranda Fraser looked stunning in a lovely peach silk creation that displayed the charming curves of her trim figure to perfection. Her shining dark hair was dressed in an upswept style, with a pretty jeweled tiara nestled in amongst her rich brown curls. Peterbloom had never seen her in such looks and he longed to feast his eyes at leisure upon every delectable inch of her.

He'd seen the young lady virtually every day since the night of the rainstorm, and although he'd barely exchanged two sentences with her, he'd found himself ready and eager to return again to the Heathrow town house the following afternoon. Never in his life had a young lady held him in such thrall. He was beginning to wonder if perhaps Keating didn't have the right of it, after all. Perhaps he was falling in love.

Peterbloom anxiously scanned the glittering ballroom in search of Miss Miranda's sweet face again. That he was at liberty to do so, ergo *not* being suffocated by a squealing gaggle of women, seemed a miracle in itself. But as this was not the first such fête he'd attended since his reentry into society, it appeared the *ton* had finally grown accustomed to seeing him out and about, and unless he desired otherwise, they now left him pretty much to his own devices. Oh, feminine eyes still cut sidelong as he strolled past, fans still fluttered coquettishly and he was smiled and winked at by scores of women whom he knew would be more than willing to admit him into their private chambers. Disinterested in that sort of casual alliance, however,

Peterbloom had neither encouraged nor accepted a single offer. He wasn't entirely certain what sort of alliance he was interested in, but stolen kisses, forbidden embraces, and illicit tumbles were definitely not it.

Unaware of the brooding look that had settled on his face as he searched for the petite figure of Miss Miranda Fraser, Peterbloom's eyes continued to scan the sea of smiling faces that stretched almost as far as the eye could see. Some distance away, he caught a glimpse of his friend Dr. Keating, who, as expected, had gravitated to the elder Miss Fraser's side. She also looked charming tonight. Peterbloom rather suspected a *tendre* was developing between the two. More than once, Keating had declared her the kindest, gentlest young lady he'd ever met. In the past fortnight, he'd been every bit as eager as Peterbloom to call upon the Fraser sisters every afternoon. Having been friends with Keating since they were boys, Peterbloom greatly admired him, and from what he knew of Miss Fraser, he thought them quite well suited.

Turning his gaze toward the dance floor again, he spotted the flame-haired Miss Lucy there. The sight of her shapely form, though well concealed tonight in a simple white muslin gown with a pale pink sash tied beneath her ample breasts, brought an indulgent smile to his lips. The little rapscallion had come a long way since that night at Almack's when she'd alarmingly whispered into his ear that she did not dance. A dark brow quirked. Miss Lucy was the type of female who, once she became aware of her seductive powers and learned to refine her skills, would develop into a rare beauty, capable of wielding great influence over a man. Her talents were raw now and therein, Peterbloom realized, lay the danger. Without a strong hand to keep her in check, to exert some control over her somewhat hoydenish tendencies today, she'd likely tumble into mischief and find herself shunned for good.

Thinking in that vein, the scowl that had formed on Peterbloom's brow deepened.

From where she stood, partially shielded by a priceless porcelain vase containing a fan-shaped array of delicate hothouse blooms, Miranda watched the Viscount Peterbloom, resplendent tonight in black evening clothes, shiny black pumps, and a tucked white silk shirt. With both arms folded broodingly across his middle, he appeared in quite a pelter as he watched Lucy and the young buck she was partnered with on the dance floor. Miranda could only wonder what sort of lurid thoughts were forming in the viscount's head.

She continued to watch the dark-haired man, being careful to duck back again behind the vase when his gaze lifted to scan the crowd. Heaven forbid he see her watching him and think *she* had the veriest interest in his whereabouts! At length, she grew bolder and began to move closer to him, slowly at first and, as her confidence grew, advancing several yards at a time, till at last she stood but a few feet away. She had no wish to engage him in conversation; not at all. She merely wished to be on hand if it appeared that he might be about to whisk Lucy into the garden, or wherever, for some evil purpose.

At length, she realized the viscount had become aware of her proximity and that he was even now striding toward her. Miranda thrust her chin up. She was not afraid of him. True, he still had the power to set her heart aflutter, and her opinion that he was the handsomest man in the world had not altered a whit, but neither had her conviction that he was the lowest form of humanity on earth. Nor that the rotter had ruined her and meant to do the same for Lucy.

"You look exceptionally charming tonight, Miss Miranda," the gentleman said, the dazzling smile on his face again nearly causing her knees to buckle beneath her.

She worked to silence the rapid pounding of her heart. She cast a frosty look at him, but said nothing.

"One wonders why a young lady as lovely as you is not dancing."

Miranda's pink lips pursed. "I am not dancing, sir, for the simple reason that I have not been asked."

He grinned. "An easy problem to remedy. Will you do me the honor, Miss Miranda, of—"

"I will not!" she snapped.

The viscount appeared somewhat taken aback, but he recovered quickly enough. "Well, then. Perhaps you'd care to take a stroll with me into the refreshment chamber? I understand the count has quite an impressive selection of wines and champagnes to choose from." He smiled agreeably and politely offered an arm.

Her chin held aloft, Miranda glared at the handsome man. And felt her breath grow short and her heart beat faster. Why was it that every time she saw him, she became so caught up in the wonder of his extraordinary attractiveness—his smooth, square jaw, his well-shaped aristocratic nose, those mysterious dark eyes, and that full sensuous mouth—that she clean forgot her purpose, whatever that purpose happened to be? It was as if his very persona so captivated her that she became drawn into him, actually became a *part* of him. She'd never felt such an overwhelming sensation before. It was so powerful as to be . . . disbelieved.

She had to shake off the part of herself that wished to run full tilt ahead, to leave behind her quest to trap him before he trapped Lucy and give herself up to the pleasure . . . yes, the *pleasure* of his . . . well, perhaps not the pleasure of *his* company, she told herself sharply, but, at least, the pleasure of being on the arm of such an attractive gentleman at this extraordinarily fashionable fête. Her chin inched up another notch. She felt a bit like Lucy in that she could hardly wait to tell her friends back in Halifax about the . . . Her eyes narrowed suddenly. Thanks to *this* particular gentleman, she might never see her friends back in Halifax! "I think not," she responded tartly. She turned her face forward again, a cool gaze directed straight ahead.

"Ah. Well, then. Perhaps we might simply stand here together and chat a bit." He clasped both hands behind his back . . . and stood there. Silently. After standing a good bit longer, he said, "Miss Lucy appears to be enjoying herself. I daresay your aunt and Lady Jersey are quite proud of themselves."

Miranda turned a sidelong look on him. "Proud of themselves?" she repeated.

"They have done an excellent job preparing her."

"Preparing her . . . for what, sir?"

A pleasant smile on his lips, Lord Peterbloom gazed down at the young lady beside him. "For whatever role she may take on." His elegant shoulders lifted and fell. "The wife of a duke, an earl"—he grinned disarmingly—"a viscount."

Miranda's stomach clenched.

"I rather expect Miss Lucy will be successful in landing whomever she sets her sights on," he went on, blithely unaware of Miranda grinding her teeth beside him. "Your sister is a beguiling young lady."

Miranda's nostrils flared afresh as she worked to push down the white-hot anger boiling inside her. Was there no end to this man's mischief? Suddenly, it occurred to her that if she herself remained glued to the viscount's side, he would be unable to lure Lucy into the garden, or wherever he meant to take her so that he could . . . she gulped from the sheer distaste of it . . . force himself upon her.

"On second thought, sir"—she smiled sweetly—"I believe I would like a glass of champagne. As it happens," she confessed before she caught herself, "I have never tasted champagne before." Tilting her head to look up at him, she curled her fingers around the viscount's forearm and then . . . swallowed convulsively as the warmth and strength emanating from it seemed to burn clean through to her fingertips. Her pulse quickened and, once again, she nearly forgot why she'd agreed to accompany the gentleman in the first place.

It took the attractive pair a good bit of time to slowly wend their way through the crowded ballroom to the anteroom where drinks and refreshments were laid out in advance of the elaborate supper that would be served at midnight. Once there, Miranda took several generous sips of the sparkling brew from the long-stemmed crystal goblet that Lord Peterbloom handed her. A few minutes later, she became aware of Katie and her companion, the good Doctor Keating, standing close by.

"Cheers," the doctor said, raising his glass in a salute as he and Katie strolled over.

Beside the tall, mustached man, the smile on Katie's face was the brightest Miranda had ever seen.

"Is it not a wonderful party?" Katie breathed, her voice containing a strange dreamy quality.

One of Miranda's finely arched brows lifted.

"I do so wish Mama and Papa could be here," Katie went on. "Mama especially. She would be so very proud of Lucy."

Miranda's spirits dipped a trifle lower. "Indeed." She sniffed. "Mama would be proud." But Papa, it suddenly occurred to her, would be doing the exact same thing she was doing. Endeavoring to protect Lucy from whatever harm might befall her.

"Even Elinor is enjoying herself," Katie said. "I last saw her dancing with that nice Mr. Dunworthy."

"The poet," Miranda murmured. She absently swallowed another sip of her champagne, and then another. And then noticed that suddenly the world was becoming a fuzzy blur. What did it mean? She'd never experienced such a phenomena before! She glanced at the pale amber liquid in her glass and blinked. Then blinked again. It was as if she could not quite clearly focus upon anything. Though it was not an unpleasant sensation, it was a trifle disconcerting. She raised her head to glance curiously about. Everyone in the room seemed now to be moving in slow motion, the bright smiling faces melding languidly into the glittering images of candlelights and sparkling jewels. Actually, the sight was quite pretty, but . . .

She tried to focus a look on the devilishly attractive gentleman standing beside her. The viscount stood just beyond her right shoulder conversing with Dr. Keating. She could hear the deep timbre of Lord Peterbloom's voice, but could not clearly distinguish the gentlemen's words. Instead, the entire chamber and the ballroom beyond it was now a buzzing mélange of voices, music, and tittering laughter. Was her hearing also being affected by the strange malady? She glanced again at the few remaining droplets of champagne in her glass. As if compelled, she drew the goblet to her lips and swallowed the last of the liquid floating in it. The fruity wine slid down her throat like silk, leaving in its wake, a tangy, tingly aftertaste that was quite delicious and not . . . unpleasant.

A crooked little grin appeared on Miranda's lips as she turned to address Katie. "Thish wine is quite good, Katie. Wouldn't chew like to try some?"

Katie smiled serenely. "I feel quite lightheaded enough, Miranda." She eyed the depleted glass in her sister's gloved hand. "You do recall papa warning us about strong drink, do you not? Perhaps one glass is enough for you. You are quite small in stature, you know. A bit more is apt to go straight to your head. It would not do to become . . . under the influence," she concluded on a whisper.

"Oh, it ishn't the least bit strong. It tashtes quite like—" Miranda's lips became a lopsided grin, "Well . . ." she giggled, "I don't know what it tastes like!" That struck her as inordinately funny and she giggled again. The lilting sound of her laughter caught the viscount's attention and he glanced up and continued to stare at Miranda even as he resumed his conversation with Dr. Keating. When a servant silently appeared at Miranda's elbow, she set her empty glass on the tray he carried and helped herself to another glass. And drank it straight down.

"Really, Katie," she enthused, "itsh *very* good."

Because Katie had already moved to stand next to the doctor, she said nothing. Miranda, still wearing the crooked little grin on her face, next noticed a somewhat fuzzy image of Lucy bearing down upon them. Watching Lucy make a beeline for the viscount, something tugged at her thoughts for attention.

"Lord Peterbloom," she heard Lucy say shrilly, "the next set is to be a waltz. I have so longed to dance the waltz with you!"

The viscount nodded gallantly. "Then the dance is yours, Miss Lucy." He set his half-full glass of wine down on a silver tray and touched Miranda's elbow. She did not clearly comprehend the few words he murmured to her before off he went on Lucy's arm.

Watching the two of them, Miranda managed to blink herself to some semblance of awareness. *She was supposed to do something, wasn't she? Something important? Ah, yes. She had vowed to ensure that Lucy was not ravished to pieces by the wicked Lord Peterbloom.*

Well, then . . . do something, she would!

Sixteen

Miranda hurried to Katie's side and placed a hand on her arm. "Lucy is dancing with Lord Peterbloom, Katie! We must watch them!" She fairly dragged Katie with her into the ballroom.

Flinging a bewildered glance at her sister, Katie offered no resistance. Beside her, Dr. Keating merely smiled, and fell into step behind the sisters.

Once the three were positioned on the edge of the dance floor, Miranda pointed an unsteady finger at the whirling figures of Lucy and the Viscount Peterbloom. "Don't you see, Katie, itsh a waltz!" Her tone was agitated.

"Indeed, it is." Katie nodded. "Lucy appears quite adept. And the viscount is a superb dancer. How romantic they look in one another's arms," she added dreamily.

Miranda turned a stricken look on her sister. "Thatch precisely my point, Katie!"

"You are acting very oddly, Miranda. The champagne has indeed gone to your head."

"Wine has nothing to say to thish, Katie. Don't you see? Ish just as the book said."

"What book? What are you talking about, Miranda?"

Miranda stamped her foot impatiently. "The new Minerva novel we read last week. In the book, Gabriella's mother told her that a gentleman's passions become inflamed quite easily, often with no more than a look or a touch, and it can lead to disastrous results for a young lady. Just look how the viscount is embracing our Lucy!"

Miranda again wagged a wobbly finger at the handsome pair twirling on the dance floor. The viscount's arm was clasped tightly about Lucy's trim waist. Her right hand was pressed into his strong shoulder and their left ones were intimately intertwined. As they executed a particularly intricate turn, the viscount pulled Lucy even deeper into his chest, causing Miranda to sputter with alarm.

"It is scandalous, Katie!" she cried. Other than the dance master demonstrating the waltz in Aunt Isobel's drawing room, this was the first time she'd actually seen the dance performed.

Katie flung another perplexed look at her sister.

"Well, it is!" Miranda exclaimed hotly. Several onlookers standing nearby glanced at her.

"Do lower your voice, Miranda. You are near to causing a scene far more scandalous than Lucy dancing the waltz with Lord Peterbloom. Actually, I think they look quite smashing."

"Oh!" Miranda gazed with horror at her sister. Katie had read the book. She should have a very good idea what sort of evil thoughts were taking shape in the viscount's mind! "The rogue is near to ravaging her!"

Katie stared at her sister with puzzlement. "Promise me you will have nothing more to drink, Miranda."

Katie turned to take the doctor's arm, and the pair of them strolled off as if nothing were amiss. Dumbfounded by her sister's nonchalance, Miranda realized there was nothing for it but for *her* to put things to rights.

Her eyes again sought out the viscount and Lucy. Spotting them, she watched intently until the music ceased. Then, when she noted the gentleman's hand still lingering intimately at Lucy's back as he guided her from the dance floor, an alarmed gaze traveled beyond the pair to the row of double French doors that gave onto the terrace. It was just as she feared. His passions were fully enflamed and he meant to lure Lucy into the garden, where he would subject her to . . . to unspeakable indignities!

She scurried after her sister and the rakehell, but lost sight of them as a fresh crush of people flowed onto the dance floor to form the next set. Undaunted, Miranda managed to elbow her way past all of them and onto the dimly lit terrace.

The gust of fresh air that greeted her outdoors felt cool on her flushed cheeks and had the additional effect of sharpening her focus. She flung a wild gaze about and was certain she spotted the viscount and Lucy, or was it simply the viscount alone, *without* Lucy? Several other guests were strolling about on the terrace and the grounds and she could not tell from this distance if the viscount was alone or not. Perhaps he had cunningly suggested that he and Lucy separate and then meet again at some designated spot in the garden. Yes! That would be his devious plan.

Miranda scampered across the wide terrace to the balustrade and down the marble steps that led into the garden. Skirting past the ornamental statuary and the flower beds, she reached the graveled path that led to the maze in the middle. Pinpricks of pain shot up her legs as her feet, shod in the thinnest of satin slippers, trod upon the sharp pebbles and uneven stones.

Ignoring the discomfort, she pressed on, guided by the steady crunch of the viscount's footfalls ahead of her. Eerie shadows danced in front of her as tall, leafy poplar trees undulated on either side of the narrow footpath. Despite the bright shafts of moonlight illuminating the many twists and turns, Miranda knew it would still be perilously easy to become lost in the confusing labyrinth.

At last, they emerged into a large circular area where

an imposing fountain spewed sparkling water into a silvery pool at its base. Across the way, Miranda saw the shadowy figure she'd been following come to an abrupt standstill. Ducking behind a clipped hedgerow, she watched the Viscount Peterbloom withdraw a handkerchief from his waistcoat pocket and swipe at his apparently fevered brow. Her nostrils flared. The man's passions were, indeed, aroused to the hilt!

Not wishing to waste a precious second before Lucy appeared for the assignation, Miranda fairly ran to where the gentleman stood and boldly announced, "You may kiss me, sir."

The Viscount Peterbloom could not imagine what manner of good fortune had smiled upon him this evening, but, being a warm-blooded man, actually, at the moment, a *very* warm-blooded man, who was dashed attracted to this particular female, he didn't waste a single second in obliging her.

Hastily stuffing his hanky back into his waistcoat pocket, he moved a half-step forward, and well, did precisely as she asked.

A moment later, his breath ragged, he dragged his quivering lips from her trembling ones and watched with fascination as Miss Miranda Fraser's sea-green eyes fluttered open. Indeed, he had not been dreaming! She was standing right here before him, her sweet, soft body cradled in his arms.

Gazing down at her, he grinned crookedly. "If I may be so bold, my dear, what exactly . . . prompted you to . . . ?"

Her lips pursed primly. "For Lucy's sake, of course."

"Ah. For Lucy's sake." She was making no sense whatever, but what the deuce? "Well, then." His eyes dropped again to the tantalizing bow of her mouth. "Perhaps . . . for Lucy's sake . . . we should . . ."

She tilted her chin up invitingly. "Very well, sir."

Dashed good luck! Peterbloom lowered his lips to hers again. When he felt her small arms slip round his neck, he took the liberty of pressing her body closer to his and deepening the kiss.

At length, however, a prick of guilt prompted him to draw away. The little minx obviously had no idea how her kisses were affecting him. Still, despite his quickened breath and . . . other discomforts, he found it dashed difficult to release her entirely. For a long moment, he stood relishing the sensuous feel of her sweet breasts pressed to his chest as he gazed deeply into her glistening dark eyes.

She was loveliness itself. He'd never felt so drawn, so intrigued, or so fascinated by a woman before in his life. The fiery sensations coursing through him now were more intense than anything he'd ever experienced. He could think of nothing to account for the strange phenomena except that . . . No, it couldn't be. He had not fallen in love with her. Had he?

She surprised him again when she suddenly pulled away and said, "I was right all along, was I not?"

He blinked. "Right? About what, Miss Miranda?"

Her head tilted to one side, causing the moonlight above their heads to dance like diamonds in her eyes. "You are a rake and a bounder," she announced matter-of-factly.

Peterbloom grinned. "So, you have found me out." He reached for her once more, but she again wrenched away.

"You do not deny it?" she declared hotly.

He cocked a brow. This was perhaps the oddest conversation he'd ever had, but . . . having just been invited to kiss the most delectable little spitfire he'd ever met, by the little spitfire herself, nothing she said or did could shock him now. "I deny nothing, my dear."

Miranda eyed him with abject loathing. "I have dreamt of this moment," she ground out.

Peterbloom blinked afresh. "Dreamt of it?" *By jove!*

"Many, many times," she added through clenched teeth.

Totally confused now, Peterbloom reached to pull her close again. It quite delighted him when, this time, she offered not the least bit of resistance.

Instead, she tilted her head up and murmured with resignation, "You may kiss me as much as you like, sir, so long as you do not touch Lucy."

His lips already pressed to hers, Peterbloom did not hear the last part of her reply. The Important Part, the part about kissing her as much as he liked had set his blood racing through his veins again.

When he felt the pretty little wench arch her back and press her body close to him, her arms wound tightly around his neck, sparks of pleasure exploded in his brain. One hand cupped the back of her head and his fingers crushed the silken dark curls he found there. *By God, he was on fire!* His other hand slid hungrily down over the curve of her hips and fanned out over the gentle swell of her buttocks. He'd never wanted a woman so much in his life!

Never had one felt so right in his arms before! It was as if his lips already knew hers, as if the sweet nectar of her mouth was a taste he'd been yearning for and now that he'd found her, he could scarce get enough of her. When, at last, he dragged his lips from hers, he was more fully aroused than he thought possible. *He must have her!*

But, no . . . no, of course, he could not take her. She was an innocent and he could not, would not, take advantage of her, no matter how compliant she was being at the moment. He could recall a time, however, when he might have behaved differently, but he was not the same man now.

Gasping for control, he thrust her from him and, lest she become embarrassed when she glimpsed the bulge in his trousers, he took a step backward into the shadows. Though it was quite dark, he could still see the sudden flash of anger that darkened her eyes.

"You are through with me then?" she spat out.

Peterbloom swallowed convulsively as the throb in his groin reached a fever pitch. She had no idea what a temptation she was presenting to him, or the difficulty he was having in resisting her. "Get the hell out of here!" he said brusquely. "You are behaving quite unseemly."

He should have known she would not obey.

Her green eyes flashed fire. "You are a fine one to talk, my lord Peterbloom!"

"I'm warning you, Miranda, get out of here before I"—he gulped for breath—"before I . . ."

"Before you, what?" She tossed her head up defiantly. "Before you steal another kiss from me?"

A snort of derision escaped him. "I can hardly be accused of stealing kisses from you, my dear. I clearly recall you freely offering them to me. And it was a dashed reckless thing to do, if I may say so."

"Well, it was not as if another kiss would matter, would it?"

He glared at her. "What are you talking about? I have never kissed you before tonight." He paused. "Have I?" It was . . . possible, he supposed. He frowned when a sudden image of that infamous night five years ago flashed through his mind. The night he'd wagered he could kiss fifty young ladies before the sun came up the next morning. Had Miranda been . . . ? "I did not . . . you were not . . ."

She continued to glare hotly at him, her slim arms folded tightly across her small breasts.

"No-o . . ." he groaned aloud.

"I was fifteen," she began softly. "You accosted me one night in my uncle Oliver's garden." Her voice fairly quaked with emotion. "I—I have never forgiven you, nor have I forgotten the fear, the indignation, I felt."

"Oh, Miranda," he breathed. "I am so very, *very* sorry." His eyes squeezed shut and one hand raked through the thick waves of his dark hair. He longed to gather her into his arms and comfort her now. "You've no idea how deeply I regret my actions of that night. My behavior was unconscionable. Can you ever . . . forgive me?"

Miranda bit her lip. "Per-haps. If you promise you will never subject my sister, or any other young lady, to the same sort of despicable treatment."

"That's what this was all about? You feared I would . . . compromise Lucy, is that it?"

Miranda nodded. The deep hurt in her eyes tugged at his heart. Considering how she felt about him, Peterloom knew it had taken a great deal of courage for her to offer herself to him in order to protect her younger sister's virtue. For that, he admired her greatly.

"Please believe me, my dear, when I say your sister is in no danger from me. I would never force my attentions upon her, or for that matter, upon any young lady who is not willing." When Miranda said nothing, he continued. "Have I given you any cause for unease of late? That is, aside from . . . just now."

When she still did not reply, he added, a rakish grin beginning to play about his lips, "You are a taking little thing, Miranda. And you did offer yourself."

"And if Lucy offers?" she parried.

He shook his head emphatically. "I would never allow it where Miss Lucy is concerned."

"But you kissed me, sir. Why did you kiss me?"

Thinking it best to stick to one charged subject at a

time, Peterbloom elected not to address that topic. "I assure you Miss Lucy is safe," he said again.

Miranda sighed. "Would that I could believe you."

"Of course you can believe me. In these last weeks, have I said or done anything that has given you cause for alarm? Have I done anything that could be construed as improper or . . . beyond the bounds?"

"You . . . you *looked* at me," she said accusingly.

His lips twitched. "As I said before, Miss Miranda, you are a taking little thing. You have quite a sweet smile, at least that is how I remember it, considering how rarely you favor me with one. And . . . your eyes—" Suddenly his voice grew hoarse. "Your eyes . . . quite compel a man to look at you." He fought an almost overpowering urge to draw her into his arms again.

Gazing up at him, she finally murmured solemnly, "I can think of nothing improper that you have done these last weeks, my lord."

"Well, then." He drew a relieved breath. "There it is. I own that I feel a good bit responsible for Miss Lucy. She does need someone to look out for her, and—"

"And you wish to take on the task?" Miranda asked eagerly.

He shrugged. "I will not shrink from it. I am, after all, the first gentleman she met in Town . . . even before she arrived in Town. In part, I feel Miss Lucy is my discovery." He paused. "When one considers all that has happened to bring us together since, indeed, it is no wonder that I feel protective toward her, as I do toward each of you."

Studying the tall gentleman, Miranda wished with all her heart to believe him genuine. Though she felt reluctant now to say it, that is, now that she had kissed him again and it had felt so very, *very* . . . She thrust the delicious memory aside and fought to pull her thought back to the matter presently under discussion. If Lord Peterbloom did, indeed, mean what he said, that he wished to protect Lucy, to marry her, she would not stand in the way. Surely, once they were safely wed, she and Katie would be allowed to return home to Halifax. That is all she wanted. Wasn't it?

"You three young ladies are essentially alone in the world," Peterbloom said quietly. "I've no desire to see harm befall any one of you. You have my word on that, Miss Miranda. I will let nothing happen to any of you, nor will I see Miss Lucy disgraced. By anyone."

Because his tone had grown raspy again, Miranda took it as a further sign of his sincerity. He seemed quite moved by his concern for Lucy. She longed to ask him about his plans for Fraser Cottage, but decided against it just now. There would be time enough for that later. His declaration to care for Lucy was enough for now.

"I trust I have put your mind at ease," he said. "Had I known what your true concerns were tonight . . . I'd have never . . . I would not have touched you. I fear I have behaved abominably again. I humbly beg your forgiveness."

A sincere smile tugged at the corners of Miranda's mouth. "Of course I forgive you. If you can forgive me, sir, for throwing myself at your head. When I saw you waltzing with Lucy tonight, I . . ." Her small white shoulders lifted and fell. "Perhaps Katie had the right of it. Perhaps the wine did go straight to my head. I had never tasted champagne before. It tastes quite good, actually."

He blinked with apparent surprise. "Well, there you are. Had you your senses about you . . . you'd never have followed me out here, or flung yourself at me." He stood gazing down upon her, an indulgent smile playing at his lips again.

Gazing up at him in the moonlight, Miranda again had to thrust aside the delicious memory of those lips pressed to hers a scant second ago, and the delightful feel of his strong arms clasped about her. His kisses tonight had been nothing like the hurried peck he'd planted on her lips five years ago in Uncle Oliver's garden. No, this kiss was more . . . She sucked in an uneven breath. She must not think on that! *Not ever again!*

"Come," he said. "I will escort you back to the ballroom. We have been away a considerable length, although considering the multitude inside, perhaps no one has noticed our absence."

Miranda let the gentleman take her elbow and guide her back through the maze. Pinpricks of bright light from above glittered on the rustling leaves of the poplar trees as they walked beneath them. Drawing closer to the brightly lit house, she could hear soft strains of music from the ballroom wafting toward them on the breeze.

As they emerged from the garden and neared the marble steps that led to the terrace, the viscount said gravely, "I think it best for all concerned if you and I never speak of this to anyone."

Miranda gazed up at him. Since her ill-fated encounter with Lord Peterbloom five years ago, he was, indeed, a changed man. He was all that was proper now; just the sort of man any girl would wish to marry. "I quite agree with you, my lord," she said quietly.

A quarter hour later, it was without a qualm that Miranda watched Lord Peterbloom escort a beaming Lucy into supper. Without a qualm, she realized, but not without a great deal of envy.

Seventeen

Over the next several days, Miranda became more and more certain that Lord Peterbloom's affections for Lucy were genuine. He and Dr. Keating called on the young ladies several times, took them for numerous drives in the park, and Lucy said he was quite attentive at a soirée hosted by the Princess Esterhazy which neither Miranda nor Katie attended.

One afternoon following another outing to Hyde Park, Miranda and Lucy were headed abovestairs to remove their bonnets and gloves.

"Did we not have a wonderful time, Miranda?" Lucy asked. "I declare, I fall more and more in love with him each time I see him. Did you note how the other ladies looked at us with envy? Especially me, since it was I who was sitting next to him. Perhaps he will offer for me at my birthday party at week's end, at Lady Jersey's. Do you think he will, Miranda?"

Wearing a somewhat wan smile on her face, Miranda said nothing as she followed her chattering sister up the stairwell. So far as she was concerned, Lord Peterbloom had already declared his intentions toward Lucy the night of her come-out ball. True, he had not yet approached Uncle John, but he had as much as said he meant to marry Lucy when he said he would not "shrink from the task of looking after her." What else could those words mean?

She also vividly recalled certain . . . *other* events that had transpired between herself and the Viscount Peterbloom that night. The feel of his strong arms wrapped tightly about her, his full, sensuous lips pressed to her own. Just thinking on it now, she was beset once again by the same tingly, breathless sensation that had washed over her then.

It was a most unsettling feeling, and one that, try as she might, she could not make disappear. Other times, of late, when Lord Peterbloom reached to take her hand to assist her from the coach to the ground, her knees would go weak beneath her skirt and her heart thump so wildly in her breast, she feared he could hear it. In truth, she had never felt so miserable in her life, but she also knew she had no one to blame for her misery but herself.

It had been quite foolish of her to follow Lord Peterbloom into the garden that night and beg him to kiss her. Her cheeks burned with fire now as she contemplated the brazenness of her actions. Her sisters and aunt would think her quite mad if they knew. Uncle John would, no doubt, insist the viscount wed her! Despite the selflessness of her motives in doing so, she prayed no one ever uncovered the horrible truth. She would die of humiliation! Over and over, she had begged her Heavenly Father to forgive her scandalous actions which she felt certain stemmed from the vast quantity of wine she'd consumed earlier. She had begged forgiveness for that, as well. Papa had been *so* right about the evils of strong drink. Katie, too.

If only she could keep a tighter rein on her emotions and recall *before* her temper flared out of control that Divine Providence was looking out for them, that *she* did not have to force things to turn out right. If only she could be more like Katie and remember all that Papa had taught them. Katie was even now falling in love with Dr. Keating, and did not yet know for certain if that gentleman returned her affections. Yet, she was as calm and serene as ever, certain that all would turn out well in the end. Why could *she* not also remember that?

"Do you think he will?" Lucy's heartfelt plea jarred Miranda's senses round.

"Do I think he will w-what?"

"Lord Peterbloom. Do you think he will offer for me the night of my birthday party?" Lucy repeated impatiently. "At Lady Jersey's."

Miranda tried for a cheerful tone. "I am certain he will declare himself quite soon, sweetheart. You've only to be patient. Everything will turn out right in the end, you'll see."

Lucy sighed. "That is what Katie says."

"Well, Katie is right."

The following morning at breakfast, Walker delivered a note to the eldest Fraser sister. After reading the contents, Katie turned a bright smile on the circle of women gathered around the breakfast table. "Lord Peterbloom and Doctor Keating wish to take us to Astley's Amphitheater this afternoon," she said.

"All of us?" Lucy asked. "Or just you and me?"

Katie retrieved the sheet of linen and flicked it open again. "All of us. Elinor, too."

Across the table from her, Elinor's light-brown curls shook. "I am expecting Mr. Dunworthy to call this afternoon. We are to exchange poetry volumes, my Lord Byron for his Keats."

"Perhaps your Mr. Dunworthy would also like to go to Astley's," Lady Heathrow suggested. She pressed an agreeable smile on her only daughter. Miranda knew her aunt was pleased beyond words that Elinor at last had a suitor.

"That would be lovely indeed!" Katie exclaimed. "We shall make a party of it; Doctor Keating and myself, Elinor and her beau, Lucy and the viscount, and . . ."

A small set smile on her lips, Miranda was already shaking her head. "I shan't be going." She glanced at Lady Heathrow. "Katie will be sufficient chaperone for Lucy and Elinor. I would . . . only be in the way."

"Rubbish!" Katie protested. "The gentlemen invited all of us. It will be such a lovely treat, Miranda. We have never been to a circus before."

"Well, I think Miranda is right," Lucy put in importantly. "She would be in the way. She'd be the only unescorted female amongst us."

Miranda bit her lower lip and fixed a gaze on her plate.

"Besides," Lucy prattled on, "I have noticed of late that Lord Peterbloom spends an inordinate amount of time attempting to draw Miranda out. When she finally began to talk yesterday, they spent all afternoon discussing their silly old herbs. It was most exhausting and I don't mind saying *I* felt totally excluded. If we had not stopped to stroll along the Serpentine and met up with Lord Chesterton and Sir Richard, I should not have had anyone at all to talk to. I do not like it when Miranda comes along."

"The gentleman is merely being polite," Lady Heathrow said. "You are both very charming young ladies and I am quite certain the viscount thinks it polite to converse with both of you."

"Well, in any case, I don't see why I am not permitted to go about with only a maid for chaperone. Betsy accompanies Elinor when she goes to Hatchards with Mr. Dunworthy. And Elizabeth and Anne are both permitted to be with their gentleman friends with only an abigail along. I feel like a child with Miranda constantly by my side."

"Lucy!" Lady Heathrow scolded. "I think it quite splendid that Miranda is at last in charity with your young man. And I expect he is delighted to have, at last, gained her approval. You should be grateful, my dear, that she agrees to accompany you at all."

Lucy pouted. "I shall soon be seventeen. I shall hardly

need a chaperone then. I am very nearly a married woman."

Lady Heathrow's eyes again cut round sharply. "You are not yet affianced, dear. An unmarried girl of seventeen, whether she is betrothed or not, still requires a chaperone." That said, she turned a look on Miranda. "Since Miranda does not feel up to the circus this afternoon, Katie's presence will suffice."

Suddenly, Miranda sprang to her feet. "If I may please be excused, Aunt Isobel?"

"Are you feeling unwell, dear? You look a bit pale. Does she not look pale, Katie?"

Katie gazed with concern at her sister.

"I . . . did not sleep well last night," Miranda lied. "Please extend my apologies to the gentlemen. I will . . . I prefer to spend the day in my room."

Before the morning was out, a huge bouquet of flowers arrived for Miranda from Lord Peterbloom. A card was attached in which he expressed both his sincere concern for her health and well wishes for a speedy recovery.

After reading the hand-penned note at least a dozen times, Miranda carefully tucked it into her Bible. It was the first note she'd ever received from a gentleman. She feared it might also be her last.

Three evenings later, Katie and Lucy, and Elinor, were still talking about the daring performances and extraordinary wonders they'd witnessed at Astley's Circus when the Heathrow party climbed into the carriage to make their way to Lord and Lady Jersey's lovely home for Lucy's birthday party. The celebration was to begin with an intimate dinner for a dozen guests of Lucy's choosing, most of them young people who had become her especial friends—among them, the Countess Lieven's niece Elizabeth, and her friend Anne, Sir Richard and Lord Chesterton, Mr. Dunworthy, and, of course, Lord Peterbloom. Additional guests would arrive after dinner for dancing and card playing.

Wearing her pretty new dimity gown with the frilly puffed sleeves, Miranda was trying, for Lucy's sake, to be cheerful and light of heart. All of them, Aunt Isobel, and even Uncle John, Miranda assumed, expected Lord Peterbloom to offer for Lucy before the night was over.

"If the gentleman so much as whispers in your uncle John's ear," Lady Heathrow said with a gay laugh as the carriage jounced beneath them, "I shall inform you of it straightaway, Lucy dear!"

Lucy beamed joyfully, whilst beside her, Uncle John merely set his jaw and turned to stare from the carriage window.

"It will be a wonderful party," Katie said, even though her special friend Dr. Keating was not amongst the invited guests. "Even if the viscount does not offer for you tonight, Lucy dear, we've still a great deal to be thankful for." She turned a charming smile on her aunt and uncle and reached to pat Elinor's small gloved hands, which were neatly folded in her lap. "We shall never forget our wonderful trip to London and the delightful times we've had here."

"Lucy's come-out has, indeed, been a smashing success," Lady Heathrow remarked brightly. "I only wish Maryella were here to see it." She blinked back the droplet of moisture that sprang to her eye and turned an indulgent gaze upon the prettiest of her three nieces. "You are the image of your mama tonight, Lucy dear."

Miranda felt tears begin to cloud her vision, as well. Lucy did look beautiful tonight. With her thick auburn hair piled atop her head, she looked exactly like Mama. What man would not be smitten with Lucy's beauty?

* * *

That night, Lucy's birthday dinner began with a dish of shellfish soup and went on to include sumptuous servings of Florentine of Veal, Lancashire hotpot, dressed crab and potted lobster, pickled oysters and mushrooms, numerous vegetable dishes, and several rich, creamy puddings. The meal, served with a choice of delicate wines and champagne—which, of course, Miranda refused—was more delicious than anything she had ever eaten.

Moments after the last remove—a three-tiered cake, the icing set ablaze with brandy and brought flaming to the table—Lord Peterbloom, who'd been sitting next to Lucy, rose to his feet and clinked the side of his glass with his spoon in order to gain the attention of the boisterous crowd before him.

Her heart suddenly in her throat, Miranda gazed up at the handsome gentleman, resplendent tonight in a rich claret coat over fawn pantaloons and a richly embroidered, pale rose waistcoat. He was, indeed, the most handsome man in the world and also, she realized now, the kindest. Of late, he could not have been more attentive, or solicitous, toward all of them.

She thought back to the night they had first made his acquaintance at the inn in Wolverton. Apart from instantly recognizing him as the rake who'd stolen a kiss from her, she'd been quite surprised then by the marked change in his bearing. He had looked and acted the pattern card of respectability. Now, she knew him to be all that and more. That he had begged her forgiveness for his actions of five years ago had elevated him immeasurably in her eyes. Lucy was a lucky young lady, indeed, to have snagged such a fine gentleman.

Before she thought ahead to what she'd say to congratulate the pair upon their forthcoming nuptials, the viscount began to speak.

"I should first like to wish our lovely guest of honor, Miss Lucy Fraser, a very, *very*, happy—" He gazed straight into Lucy's glittering blue eyes. "How old did you say you were, sweetheart? Twenty-seven?" When Lucy squealed with delight and several of her young friends called out "Seventeen!", he recounted. "Ah, yes, only seventeen. My, my—" His dark head shook appreciatively. "One can only imagine the number of hearts this lovely young lady will break in the next decade. Happy *seventeenth* birthday, my dear."

While everyone seated round the table applauded roundly, he gazed with genuine affection at the beaming Lucy and raised his glass. "A toast," he said. But suddenly, he turned and looked straight at Miranda, "To the three, very lovely Fraser sisters, whom we are all, indeed, quite fortunate to know. A toast to the future happiness of each of you."

Though everyone at the table cheered, Miranda did not fail to note the crestfallen look that appeared on Lucy's pretty face. She saw Katie reach to place a comforting hand on their sister's arm and she gave Lucy what, she hoped, was a reassuring smile. Perhaps Lord Peterbloom meant to speak to Uncle John first. It would be the proper thing to do.

When dinner had concluded, all the guests drifted into the drawing room to await the late arrivals and for the servants to move the massive furniture in the dining chamber aside and roll up the rug in preparation for dancing.

Because Miranda had decided she did not wish to take part in that activity, she slipped quietly from the elegant drawing room into the long, carpeted corridor. Here, the walls were lined on either side with portraits and landscape paintings of every size and shape. Gazing up at them, she ruefully recalled her previous excitement over the prospect of being invited to the Countess Lieven's fashionable home the night of Lucy's come-out ball. But, once there, she'd been so intent upon her quest to run Lord Peterbloom to ground that she'd failed to take note of anything of grandeur beyond the ballroom . . . and the garden.

As usual, that memory caused her cheeks to burn and her heart to flutter, but she refused now to dwell on the sensations. The intimate moments she'd shared with the Viscount Peterbloom should never have happened and she simply must learn to thrust those memories aside. Over a week now she'd lived in fear that the wellspring of emotion that was building within her would erupt, that she'd do or say something to further embarrass herself. Lord Peterbloom was to become her sister's husband, for pity's sake. She could not spend her life rhapsodizing over him!

Lifting her chin with fresh resolve, she turned a gaze upon the elegant blue-gold-and-cream striped silk that covered the walls of the corridor. How prettily it complemented the plush Aubusson carpet beneath her feet. Blue velvet draperies tied with gold tasseled cords hung over a row of long windows. Overhead, she noted the intricately carved plaster molding that defined the edges of the high, arched ceiling.

Entering the circular rotunda, she next strolled into a spacious gallery to one side, the floor a highly polished mosaic of elegant wood and marble. Portraits of every size and shape decorated the walls here. Inspecting them a bit closer, she noted a marked resemblance in many of the faces to either Lord or Lady Jersey.

At length, she stepped from the picture gallery and moved up a wide sweep of stairs at the far end of the hall. Because a few other guests were also milling about on the landing, she did not feel she was trespassing, so continued onward to the next floor of the large house.

Once there, she peeked tentatively inside several chambers whose doors were standing open, and coming upon an exquisitely appointed drawing room complete with a pretty pianoforte in one corner and an elegant, carved golden harp beside it, she stepped inside. Would Lucy and

Lord Peterbloom have just such a lovely home one day? she wondered. Noting the pages of sheet music propped up before the pianoforte and harp, she wondered if they, too, might pass a pleasant evening in the quiet pursuit of music. Lucy was quite talented on the pianoforte.

At length, she turned with a sigh, and near the end of the corridor, stepped cautiously into the final chamber. The wainscoted walls here were a deep, rich walnut with burgundy velvet draperies hanging at the windows. A low fire burned in the hearth. Noting the vast quantities of books in long cases, she decided this must be Lord Jersey's study. Just as she was about to hastily exit the room, she noticed what appeared to be a collection of wartime memorabilia on a large loo table. Curious, she stepped toward it, bending to inspect the dozens of exquisitely carved soldiers, ships, and cannon. She'd never seen such intricately carved pieces before.

"Interesting, are they not?"

Startled, Miranda whirled about to find the Viscount Peterbloom standing by her side. In a small alcove that she had not noticed before, she spotted Lord Jersey replacing a billiard cue in a wooden rack on the wall.

"P-please forgive me, sir," she stammered, "I did not mean to intrude."

"We have finished our game and were just going down," Peterbloom said easily. He glanced at the delicately carved figure of a British soldier that Miranda had been studying.

"It's made of human bone, you know."

"Bone?" Miranda gasped, her eyes widening with alarm.

Peterbloom laughed.

"Entire set is made from human bone," Lord Jersey said, ambling toward them, a wide smile of greeting on his face. "French prisoners-of-war carved the entire set whilst incarcerated on British hulks in the harbor. The castle and the walled-fortress"—he pointed to several larger pieces—"are ivory. The fleet of ships, just there, is made from wood."

"Seems a bit sad, doesn't it?" Peterbloom mused.

"Yes," Miranda said quietly, not thinking to question why he felt as he did. "It is sad that such rare talent could not have been put to greater use."

Lord Jersey laughed. "Well, someone profited from it. I can assure you I laid out a good bit of the ready in order to acquire these little gewgaws. Pieces are widely collected now. I understand some of the prisoners even take commissions." He laughed again. "Which seems a bit sad to me. Prisoners making a profit at our expense."

Peterbloom laughed as well. "One never knows what manner of commerce war will spawn."

The three of them fell silent a moment, then Lord Jersey said, "You coming, m'boy?"

The viscount nodded. "I'll be along shortly. I thank you for the game, sir."

"My pleasure." Lord Jersey exited the room.

Miranda glanced back at Lord Peterbloom who was now striding toward the alcove where the billiard table stood in order to replace the long cue stick he'd been holding.

From there, he asked Miranda, "Do you play?"

Her gaze fixed on the handsome man, she smiled. "No. I confess I know nothing about the game."

Peterbloom's eyes twinkled merrily. "I'd be happy to teach you."

Thinking he was larking with her, Miranda laughed. "A skill that would most certainly ensure my success at *ton* parties, correct?"

Peterbloom grinned. "I daresay it would add consequence"—his dark eyes pinned hers—"where none is needed."

Despite the rush of warm color that Miranda felt rise to her cheeks, she tilted her chin up tartly. "Very well, sir. If you do not think a young lady caught playing billiards would be thought fast."

Peterbloom watched her walk toward him. "No faster than a young lady caught kissing a lord in a garden," he said pointedly. And was certain he saw a rush of color flood her cheeks as her eyes darted quickly away.

"I thought we had agreed never to speak of that again," she said quietly.

Peterbloom said nothing for a long moment, though he longed to. The past week had been torturous for him. Near every day in Miss Miranda's company, but always with Miss Lucy between them, meant that not once had he had the opportunity to exchange a private word with Miranda. He had experienced some success in drawing her out, and he'd quite enjoyed their talks on everything from herbs to the war and her views on political concerns, but there was a great deal more he wished to know about her. In fact, he wished to know everything. She was the most fascinating young lady he'd ever met.

Her disclosure that she'd been one of the innocent young girls he'd pressed himself upon those many years back helped him understand her reticence toward him the first few weeks the young ladies were in Town, but he was at a loss now to understand her aloofness.

He had not been so very long from the company of women to not know when one found him to their liking. The sharp intake of breath when their eyes met, the guarded looks, the shy smiles. Generally these were all telling signs. Signs he thought he'd noted in Miranda. But, with her, he was learning that nothing seemed to be what it really was. This past week, he'd tried his best to openly exhibit his growing interest in her, and at the same time keep Miss Lucy out of mischief. He wondered now if lack of use had caused his courtship skills to grow a trifle rusty.

Though he vowed to try again now, with such contrivances as a hand brushing against hers as he taught her the rudiments of the game, he finally concluded that neither the setting nor the nature of the activity was conducive to romance. In less than a quarter hour after they'd begun to play, they were both laughing uproariously over her unskilled attempts to skillfully sink a billiard ball into a pocket.

"Any pocket will do!" he finally said, shaking his head with unrepressed mirth.

"I am trying, my lord, truly I am!"

"Try holding your hand . . . thusly." He bent over her once again, his dark head close to hers as his large hand wrapped her delicate fingers around the slim cue. "There."

He thought he felt her fingers tremble beneath his, but he could not be certain. It was with great reluctance that he moved away.

When again the ball went vastly awry, they again dissolved into fits of laughter.

For a lark, Peterbloom began to tease her by proclaiming great lots of money he'd put up if she could sink just one ball.

"Twenty thousand pounds on this one, my dear. Forty, if you sink it, twenty if I do."

In no time at all, Miranda was into him for upward of sixty-three thousand pounds.

Delighted over the many pretty smiles he'd coaxed to her lips, he wished to extend the game indefinitely, but, at length, she firmly declared it at an end.

She handed him the cue stick. "I fear I shall never be able to pay you what I owe you, sir," she said, though she was still smiling prettily.

However, Peterbloom detected a trace of sadness in that smile, and wondered at it. His eyes held hers a long moment, then he said, "I will cancel the entire debt, Miss Miranda, if you will—"

He had been about to say "if you will kiss me again,"

but at precisely that moment two gentlemen came striding into the room, apparently intent upon playing a game themselves.

Taking a thought for the young lady's reputation over being caught alone with him, Peterbloom quickly said, "Thank you for delivering the message to me, my dear, I will come at once."

He hastily escorted his charming partner back down stairs. Although he was still at a loss to understand her bouts of odd behavior, he had quite enjoyed their silliness. Though they'd not spoken sensibly on any topic, the interlude had given him a glimpse of yet another side to her charming personality, one that he found quite to his liking.

On the way home from the party that night, Miranda's pleasant memory of her few moments alone in the viscount's company was shattered when Lucy announced that the gentleman had promised to take *her* to Gunter's tomorrow afternoon for a birthday ice.

"It is to be a special treat, especially for me," she declared proudly. "With no one to accompany us but Betsy."

Lady Heathrow cocked a brow of displeasure, but the stab of pain Miranda experienced over Lucy's pronouncement could not have been more fierce had Lucy announced that she and the viscount were to be wed on the morrow.

And what was worse, she could think of no plausible reason to account for the feeling.

Eighteen

Miranda was happy for Lucy and thrilled that she was to wed the Viscount Peterbloom. It was the very thing they all wanted. Though she still had not yet brought up the subject of their home in Halifax with him, she fully expected him to grant her and Katie permission to live there once he and Lucy were wed.

Quite convinced of that, it came as a shock when the day after Lucy's birthday party, the Viscount Peterbloom never appeared to take Lucy to Gunter's.

"But, he promised!" Lucy cried. "He did!"

"Perhaps you misunderstood him, dear," Lady Heathrow said. "Or perhaps he will still come. She cast a glance at the bracket clock atop the mantel. "No, I rather expect six of the clock is a bit late for an ice."

The ladies of the Heathrow household were scattered about the drawing room, Miranda, reading a new penny novel; Katie, embroidering the edge of a scarf she was making as a gift for Aunt Isobel; Elinor, quietly turning the pages of a book of poetry lent to her by Mr. Dunworthy, and Lucy, pacing fretfully before the hearth. Lady Heathrow was sipping on her third or fourth cup of tea since teatime.

They'd all spent a quiet day, not a one of them arising before noon or accomplishing much of import since. Lady Heathrow had roused herself enough to sift through the stack of calling cards that'd piled up throughout the day on the silver salver in the foyer. Stifling a yawn now, she reached again for the basket into which Walker had unceremoniously dumped the last handful of cards that had been delivered.

"Ah! Just look at what I've uncovered!" she cried. "I must have overlooked it earlier."

Lucy dashed to the sofa and perched on the edge of it beside her aunt. "Is it from him? He was here, was he not? I knew he would come, I knew it!"

"Oh, dear." Lady Heathrow frowned. "I'm afraid the corner is not turned down." Which, of course, meant that the gentleman had not called in person, but had, instead, had his card sent round. "But"—Lady Heathrow flipped the card over—"there is a note scratched on the back."

"Do read it! Please, Aunt Isobel!"

"He says . . . he enjoyed the party last evening . . . and hopes you have a pleasant day."

Lucy's blue eyes widened. "Th-that's all?"

Her aunt slowly nodded.

"Oh-h-h!"

When the rest of that week slipped by with no further word from the Viscount Peterbloom, Miranda grew quite alarmed. Something was definitely amiss.

"I cannot think what this could mean, Katie," she said. She and her older sister had settled into the small upstairs sitting room, prepared to spend a quiet evening alone whilst Lady Heathrow, Elinor, and Lucy attended a musicale at Lord and Lady Chalmer's. "Lucy says she has not seen the viscount at any of the functions she's attended this week. We were so certain he meant to offer for her . . . and now . . . nothing. Has Doctor Keating mentioned anything that might account for the viscount's whereabouts?"

Katie shook her head. "I've hardly seen him either. He has been excessively busy. There was an outbreak of influenza at the hospital, you know."

"Oh, dear. I do hope Lord Peterbloom has not contracted it. Or his mother. Perhaps he is caring for her. What do you think, Katie?"

Katie sighed. "I expect the viscount and Reginald—" She blushed. "I mean, the viscount and Doctor Keating have both been quite busy. It takes a good bit of time to prepare their herbal remedies and to dispense them. And the viscount maintains quite a full schedule at the House. Uncle John has attended a good many meetings this week. I expect the same is true for Lord Peterbloom."

"I expect you are right, Katie," Miranda agreed. "I suppose we should be thankful that Lucy has had plenty with which to occupy herself. Otherwise she'd be excessively cross."

"She does have a good bit to do. I delivered several letters to her only this morning from her friends in Halifax. There were two from Theodore O'Malley." She smiled maternally. "Despite what Lucy says, I am quite certain she misses everyone at home."

"I don't believe our sister had any notion what becoming a darling of the *ton* entailed," Miranda said thoughtfully.

Katie nodded. "The sheer number of morning calls is tedious enough, to say nothing of the vast number of breakfasts and teas and dinners one is obliged to attend." Her head shook. "For my part, I feel fortunate that I may cry off from time to time without incurring censure."

"As do I," Miranda murmured. A moment later, she said, "I do hope we have not been led astray, Katie."

Katie looked up from her embroidery. "It does seem

a bit odd that Lucy has not seen the viscount anywhere about the City this week."

"It is *quite* odd," Miranda exclaimed. "Especially when one considers that less than a fortnight ago, he was seen at every rout and soirée in Town. It is as if he has simply vanished from sight. Again."

A somewhat anxious frown creased Katie's brow. Presently, she said in a low voice, "I had rather thought we would be on our way back to Halifax by now."

Miranda's ears snapped to attention. "As did I. You realize that if the viscount has, indeed, vanished from sight again, Katie, it means that we have been left out to dry!"

Katie took that in, but very quickly her worried countenance again grew serene. "I am certain he will turn up, Miranda. He cares a great deal for Lucy. We are oversetting ourselves needlessly."

Miranda said nothing further on the subject. But the topic came up again three days later.

The Heathrow household was in what could only be described as a frenzy. More than a half dozen of Lord Heathrow's relatives had descended upon them, some coming from as far afield as Cornwall. In addition to a flighty little aunt, who was constantly losing her way about the large house, there was a foppish young man, a distant cousin of eighteen or nineteen, who, after he got a look at Lucy, declared himself top over tail in love. Lucy was not the least bit flattered by the young man's attentions and was constantly flitting from one room to another in the hope of avoiding him.

In addition, one of Lord Heathrow's several sisters was accompanied by three of her offspring; a toddler, a girl of five and a boy of seven, who had brought along a school chum of his. The youngster's paternal grandmother, a woman heretofore unknown to either Lord or Lady Heathrow, spent her days complaining of the noise made by the unruly children and the steady stream of young people who still called hourly upon Lucy and the love-smitten young man.

"A person can't get a moment's peace around here!" the old woman grumbled.

Taken aback by the onslaught of Heathrow relatives, Miranda and Katie spent the bulk of their days sequestered in their respective bedchambers where the ruckus was a bit less disturbing. Although no room was safe from the children, as Miranda learned when she discovered the toilette articles atop her dressing table scattered thither and yon.

One day, as Miranda was headed belowstairs for luncheon, she chanced to overhear a heated debate going on between her aunt and uncle. Although they were within their own suite of rooms, Uncle John's thunderous voice was as loud as if he were standing on the landing beside Miranda. She had just heard him tell Aunt Isobel that he meant to remove to his club until the household returned again to normal.

"I will not be left here alone, John. I will not!"

"Then, do as I say and clear some of the riffraff out. Your nieces have definitely overstayed their welcome," he declared firmly.

Against her will, Miranda edged a step closer to the Heathrow suite.

"But you, yourself, gave the girls leave to stay here as long as they wished," Lady Heathrow retorted.

"That was then, this is now."

"The girls have no place to go, John."

"It is none of my concern."

Miranda bit down so hard on her lip it almost bled.

"We cannot simply turn them out, John. The house is indeed quite full, but I daresay we are comfortable enough. Katie has moved in with Elinor, and Lucy and

Miranda are sharing a suite. I expect Elinor to receive an offer any day now."

"Dunworthy chap?" Lord Heathrow snorted. "Fellow hasn't a feather to fly with. If our girl marries him, no doubt he will expect to reside here, as well."

"But he is a suitor, John. And we have my nieces to thank for it. Before they came, Elinor hadn't a one. Lucy, as well, is near to becoming betrothed," Lady Heathrow added with satisfaction.

Lord Heathrow snorted again. "If you women think Peterbloom means to come up to scratch in that quarter, you've another think coming! Mark my words, he doesn't have the least notion of saddling himself with those three penniless chits."

Miranda's eyes widened with horror. Not wishing to hear another word, she hurried belowstairs in search of Katie. Drawing her sister into the corridor beyond a small sitting room where she and Elinor had taken refuge, she blurted out all that she had just heard.

"We've no choice, Katie, but to call on Lord Peterbloom ourselves. Our situation has become desperate! I am prepared to beg him to—"

"To marry Lucy?" Katie gasped.

"No. To allow us to return home to Halifax. He has yet to see Papa's grant, but I am certain once he sees it, and . . . and"—her voice nearly broke—"surely he will relent, Katie. He *must!*"

A worried frown began to replace the placid look on Katie's face. "I—I don't know, Miranda. You are quite overset now, perhaps—"

"We've no time to waste, Katie. Uncle John says the viscount has no intention of offering for Lucy! We should have known something was amiss when he did not turn up to take her to Gunter's."

"I am certain there is a reasonable explanation for his absence, Miranda. Lord Peterbloom is a gentleman."

Miranda worked to calm herself. She did not wish to believe the worst of him; truly she did not. Especially not now. She wished to do nothing to spoil the friendship that had sprung up between them. But, perhaps he had already spoiled it. She thrust her chin up with resolve. "Well, then, I . . . expect we shall soon find out if he is a gentleman or not, shan't we?" She turned to hurry up the stairs and paused only when Katie caught up to her.

"Perhaps I should be the one to handle this, Miranda. I am the eldest. And I shouldn't want you to . . ." Her voice trailed off.

"I will not lose my temper, Katie!" Miranda cried hotly.

"I was not suggesting that you would, dear. Although . . . you must own, that, under the circumstances, the possibility looms . . . quite great."

Miranda's lips pursed. "I will loose control only if I find that he has purposely misled our Lucy. Otherwise, I am determined to remain calm." After a pause, she added, "You must own that it would be insupportable of him to have toyed with her, and considering the seriousness of our situation now, it would be equally insupportable of him to have misled us."

"Indeed, it would be," Katie agreed. "But I cannot believe that that is the case. Reginald has invited me to take a drive with him this afternoon, Miranda. Perhaps I can find a way to broach the subject with him. He and the viscount are quite close, you know. Perhaps he will be able to shed some light on the matter. Although," she hesitated, her brows drawing together thoughtfully, "I shan't wish to make our circumstances appear so very desperate that he will think I am trying to force *his* hand. Still . . ." she smiled with assurance, "I am certain I can manage. Reginald is quite easy to talk to."

Miranda studied her sister. "You care a great deal for him, do you not, Katie?"

Katie smiled wanly. "A very great deal, Miranda. He is the most wonderful man I have ever met."

Suddenly, it struck Miranda that, until a few moments ago . . . she had felt the exact same way about Lord Peterbloom. The thought thoroughly unsettled her.

"I cannot imagine . . ." Katie began, her lashes fluttering nervously. "I—I was about to say that I cannot imagine living my life without him, but . . ."

"Oh, Katie. You do love him! And he must feel the same about you. Reginald will help us, I am certain he will."

Katie nodded tightly. "I am certain he will, too, Miranda."

Later that evening, Dr. Keating paid a call on the Viscount Peterbloom. The two men were sharing a drink in the viscount's study.

"The ladies think *what?*" Peterbloom sputtered.

"They are waiting for you to offer for Miss Lucy," the good doctor repeated.

"My God!" Peterbloom ran a hand through his dark locks.

"They became concerned when you failed to take Lucy to Gunter's for an ice."

"When I failed to what?"

"Apparently the girl told them that, as a special birthday treat, you'd promised to take her there for an ice."

Peterbloom shook his head with disbelief. "I recall promising nothing of the sort, Reginald. I am a man of my word. If I had promised, I'd have taken her." He pushed himself up from the overstuffed chair where he'd been sitting and strode across the room to the large kneehole desk that sat beneath a window. "I shall send my apologies at once."

Dr. Keating followed him. "Forgive me if I am speaking

out of turn, Peterbloom, but Miss Fraser also mentioned some sort of entailment the girls have on a piece of property you own in the country. Seems the Heathrow household is crawling with relatives and the young ladies feel . . . well, they feel a bit . . . in the way." He paused, then said, "I do hate to see the ladies leave Town, but—"

"I have withheld my approval of their petition for the selfsame reason, Keating."

"Ah." The doctor nodded.

Lord Peterbloom's head was bent over the desk, the pen in his hand scratching furiously as he talked. Straightening, he said, "I shall have this delivered straightaway. In the meantime, you have my leave to inform Miss Fraser that the young ladies have nothing to fear."

Abandoning that subject, the gentleman turned their attention to other matters, one of which was to look in on Lady Peterbloom, who had indeed contracted a mild case of the influenza, but whose health was now improving. Peterbloom fell into step again beside his friend as he and the doctor descended the stairwell to the foyer.

"I appreciate the call, Keating. And thank you for looking after the young ladies in my absence. I expect I should have told one of them that I would be out of pocket for a few days. The herbs I collected on this trip to Derbyshire should round out our collection nicely."

"The ladies will be overjoyed to receive the good news, Peterbloom. Though, I—I will regret seeing Miss Fraser leave Town," he said again.

"As will I," Peterbloom muttered. "Though I suppose it cannot be helped. Good day, Keating."

"Lord Peterbloom gave Reginald leave to tell us that we have nothing to fear, Miranda!"

"Oh-h." Miranda's eyes squeezed shut. She should

never have doubted him. He was the most wonderful man in the world.

"The viscount had simply left town for a few days in order to collect cuttings of some herbs. Reginald said he had no recollection of promising to take Lucy to Gunter's. But, he sent a letter of apology to her all the same. And, he has invited all of us to go there tomorrow for an ice."

"All of us?" Miranda queried.

Katie laughed. "Lucy was not the least bit pleased until I reminded her that she will have the remainder of her life to spend alone with the Viscount Peterbloom."

For some reason, that particular remark did not particularly please Miranda.

Nineteen

At Gunter's the following afternoon, the three Fraser girls sat clustered about one of the small tables in the fashionable eating establishment while Lord Peterbloom stood nearby, one booted foot crossed over the other as he leaned against the wall.

Although Lucy looked pretty as a picture in blue sprigged muslin, she was behaving a bit snappishly. "Why does he not come and sit with us?" she demanded in a hushed tone.

"There is scarcely room for the three of us at this tiny table," Katie remarked, also keeping her voice low, "let alone a gentleman of such height and . . . bearing."

Lucy's lips pursed petulantly. "Well, I still do not see why he invited all of us. I wished it to be *my* special treat."

While Miranda was inordinately pleased that everything was turning out as it should, she, too, had noticed the viscount's aloofness this afternoon and thought it a bit odd. He wore a dark brooding look on his face now, and despite the pleasant greeting he'd given them when he arrived to collect them, he hadn't said two words since.

After they'd all climbed again into the viscount's elegant maroon barouche, Miranda and Katie sitting opposite Lucy and Lord Peterbloom, Lucy kept up a running chatter telling the gentleman about all the society events she'd attended since last she'd seen him. Since Lucy had been occupied nearly every minute of every day, she had a good deal to talk about.

"Will you be attending the Hamilton's ball at the end of the week, Lord Peterbloom?" she finally asked. A flirtatious smile on her lips, she tilted her auburn head coquettishly as she gazed up at him.

The gentleman did not reply straightaway; instead, his dark eyes cut round and he directed a penetrating look at Miranda.

It was so piercing, she felt a blush creep to the roots of her hair.

"Will all three of you young ladies be attending the ball?" he finally asked.

"Oh, yes," Lucy replied, "as will Uncle John." She giggled self-consciously.

One dark brow lifted. Crystal clear to Peterbloom was the fact that he had got himself embroiled in a prickly situation. Apparently, the girls had perceived his attempts to look out for Lucy's well-being as having considerably more meaning than he'd intended. Since the chit's come-out ball, when he'd promised Miranda that he'd keep an eye out for Lucy, he'd purposely invited her along on every outing so as to ensure that the little hoyden did not inadvertently land in the basket. The girl had more hair than wit and, in the last weeks, he'd seen and heard enough from her to lead him to believe she was never more than two steps away from complete ruination. Both she and Miranda needed someone to look after them. But, of course, he had a different reason for wishing to be near Miss Miranda.

He slanted a sidelong look at her now. She looked delightful this afternoon in a pretty lavender round gown picked out in blond lace. Atop her dark curls was a charming little pouffed bonnet edged with the same trim. Apparently she had finally relented and allowed her aunt to trick her out properly. He smiled to himself. Had he been alone with Miranda now, he'd have teased her soundly about it. He quite enjoyed making the little minx laugh. He had missed seeing her this past week, had missed her spirit, her snapping green eyes and her charming smile. He'd even missed the sight of her shiny dark curls, and the disarming scent she wore. Roses. Miranda always smelled of roses.

He shifted uncomfortably on the bench. Fully acquainted now with the young lady's volatile temper, he realized he'd have to find a way to crawl out of the bumblebroth he'd landed in without losing any of the precious ground he'd gained with Miranda or causing Miss Lucy undue embarrassment.

He spent the remainder of that day and most of the next considering the options open to him. With considerable chagrin, he realized there weren't many. However, a rather startling conclusion did come to light, that he did, indeed, care a great deal more for Miss Miranda Fraser than he'd realized. He cared a very, *very* great deal for her.

He had never known a woman like her before, one who left *him* feeling breathless, one who shared his absorbing interest in horticulture, and one whom he found clever, charming, *and* enormously appealing. It quite astonished him to realize he could easily imagine spending the remainder of his days with the captivating Miranda by his side. Though he'd never expected this to happen to him, the bald truth was, he had fallen deeply in love with her and he wanted nothing more than to make her his bride.

But how was he to convince her of that . . . now?

He finally decided that the only course open to him was to tell her straight out how he felt about her. Then he'd find a way to break the news gently to Miss Lucy. He did not believe that she truly loved him. No doubt what she felt was more on the order of a schoolgirl infatuation.

The sooner he accomplished this feat, the better. The Hamiltons' ball would serve, he decided. All the young ladies would be in attendance. He had never shared a dance with Miranda before. He would ask her to waltz. The steps of that dance afforded the best opportunity to speak privately with one's partner. Whilst he held her in his arms, he would whisper into her ear that he found her enchanting, that he loved her dearly, and that he wished to marry her.

On the evening of the Hamiltons' ball, Miranda and her sisters were quite atremor as they dressed for the festive occasion. All of them sensed that tonight would be especially important for them. Katie had earlier confided to Aunt Isobel that the viscount had given the doctor leave to tell them they had nothing to fear. Lady Heathrow, as well, took that to mean Lord Peterbloom was ready to declare his suit. Now that he was back in Town and had commenced to call again, such an announcement was imminent, she said.

"Did I not tell you everything would turn out splendidly?" she exclaimed as she fussed with the flounce on Miranda's gown and adjusted the bow at Lucy's back. "You all look so very pretty tonight. I declare I love each of you as if you were my own!"

Miranda and Katie both turned warm smiles on their aunt.

Gazing at her reflection in the cheval glass, Lucy said, "When I am married to the viscount, Aunt Isobel, I shall become a 'lady' just as you are. We shall be able to see one another whenever we wish, shan't we?"

Lady Heathrow reached for a scrap of linen and began to dab at the moisture that had sprung to her gray eyes. "Yes, my dear. Just as your sweet mama and I should have." She swiped at the moisture that trickled down her cheek.

"How can we ever thank you for all you have done fo

us?" Katie asked, moving to embrace her nearly overcome aunt.

Her own chin trembling, Miranda did likewise. "We hall always be grateful to you, Aunt Isobel."

Some moments later, they all regained themselves and were in especially high spirits as they set out. Lord Heathrow's aunt and sister accompanied them to the oirée, so it was a large party that alighted from the Heathrow carriage and made their way into the foyer of Lord and Lady Hamilton's lovely home. A liveried footnan showed them into the ballroom, which stretched cross the back of the house, a row of double French doors giving onto a sweeping terrace and a beautifully aid-out garden beyond. It was quite a warm night, and nce the ballroom had filled to capacity with people, the ir inside grew quite oppressive.

It felt especially heavy to Miranda, who, for some reaon, had begun to experience odd pangs of anxiety again. Before the evening was over, she fully expected Lucy to ecome a betrothed woman, which meant that she and Katie would be free to return home to Halifax. Which, f course, made her exceedingly happy, so why did she uddenly feel so . . . uneasy?

Unable to think of a reason for her strange mood, she ied to fix her thoughts on her surroundings: the beauful music coming from the orchestra, the crush of splenidly attired people squeezed shoulder to shoulder in the allroom, the glittering jewels, and the flicker of hunreds of candles in the chandeliers overhead.

Instead, another thought seemed to take shape in her mind . . . that once Lucy and Lord Peterbloom were wed nd she and Katie had removed to the country, she would o longer be able to see the viscount every day. And hat . . . that she would miss him dreadfully. But, of course, he did not really feel that way. Lord Peterbloom would

be her brother-in-law and she and Katie would, no doubt see quite enough of him . . . at family gatherings and such
Although she had not seen the illustrious gentlemar yet this evening, she was certain he must be here. Fron the look of it, most of London was here. Katie stood a few feet away, looking quite content with her hand drapec over Dr. Keating's arm. Elinor looked pretty tonight in a pale pink satin slip with a matching silk overdress. She was grinning ear to ear as she and Mr. Dunworthy wen through the patterns of a quadrille. And Lucy . . . yes there she was, also on the dance floor happily chattin up one of her most ardent suitors, Sir Richard Andover
"I understand the next set is to be a waltz," suddenl came a deep voice near Miranda's ear.

She spun about. *It was he!* And he looked startingl handsome tonight! She felt her heart begin to pound ir her ears and her cheeks to burn with fire. He had so stunned her, she could think of nothing at all to say. A silly grin on her lips, she stood gazing up at him like witless ninnyhammer.

"I would be honored if you would consent to danc the waltz with me, Miss Miranda."

The smile on Miranda's lips wavered nervously. "I . . uh . . . have never danced the waltz before, sir. I am nc nearly so proficient as Lucy. I fear I could not keep up.

Peterbloom laughed, the deep throaty sound sendin quivers of delight through Miranda's veins. The gentle man looked dazzlingly handsome in dark evening clothe an elegant froth of linen cascading down his gleamin white shirtfront. Miranda's heart fluttered wildly as sh recalled the sight of him dancing the waltz with Lucy. H had embraced her in quite an intimate fashion. Coul she bear to have Lord Peterbloom hold her in such way? Oh, my! She feared she could not.

He was smiling down at her in so beguiling a mann

that she was completely unaware she had nodded in agreement to his second request for her to stand up with him.

In a foggy daze, Miranda allowed the dashing gentleman to guide her onto the dance floor, and from somewhere far, far away, she heard the orchestra begin to play. When Lord Peterbloom's hand slipped round her slim waist and he drew her small body close to his, she very nearly swooned from the pleasurable feelings racing through her. Instead, they seemed to float across the floor, one body instead of two, in perfect harmony with the steady three-quarter time. The room began to swirl faster and faster, a glittering, brilliant whirl of color and music and light.

From an even greater distance, she was vaguely aware of the deep timbre of Lord Peterbloom's voice. He seemed to be leaning toward her, whispering something that sounded very like pulsating chords of music into her ear. She had no idea what he was saying and, in truth, did not care. She was gloriously, deliriously happy. She was in the arms of the man she lov—No! *No!* What was she thinking? With a jolt, she drew away from him. The gentleman was still talking. She could feel the soft puffs of his breath fanning the flaming skin of her cheek.

". . . never felt so warmly toward a woman before . . ."

Ah, yes, he'd been telling her how very much he loved Lucy!

". . . had not considered that I would ever marry . . ."

He was telling her he wished to marry Lucy! Yes! Oh, yes!

When again, the gentleman drew her body close against his chest, the waves of exquisite current that trembled through Miranda were more intense than anything she had ever felt before! It brought to mind far more intimate things a man and a woman might do together. But . . . she dared not think about that! *Dear God.* Waltzing was, indeed, a scandalous experience!

When suddenly, the music halted, an enormous sigh of relief escaped Miranda. She turned a shaky smile upward as Lord Peterbloom led her off the dance floor.

"Thank you ever so, sir," she murmured. That her breath was still coming in fits and starts alarmed her further. *They were no longer dancing and still she felt as if they were!* "This has been the most . . . thrilling experience of my entire life," she added breathlessly.

Lord Peterbloom turned to look into her shining green eyes. The liquid warmth Miranda saw in his set her on fire all over again.

"Thank you for making it so easy for me to tell you how I feel, Miranda. You do not mind if I call you Miranda, do you?"

"No . . . of course not." She laughed nervously. Indeed, he had just confided to her that he loved Lucy with all his heart and wished to make her his bride. "We are to be family," she murmured. "I expect you mean to speak with Uncle John straightaway?" she asked, beginning to feel somewhat stronger at last.

Peterbloom blinked as if taken aback. "I . . . well, yes, of course, if that is your wish, my dear. I had thought we might . . . wait a bit, but if you . . ."

"Oh, I see no need to wait a single day longer. When two people are certain they love one another, there is truly no need to wait, is there?" She gazed up at him, quite a relieved smile now curving her pretty lips.

"Indeed not." Lord Peterbloom reached to give her gloved fingers, which were still draped over his arm, an affectionate squeeze. "We shall deal very well together, Miranda, I am certain of it."

"I am certain, as well," Miranda said with conviction. "Aunt Isobel will need a bit of time in which to plan a lovely wedding, but beyond that, I . . . I see no reason why a . . . d-d . . . Why a d-date—" Suddenly, a queer tightness gripped Miranda's throat. It was so intense, she could scarcely draw breath! *What was happening to her?* Why was the matter of setting an actual date for Lucy's wedding to Lord Peterbloom causing her such distress?

She turned a terrified gaze on the gentleman. "Sir, I really must . . . If you will please excuse me!"

Without waiting for a reply, she bunched her skirts in her hands and darted from the gentleman's side. She did not stop running till she'd left the stuffy confines of the ballroom behind and gained the clear, cool air of the moonlit terrace.

Air! She flung her head back and drew in great, gasping gulps of it. Down, down, down into her painfully tight lungs.

What had come over her just now? Lord Peterbloom had finally declared his suit. It was what they all wanted. In a week's time, maybe less, she and Katie would be on their way back to Halifax. Everything had turned out perfectly. *So, why . . . ?*

Feeling an unwelcome rush of hot, stinging tears suddenly brim to her eyes, Miranda squeezed them shut and curled her fingers around the stone railing of the balustrade where she stood. She clung so tightly to the railing, her palms grew numb. *Why was she so overset?*

She stood thusly for quite a length, trying valiantly to understand the strange mix and stir of emotions whirling within her. Presently, she became aware of the gentle murmurings of other guests strolling about on the terrace around her. She also began to hear the sound of voices coming from a few feet below her in the garden. But the exact words the gentleman and his lady friend were saying were obscured by the thick jasmine vines that grew between the balustrade and the ground below it.

She knew she should not be listening to the private conversation, but as the voices grew more insistent, her attention seemed to fix more intently upon them.

"Please, milord, just *one* kiss," the lady pleaded. "Surely you have not forgotten all that we shared."

She really should move away, Miranda told herself

firmly. Instead, she leaned even closer over the railing to listen for the gentleman's reply.

"I recall that one kiss was never enough to satisfy you." The gentleman's tone was barely above a whisper. Still, Miranda detected a familiar quality to it. Perhaps it was that of Lucy's many suitors.

A long pause followed, during which Miranda assumed the gentleman was doing as the lady asked. At length, the feminine voice purred, "There was that not . . . ? Hmmm. Now, just one more, sir. Please."

"You asked for only one kiss, my dear, and I obliged.

"Pl-lease."

"Very well," the gentleman said with resignation, "but you must promise to return to the ballroom without causing a scene?"

The silence that then ensued was a good bit longer than the previous one. It, too, told Miranda the deed was being done. Again. She smiled a bit sadly as she dragged her attention away and sucked in another refreshing breath of cool night air. Were she to be completely honest with herself right now, she would have to admit to a lingering desire for one last kiss from the Viscount Peterbloom. But, of course, she was being foolish, wasn't she?

With another melancholy sigh, she pushed away from the railing and was about to turn and make her way back inside when she heard the young lady in the garden say, "Ah, was that not delicious, my lord Peterbloom?"

Miranda's head jerked up. *Peterbloom!*

Blinding hot rage seared through her as she lifted her skirts and tore down the stone steps of the terrace and around the circular path till she came face-to-face with the amorous pair . . . *still locked in one another's arms!*

"How dare you?" she cried. "How dare you profess your love for my sister one minute and make love to another woman the next!"

"M-miranda!" was all the stunned gentleman could say.

The voluptuous brunette in his arms drew away. She tossed an amused glance at the angry young lady with the blazing green eyes. "Well, my lord Peterbloom. I see very little has changed in the past five years."

Miranda glared daggers at the now laughing woman, and when Lord Peterbloom began to speak, she turned a seething glare on him.

"I had come to the garden in search of you, Miranda, and I—"

"How dare you insult me with your lies! You are a loathsome creature, sirrah!" She ripped one long white glove from her arm and flung the soft kid against his cheek. "You leave me no choice but to demand satisfaction for my sister's honor!"

Peterbloom regarded her with disbelief, then he threw his dark head back and he and his lady friend both dissolved into laughter. Peterbloom laughed so hard, tears streamed down his cheeks.

"How dare you make sport of me!" Miranda sputtered.

When he managed to contain his mirth long enough to speak, he said, "You are the most delightful young lady I have ever met, and I love you dearly!"

"Oh!" She glared at him with horror. "You are a rake and a womanizer and a . . . a *blackhearted scoundrel!* From the outset, you have insulted me and my family with nothing but lies and empty promises! Well, sir, you have pulled the wrong pig by the ear this time!" She thrust her head up. "You will receive my cartel before sunup."

That said, she hiked up her skirts again and vanished from sight.

It was a few moments later before Lord Peterbloom realized that he had, indeed, landed in high thicket this time.

Twenty

"Oh, Miranda, how could he?" Lucy wailed.

In the ballroom, Miranda hurriedly told her sisters part of what had just transpired, the part about Lord Peterbloom's declaring his love for Lucy and then rushing straight into the arms of his ladybird. Her heated reaction to the fracus, she purposely failed to mention.

"I want to go home!" Lucy cried. "Where is Aunt Isobel? I refuse to stay here a second longer!"

Though he was not apprised of the details of the matter, Dr. Keating gallantly offered to see the girls safely home. Once there, he administered a sedative to Lucy.

"She will sleep soundly now," he said. "I will call to see how she is in the morning."

A worried look on her face, Katie turned to accompany the doctor back down the stairs. After thanking him profusely, they exchanged a private moment, then she returned abovestairs in search of Miranda. Spotting a light on in the small sitting room across from the girls' bedchamber, she peeked inside.

Miranda, still dressed in her ballgown, was seated at the small writing desk in the far corner. She did not hear her sister enter the room.

"Who on earth are you writing to at this hour?" Katie asked.

Miranda did not look up. "Lord Peterbloom. I was so

angry when I discovered him in the garden . . ." She turned a blazing look on her sister. "He was actually *kissing* that woman, Katie. Kissing her! Anyhow, I was so angry, I called him out and now I am—"

"You did *what?*" Katie stared aghast at her younger sister, the joyful news she had wished to impart all but forgotten.

Miranda was again furiously writing. "There is no cause for alarm, Katie. I admit I should not have lost my temper, but the rakehell drove me to it and the deed was done before I—"

"Well, I hope he will accept your letter of apology, Miranda, for that is the only acceptable—"

"Oh, this is not an apology, Katie. It is my cartel. Duels are quite commonplace, you know. Lord Jersey is constantly being called out over such trifles as Lady Jersey refusing to extend a voucher to Almack's or an invitation to a ball. You will own that this is a good deal more serious than that." Miranda bent her head lower over her work.

"Miranda, you will cease this nonsense at once!"

Miranda's lips pursed as she flicked an impatient gaze at her sister. "I told the viscount he would receive my cartel before sunup, Katie. You will serve as my second, will you not? I rather expect the viscount will choose Doctor Keating, don't you?"

"Miranda!" Her eyes wide with horror, Katie made as if to snatch the piece of paper from Miranda, but was unsuccessful, so instead, she parked both hands on her hips. "Have you gone daft? You cannot fight a duel with the viscount. He may have disgraced our Lucy, but that does not give you leave to . . ."

Miranda lifted her chin, a long-suffering look on her face. "I said there was no cause for alarm, Katie. I have no intention of killing Lord Peterbloom. Although, I declare, I am quite mad enough to shoot the blackguard! At any rate, how would I fight a duel when I know nothing of guns or swords?" Satisfied when Katie said nothing, Miranda's green eyes suddenly began to sparkle and a delighted grin lit up her face. "Oh, Katie, just wait till you hear my clever scheme."

Katie's eyes narrowed. "How many glasses of champagne did you drink tonight, Miranda?"

"I drank none at all. You may rest assured, I have learned my lesson where strong drink is concerned. Why, I should never have been able to think up such a brilliant plan if my thoughts were in a muddle. There." She laid her pen aside. "Do you not wish to hear it?"

Katie's lips thinned. "I expect you will tell me whether I wish to hear it or not."

Miranda took up the page she'd been writing upon and in a self-satisfied tone began to read.

"Hummph. Dashed clever of the little minx," the Viscount Peterbloom muttered, a look akin to admiration forming on his unshaven face. Dawn had just begun to peek over the horizon when a sealed missive that smelled faintly of roses had been delivered to him. He'd had to hurriedly don his dressing gown and answer the summons himself since the elderly retainer who butled for him was still abed.

An hour later, Dr. Keating arrived and the two men sat down to breakfast together.

"I fail to see where Miss Miranda tossing the gauntlet at your feet can be called clever."

Peterbloom reached for his coffee cup and took a satisfying sip. "That wasn't the clever part." His lips twitched. "The little spitfire has offered to spare my life in exchange for Fraser Cottage." He set his cup down and reached for a hot buttered scone.

Across from him, Dr. Keating seemed alarmed, to the point he had barely touched the deviled ham and eggs on his plate. "Beg pardon, old man, but I was under the impression you meant to offer for Miss Miranda last evening. I take it somewhere between your declaration of love and her answer . . . things took a nasty turn."

Peterbloom snorted. "Should have expected she'd read something contrary to what I meant in my words." A moment later, a lopsided grin split his face. "Of course, when she discovered me in the garden with—" He cleared his throat. "Well, I can hardly say I blame her."

"Still, to call you out seems a bit . . ."

"Extreme?"

Keating nodded.

"And yet, one must admire the young lady's spirit," Peterbloom remarked, no small amount of pride evident in his tone.

"I daresay you admire a good deal more than that about Miss Miranda."

Peterbloom nodded thoughtfully. "I do, indeed."

"So, what do you propose to do now, old man?"

Peterbloom shrugged. "The obvious, of course." He reached for his coffee cup and took another sip. "Refuse her offer and choose my weapons."

"Good God, man! You can't be serious!"

"On the contrary." Peterbloom scooped up a generous forkful of creamed eggs and popped them into his mouth. "You will stand as my second will you not? And you will please inform Miss Fraser that while I find her sister's offer quite generous, I cannot accept it. And then you will invite both girls for pistols and coffee-for-four at sunup tomorrow."

Keating looked stricken.

"Where we shall fight to the death," Peterbloom added with a grin.

Keating stared at Peterbloom in much the same fashion as Katie had regarded Miranda the night before. "I hope you know what you're doing, old man."

Peterbloom said no more. He knew exactly what he was doing. He was outsmarting the clever little minx at her own game.

After entrusting the note she'd written to Lord Peterbloom to a servant who had promised to have it delivered before daybreak, Miranda had climbed into bed beside a slumbering Lucy and fell at once into a sound sleep. Not even the slight shaking of the feather bed when Lucy rose long before daybreak and slipped quietly from the room disturbed an exhausted Miranda.

By the time she awoke late the following morning and discovered her sister gone, it was far too late to do anything about it.

The groom who had accompanied a determined Lucy to the inn in Wolverton had returned to London with a note Lucy had insisted he *not* deliver to her aunt and sisters until well past noon.

"I expect Lucy and Theodore O'Malley are well on their way to Gretna Green by now," Katie said, on a long sigh.

Shaken, Lady Heathrow dabbed at her red-rimmed eyes. She, Elinor, Katie, and Miranda were huddled together in the small sitting room where Miranda had only last evening penned the cartel to Lord Peterbloom.

"Teddy is a big strapping fellow, Aunt Isobel," Miranda said. "And he cares a great deal for Lucy, else he would not have been on his way to London to fetch her. I expect he missed her fiercely."

"That is what Lucy said in her note," Lady Heathrow murmured. She listlessly fingered the much-handled piece of cheap paper. "I do hope he will not . . . ill-use her."

"Teddy is a fine Christian lad," Katie said firmly. "His father, Mr. O'Malley, owns the mercantile in the village.

They are a respectable family . . . and not without means."

A horrified look appeared on Lady Heathrow's face. "The family is in trade! *Oh-h!* It is far worse than I feared! I had hoped he was a clergyman, like your dear papa." She drew forth an already soggy handkerchief and blew her nose soundly into it. "Sally and I had such high hopes for Lucy! To see our plans dashed to the ground in such a fashion is . . . frightfully disheartening." She brought the balled-up scrap of linen to her nose once more.

Miranda was as overset as both her aunt and Katie, but she had no doubt her sister was safe in Teddy's care. "Lucy was so very distraught over the viscount's betrayal last evening," she began, her tone genuinely sad. She bit her lip. She dared not tell her aunt what had transpired between herself and Lord Peterbloom as a result of that betrayal, and she was certain Katie had said nothing on the subject either. "As we all were," she added, but fell silent again when she noted the quelling look Katie was aiming at her.

"I recall Lucy saying last evening as we drove home in the carriage," Elinor put in quietly, "that Teddy O'Malley would never treat her in such a shabby fashion."

"Did she say that?" Miranda asked with high interest. She sat up a bit straighter in her chair. Perhaps Lucy had never *really* loved the viscount after all, though why *she* found that piece of news uplifting, she couldn't say. "I did not hear her say that."

"One can only wonder why," Katie muttered beneath her breath.

"But she had so many other suitors to choose from," Lady Heathrow remarked unhappily.

"And every last one of them a far sight more suitable than—"

"Miranda!"

"Well, it's true, Katie."

Katie turned to her aunt, and in a reassuring tone, said, "I am certain Teddy will make Lucy very happy."

"I do hope so." Lady Heathrow tried in vain to smile. "I can hardly bear to think of her . . ." Her chin trembled afresh. "But, of course, both of you girls are welcome to stay here just as long as you like," she concluded tearfully.

Miranda's countenance brightened. "Oh, I doubt we shall be in London a great deal longer, Aunt Isobel. I expect we shall hear from Lord Peterbloom before the day is out. Katie and I may very well be on our way back to Halifax before—"

"I shall not be returning home to Halifax," Katie put in firmly.

"But, Katie, I thought you—"

"I never told you my news last evening, Miranda." A mixture of joy and sadness appeared on Katie's face. "I am to be married."

"Married!" Lady Heathrow cried. "Oh, my dear child!" She flung her arms about Katie and crushed the girl to her bosom.

Miranda, too, beamed with pleasure. "How perfectly lovely, Katie! I am so very happy for you. When did he ask?"

Katie wiped at the tears of joy that glistened on her lashes. "Last evening, after he'd tended to Lucy. He told me just before he left that . . . he wished to marry me. I would have told you then, Miranda, but"—she pinned her sister with another recriminating look—"something came up."

Miranda stiffened. "Well, it appears I am losing not one, but two sisters."

"Well, at least I shall have *one* wedding to plan," Lady Heathrow cried gaily.

"Two weddings, Mama," Elinor put in shyly.

"What did you say, dear?"

"I said two weddings, Mama. Mr. Dunworthy spoke to me last evening, as well. He means to declare his suit to Father later today."

"Elinor!" My dear child!" Lady Heathrow's arms enfolded her only daughter. "Oh, my precious dears! You have both made me very, *very* happy!" She drew back, her face flushed with pleasure. "Come, Katie, come Elinor! We've an inordinate amount of work to do. I can't think when I've been in such alt."

Miranda watched in silence as her aunt, and a smiling Katie and a flushed Elinor, left the room. In one fell swoop, she had, indeed, lost everyone dear to her.

She dared not think what she would do if the Viscount Peterbloom refused to accept the terms of her challenge.

Moments before Dr. Keating arrived at the Heathrow town house bearing Lord Peterbloom's answer, Miranda drew Katie aside and begged her to not tell the doctor that Lucy had vanished.

"I can hardly fight a duel to avenge Lucy's honor if she has already married another!"

"I thought you said there would be no fighting," Katie retorted.

Miranda thrust her chin up stubbornly. "That depends on whether or not the viscount accepts the terms of my cartel. If he does not, then I shall have no choice."

Katie glanced toward the clock on the mantelpiece. "Reginald should be here any minute. I expect we shall very soon find out which way the wind blows."

"Promise me you will say nothing, Katie. It will not do for either gentleman to know that our Lucy has vanished." Against her will, Miranda felt her eyes suddenly fill with tears. "I only wish to go home to Halifax, Katie." She fought to keep her tears in check. "Lucy is a married woman now. And you have Doctor Keating. All that is left to me is Fraser Cottage."

Katie's heart melted. She drew Miranda into her arms and hugged her tightly. "Dear, dear Miranda, what folly hath your temper brought down upon your head now?"

Miranda was stunned to learn that the Viscount Peterbloom refused to accept the terms of her challenge. She had been so very certain he would. She had no desire to see this wretched drama proceed to some deadly end. Although she knew full well that if her temper had not flared out of control, none of this would be happening at all.

As she crawled into bed that night, she was more than ready to admit that her scheme to make things turn out right had gone askew. Of her own accord, Lucy would have refused to marry Lord Peterbloom. Circumstances being what they were, no young lady in her right mind would marry the rakehell! It was also quite possible that none of this would ever have happened if Miranda had told her sisters the horrid truth about the man at the outset.

Oh, why was Lord Peterbloom being so very cruel to her? This afternoon she had foolishly entertained the notion that Dr. Keating would arrive with the deed to Fraser Cottage tucked in his waistcoat pocket.

Oh-h-h! She moaned miserably into her pillow.

If she did not fall asleep soon, she'd be unfit to face the loathsome man over pistols in the morning. She turned over and pounded her pillow again. She had never met such a vile man! She hated him. She did!

She did!

Didn't she?

Her throat tightened painfully. No . . . she did not hate

him, she . . . Oh! She could not say it. Her eyes squeezed shut as tears of anguish and frustration gathered in them.

The awful, horrible truth was, she . . . she loved the libertine! *Oh-h!* She covered her face with both hands and tried to choke back the sobs that were strangling her. How could she feel such a lofty emotion for such an odious creature? But she did. She could not help herself.

She loved the horrid man!

Lying awake as the long hours of the night dragged by, Miranda's spirits sank lower and lower. At length, she allowed, that for the first time in her entire life, she could not think of a single way to make this faradiddle turn out right. With Lucy gone now, and Katie near refusing to speak to her, she had no one to turn to.

Miranda buried her head in her pillow and was very near to another bout of uncontrollable sobs, when instead, she slipped from her bed and fell to her knees beside it.

"Dear God . . ." she prayed.

Miranda awoke at first light the following morning with a sense of peace and serenity that was in direct contrast to the blustery weather outside. Thunder rumbled in the distance and, closer in, a harsh wind rattled the windowpanes and shutters. Miranda had no notion what would transpire this morning between herself and the Viscount Peterbloom, but in her heart, she was certain she had the strength to accept whatever the outcome was with, at least, a modicum of grace and dignity.

She hurriedly dressed in warm clothing, and after rapping lightly at Katie's bedchamber door, the two set out for the assignation.

This early in the morning, they found stealing from the house a fairly easy matter. With it still so full of people, there was generally always someone abroad, regardless of the hour. Not a one of the servants bustling about the place even noticed the girls walk around the large house to the mews and request the use of a carriage.

After they'd settled themselves inside it, Katie gave the somewhat sleepy driver the direction. The *affaire d' honneur* was to be held in a clearing beyond the viscount's home on the outskirts of the city.

A half hour later, the heavy black coach bearing the Heathrow coat of arms lumbered into the clearing and drew up behind an elegant maroon barouche already parked there. Both of the gentlemen—the viscount, looking quite dashing in an ankle-length, multicollared cloak, and Dr. Keating, a bit less fashionably dressed, but nonetheless alert—were standing nearby. In his hand, the doctor carried a square leather case, which Miranda assumed contained the dreaded weapons.

When the groom that had accompanied the girls let down the steps, Dr. Keating moved to assist them to the ground. At once, Miranda noted the thunder cloud on Lord Peterbloom's face, and those darkening the sky. Though Peterbloom's scowl caused her heart to lurch to her throat, she managed to still her uneven breath and swallow a bit of her fear. The outcome of this unfortunate matter no longer rested in her hands.

As both girls approached Lord Peterbloom, he fastened a piercing look on Miranda. "Good morning, ladies," he said, his tone especially cool. "I am pleased to see you arrived safely, it being quite early for two unescorted young ladies to be about."

Miranda nodded tightly, but said nothing. She fixed a small, set smile on her lips.

"Well." The viscount flung a gaze over one shoulder. "Appears to be cutting up nasty this morning. We'd best get to it. Shouldn't want to postpone the . . . festivities."

A cry of alarm escaped Katie. Beside her, the doctor

cleared his throat and nervously shifted the brown leather case he carried from one hand to the other.

Glancing at it, Miranda was unable to forestall the hard knot of anxiety that formed in her stomach. "I—I see you took the liberty of . . . of . . ."

"Providing the weapons?" Peterbloom said easily. "I trust you have no objection to that, or to my choice?"

Miranda thrust her chin up. "Not at all, sir."

"Lord Peterbloom, please—" Katie began, her frightened tone pleading. "Please, can't you and Miranda . . . ?"

Dr. Keating's voice cut in. "I'd feel considerably more at ease, Katie, if you'd wait out this nasty business in the carriage, sweetheart."

A look of outrage appeared on Miranda's face. "I have no intention of shooting my own sister!" she sputtered, then with a sniff, she recalled her resolve to remain calm and serene throughout the proceedings. "Katie is my second," she added quietly. "I shall tell her where to wait."

During the uncomfortable moment of silence that followed, a loud clap of thunder reverberated in the stillness.

When the disturbance had subsided, Miranda said, "You may wait in the carriage if you please, Katie."

Before scurrying back inside, Katie flung one last imploring look at the viscount, then she turned to the doctor. "Can you not stop them, Reginald?" she cried. "Please, stop them!"

"There is no cause for alarm, Miss Fraser," Peterbloom said, his tone a bit more gentle. "I am confident your sister and I shall have the matter settled in no time, with little or no harm coming to anyone." He shot an intense look at Miranda, but said nothing more.

A squeak of trepidation escaped her as she furtively glanced over her shoulder and watched Katie climb back into the coach. The doctor handed the case he was carrying to the viscount, then he, too, crawled in beside Katie.

Miranda knew little to nothing about proper dueling etiquette, but she had rather thought it involved having both seconds standing nearby, and a doctor, in case one was needed, plus some sort of official to count off the paces. Apparently, Lord Peterbloom was conducting this *affaire* according to his own set of rules. She bravely schooled her features for whatever lay ahead.

"Shall we proceed?" Peterbloom asked Miranda. His tone was near to icy now.

Since the tall grass they were tramping through was quite damp, Miranda lifted her skirts a few inches so as not to muddy them. Walking beside the tall gentleman, his top boots crunching the hay beneath his feet, Miranda realized that as disturbing as the circumstances were, she still felt acutely drawn to the man. In the cool, predawn hour with the storm threatening overhead, his strong, masculine presence felt quite comforting to her. She knew, if the need arose, he would protect her from harm. It was quite an odd sensation, and not the least bit . . . alarming.

When sudden gusts of cold air rustled the trees they were passing beneath, Miranda drew her new fur-lined witzchoura more tightly about her.

"I would offer you my cape," Peterbloom said quietly, "but I fear it would be so long and cumbersome, you would be unable to walk in it."

Miranda cast a sidelong look at him. "Thank you all the same, my lord. My wrap is quite warm."

"I suppose I could scoop you into my arms and carry you to the clearing," he murmured next, his tone becoming almost friendly.

Miranda's head whirled about. *Was he bamming her?* She cleared her throat primly. "I hardly think that necessary, sir." All the same, the notion sent a shiver of delight racing through her.

They walked in silence for a few paces more, then Peterbloom said, "We are nearly there."

A moment later, the viscount slowed his step and then drew altogether to a halt. Miranda gazed about. They had just passed beneath an arch of willowy birches and now stood in quite a snug clearing, ringed on three sides by a row of stately oak trees. Behind them was the road and carriages, but from this aspect, neither were visible.

Peterbloom moved a bit to the left, and when he did, Miranda saw the bright red cloth spread invitingly on the dew-moistened ground. On it were two damask-covered cushions and in the center, a brown wicker basket with the lid flung back. Protruding from the basket was a bottle of red wine, an assortment of breads and croissants and fruit: apples, oranges, and bunches of shiny grapes. *Were they to eat before they . . . ?* She flung a questioning gaze up at her companion.

"I thought a bit of sustenance in order before we . . . attempt to ventilate one another," he said, striding toward the setting. Miranda could not see the twitch of amusement that played at his lips.

With a resigned shrug, she followed him to the red cloth and settled herself upon it. After tucking her pretty new forest-green cape about her knees, she drew the toes of her boots up under her skirt and watched as the viscount set the brown leather case he carried in front of him. His jaw set with determination, he slowly unclasped the latch and lifted the lid.

Her face still a question, Miranda watched curiously as, instead of the pistols she expected him to produce, he instead withdrew a thin sheet of pale gray foolscap and handed it across to her.

"This, my dear," he said, without preamble, "is a fresh document, which I had my man of business draw up only yesterday. In short, it states that permission to occupy Fraser Cottage, located near the township of Halifax in Yorkshire County, is granted to Miss Miranda Fraser, for as long as she, or any of her heirs, shall live. If you deem this acceptable, my dear, all that remains to legalize it, is your signature."

Miranda gasped with disbelief. "*This* is your weapon, sir?"

Peterbloom nodded gravely, though his cool brown eyes were becoming quite warm. "The only weapon I have ever had, Miranda. I denied your petition the day your uncle came to call simply because I wished to keep you in Town."

"But . . . why?" she murmured breathlessly.

He smiled, a bit sadly. "So that I might properly court you. Send you poseys, bring you bonbons, escort you to any place in the city you'd like to go; the opera, drives in the park, wherever." He edged a bit closer to her, his gaze now fastened on the tantalizing rosebud of her mouth.

"But I thought—" Miranda murmured. She felt happy tears begin to swim in her eyes.

"I know what you thought, peagoose. You and Katie and Miss Lucy. And, while I deeply regret whatever misperception my actions may have spawned, or any pain I may have caused your younger sister, the plain truth is, I love you, Miranda. You and you alone." When she said nothing, he continued. "I began to fall in love with you the night I saw you at the inn in Wolverton, trying so valiantly to keep your rapscallion little sister out of mischief." He paused to smile into her glistening green eyes. "That, my little spitfire, is what I tried to tell you at the Hamiltons' ball as we waltzed."

A sheepish gaze fluttered downward. "Oh."

"So, now that you know how it is with me, what have

you to say?" Again, his eyes fastened on her sweet lips. "Do you not care for me a little?"

A wavery smile lifted the corners of Miranda's mouth. "Oh, my lord Peterbloom, I—"

"Grant. My given name is Grant."

Miranda wished so very much to fling herself into the handsome gentleman's arms and never let go. But she could not. Not until . . . "I . . . must know about the woman . . . the woman in the garden. What is she to you?"

Peterbloom grinned. "She is someone I knew . . . she is no one, Miranda. You, of all people, are aware of my . . . shall we say, my youthful exuberance where women were concerned. But you also know that I am no longer that same, devil-may-care fellow." His lips twitched. "And now that I am acquainted with your fiery temper, I can think of no woman worth risking my life for."

Miranda ducked her head and laughed softly.

"So . . . will you consent to become my bride?"

When, still she seemed reluctant to answer, he edged even closer to her. Cautiously, he slipped an arm about her small waist. "If you do not answer me quite soon, my dear, and with the answer I seek, I shall be forced to compromise you and then you shall *have* to marry me," he teased.

Miranda longed to give herself up to the delightful sensations coursing through her. *She loved this man dearly!* Instead, something made her thrust her chin up defiantly and say, "No. I will not marry you, my lord."

Despite the forcefulness of her reply, Peterbloom saw the playful twinkle in her pretty green eyes. "Very well, then. You leave me no choice but to—" Slowly, he reached to cup her chin and cover her sweet lips with his own.

A purr of pleasure escaped Miranda. Arching her back, she twined her arms up round the Viscount Peterbloom's neck. When next he gathered her into his arms, drawing her small body close against his strong one, she offered no resistance whatever. When at last he pulled his lips from hers, she sighed happily and nuzzled her silky dark curls into the crook of his shoulder.

"Now, will you marry me?" he asked hoarsely.

Miranda drew in a long breath of his male scent, a heady mixture of man, lime, and musk. How very dearly she loved him! "No, my love, I cannot."

She smiled impishly when she heard his sigh of exasperation. "Well, then, you leave me no choice but to continue kissing you until I receive the proper answer."

Miranda tilted her chin up saucily. "And I, my dearest Grant, see nothing for it but to accept your challenge."

Miranda's green eyes drifted shut once more as the wicked viscount's lips came down hard on hers.

When that kiss ended and he kissed her again, she snuggled even closer to him.

And closer still.

All things considered, she had no doubt now that the Viscount Peterbloom was the most suitable suitor in the world. For her.

Dear Reader,

If you are like me, you also feel an overwhelming longing to experience life as it was in the romantic time period known as the Regency. Then, a real man was a gentleman, right down to his polished Hessians, and a proper young lady still blushed when caught staring overlong at milord's broad shoulders—not to mention his thigh-hugging inexpressibles!

For me, the pull was so great I simply had to delve deeper to learn more about the past I found so intriguing. Not even traveling to London, or visiting Brighton and Bath, was enough to satisfy me. I had to know more! From this longing grew *The Regency Plume*, a bimonthly newsletter dedicated to accurately depicting life as it was in Regency England.

Each issue of *The Regency Plume Newsletter* is full of fascinating articles penned by your favorite Regency romance authors. If you'd like to join me and the hundreds of other Regency romance fans who experience Prinny's England via *The Regency Plume*, send a stamped, self-addressed envelope to me, Marilyn Clay, c/o *The Regency Plume*, Dept. 711-D-NW, Ardmore, Oklahoma 73401. I'll be happy to send you more information and a subscription form. I look forward to hearing from each and every one of you! In the meantime, I hope you enjoyed reading *THE UNSUITABLE SUITOR* and will want to read my next Regency romance! Thank you!

Sincerely,
Marilyn Clay